Matthew Prior
The Queen's
Pawn

Alan Butler

Priority Books

www.prioritybooks.co.uk

Published by Priority Books

Copyright © 2014 Alan Butler

All rights reserved.

ISBN -13:978-1503173927
ISBN-10: 1503173925

DEDICATION

This book is dedicated to the memory of my late Mother
Mary Butler and also that of her sister Isobel Redfern, a
woman who saw something in me when the world generally
did not. - Thanks Aunty Belle!

CONTENTS

Chapter 1   Page 3

Chapter 2   Page 15

Chapter 3   Page 32

Chapter 4   Page 50

Chapter 5   Page 65

Chapter 6   Page 80

Chapter 7   Page 98

Chapter 8   Page 113

Chapter 9   Page 130

Chapter 10   Page 147

Chapter 11   Page 162

Chapter 12   Page 178

Chapter 13   Page 192

Chapter 14   Page 207

Chapter 15   Page 223

Chapter 16   Page 238

Chapter 17   Page 255

ALAN BUTLER

ACKNOWLEDGMENTS

My thanks go as always to my wife Kate for her tireless assistance in every way, for her belief in Matthew and also for her continued support.

I would also like to thank Les Carver for his interest and his assistance in the reading of the manuscript.

Thanks also go to Fiona Spence-Thomas, who was another believer in Matthew from the start and who has stuck by me through thick and thin.

Chapter 1
By Royal Command.

With a final gutter the wick keeled over and the room fell into comparative darkness. Through the grimy casement cold moonbeams crept in to icily penetrate the furthest recesses of the dingy London lodging, hard by the Thames and wringing with damp. But Matthew didn't even notice. He was deep in thought and deep in debt.

"The life of a pensman is a precarious existence."

The words of his father floated up from the pewter ink pot; and why not? The inkwell had, after all, been his father's property. Matthew searched with the nib of his quill in the silver gloom until it found its mark, where it settled into the substance of unwritten words, blocking out his father's voice and putting the last full stop to a predictably dull day.

"Time for bed", he sighed, rising and opening the doors of his 'vast' boudoir, which was, in effect, little more than a cupboard in the wall at the far side of the room. Tomorrow marked the day of his birth. Thirty-five Aprils, he thought; and each one bringing him closer to oblivion and obscurity.

His head swam a little as he climbed beneath the welcoming blanket. There was still some warmth here, the remnants of the meagre fire, now little more than grey ash in the grate. Deep in his stomach the dubious concoction of mutton and ale struggled to gain a common chemistry. At least he'd eaten and drunk well – rather too well it now seemed. A bawdy repast paid for by a simple sonnet, made in a moment for a lovelorn Lancastrian, bound for a tryst by London Bridge.

The White Goose in Southwark had been crowded; old men spitting, young men coquetting, and a buxom barmaid, apple-cheeked and ready with a wink, blustering about amongst the tables, in an atmosphere as sweet as a piggery and as thick as a four day stew.

John Acres, of Lord Reckington's Men, had arrived just past ten, with a promise of work if Matthew could only force his errant brain around a new comedy, or better still a stout history to counteract the success of 'Lord Strange's Men' at the Rose.

Matthew had smiled. John was a good friend and ever ready with promises but for all his optimism, tardy when it came to parting with the tin. In any case, the muse that very occasionally alighted on Matthew's battered old oak desk was presently residing in the Americas, or at any rate far from Wyatt's Yard, where Matthew's pens and parchment presently waited for promise of fruitful use.

Already beneath the blanket Matthew rolled over and tossed his doublet onto a chair. He was struggling to remove his boots when he heard the horses galloping into the yard beneath his window.

"Hold his head!" A sharp command cracked in the quiet night. "I'll get him."

A heavy thump, thump commenced on the street door, at the top of the stairs, outside his room. Matthew crouched in the darkness and wondered which of his creditors would go to the expense of sending horsemen round in the middle of the night. He half forced a smile. They had little chance of plucking even such paltry sums as he owed from a purse more roomy than Westminster Abbey. He smiled, knowing that he wasn't successful enough to be deep in debt.

"Open up!" cried an angry voice, "Open Up - In the

name of the Queen!"

The Queen? What on earth could the Queen possibly want with him - Matthew Prior? Fearing that the ancient oak planks would part at any moment, adding to the amount he already owed his avaricious landlord, Matthew struggled from beneath his heavy woollen blanket, and grabbing his doublet once more, he hurried off down the steep steps. A split second before the old iron hinges burst inwards he had eased back the bolt and opened the door. Out in the yard, holding a torch in one hand, and the reins of three fine horses in the other, was a liveried guard, gold and silver thread on his surcoat glinting in the flickering light of the fiery brand.

Before Matthew stood the Yeoman's companion, huge, dark and dangerous.

"Would 'ee be Master Matthew Prior?" The tall man croaked in a West Country drawl.

"Why - Yes", gulped Matthew, his last hope gone of these fine fellows having come to the wrong door.

"Get your cloak", the soldier ordered. "Her Majesty the Queen has business with 'ee!"

Matthew wondered that if, in spite of his rumbling stomach and the bitter cold he had managed to get to sleep and was now partaking of a particularly strange dream.

"The Queen?" he spluttered. "What business could the Queen have with me?"

"Like as not she wants to hang 'ee for all I know." The big man, growing larger by the moment, showed a glimmer of humour and a mouth full of rotting teeth. Turning to his colleague he repeated the line and laughed. Matthew tottered, his mouth open, the scratching of the hempen rope on the flesh of his neck all too real in the fertile recesses of his fabler's mind – ironically his first glimmer of genuine creative invention in weeks.

The soldier turned back to him abruptly. "Can 'ee ride Matthew Prior?"

Matthew toyed with the idea of suggesting that he could not, but even a humble scrivener has some pride and he did not relish the prospect of entering the Royal presence slung like a side of beef across the pommel of a saddle.

"Yes," he managed in a resigned tone of voice. "I can ride".

All too soon the streets and byways were racing past them, houses and yards, shops and stables hurtling backwards as they sped onwards through the night at an alarming pace. The cold was now starting to bite and Matthew's cloak was not adequate for keeping out the chill on any journey but that from the nearest ale house to his lodgings. He shivered, from a late frost but hardly from fright, since he was so busy trying to keep his seat on the racing horse and barely had time to contemplate his fate at the Tower. The Queen's business probably wouldn't matter, he thought, as his shoulder bumped heavily on a low inn sign, threatening to dismount him. He'd be dead long before they reached the Tower.

The near full moon did at least offer some illumination. On Parsons Row Matthew's horse put a foot wrong as he struggled to keep up the pace, threatening to toss him onto the cobbles. By a stinking drain, in a maze of streets close to the bottom of Tower Hill his right foot slipped from the stirrup and he had to be hauled into an upright position by his two companions. Finally, with the shadow of the imposing bastion not far off, and at the top of Ermine Row the mutton and mead formally gave notice of their incompatibility. Leaning down from the saddle, Matthew wretched violently. The halt was fleeting, and the only satisfaction for having parted with a supper so gainfully won and enjoyed was that he had accidentally contrived to deposit the entire meal on the doorstep of a particularly loathsome money lender of his acquaintance, a man by the name of Erasmus Small. Small by name, and small by nature.

The imposing walls of the Tower of London were growing larger, and the building, many towered and silver in the glow of the moon stood like a mountain before them. The trio clattered across the metalled yard and on, up to an open and well lit doorway. Matthew slithered down gratefully. The large grey gelding turned to look at him and snorted contemptuously, obviously unimpressed by his equestrian skills.

"Don't stand there man," scolded the Yeoman. "In 'ee go. We'll catch our deaths out here on a night like this."

"And I may well catch mine in there and out of the night," Matthew heard himself mutter.

In the seventeen years he had been in London, Matthew had only rarely caught sight of Queen Elizabeth, let alone been summoned into her presence. He liked it that way - everyone did. It was well known that Queen Bess only ever came into contact with her humbler subjects, either to provide them with alms on holy days, or to have them flogged and hanged on other occasions. Holy days were rare, which was more than could be said for hangings.

The writer was pushed and bullied down a series of corridors, each hung with a collection of portraits larger and more imposing than the last and lit by smoking torches and bunches of rush lights. Finally he was urged through a dark, anonymous door and into a sumptuous room hung with tapestries and dripping with wealth. It smelled of intrigue and tobacco. The air was warm - but certainly not welcoming and a brooding silence hung over all. Matthew had time to take in his surroundings because as the door swung shut behind him, he seemed to be alone. A large table stood in the centre of the room, containing writing implements and pieces of parchment. Expensive looking gold handled pens lay on a Flemish cut glass stand and a three branch candlestick, with fine beeswax candles, cast a steady light onto the documents.

At the far end of the room a log fire crackled in an iron grate and either side of the chimney, large fire screens showed summer scenes of shepherds picked out in faded but exquisite needlepoint. The large window was shuttered against the night and above the mantle a stern portrait of Queen Elizabeth herself glowered down at him, so that despite the heat of the room, he shivered again.

"You are Matthew Prior?" A disembodied male voice floated across the room. It carried the cracks of age, but the swell of authority.

"Yes", Matthew replied hesitantly, his own voice a mere rasp and his quick eyes darting this way and that, trying to discover where the speaker was hiding. There was silence for a moment, which Matthew instinctively considered he should somehow fill.

From a doorway in the far corner, obscured by a free-standing oak screen, appeared an elderly man. In the flickering candlelight his skin looked the colour of aged velum. He was gaunt and sported a wispy pointed beard, which fell awkwardly across a large starched ruff. His clothes were dark forests of black material, carrying only some colourful badge of office to break the solemnity. The man glowered at Matthew, who at last found the courage to speak.

"I wonder sir? Do you know why Her Majesty has summoned me?" he finally managed and then added,

"Am I to see her here?"

The old man's solemn countenance faltered as he managed a sort of laugh.

"Good God Man", he said, eyeing Matthew up and down and obviously unimpressed by the shabby attire and worn boots, "What on earth do you think Queen Elizabeth would want with you?"

Thinking the old man to be some sort of servant, and feeling indignant, because whatever law he had broken must be serious indeed to involve recourse to the Queen herself, Matthew managed.

"But two Yeomen came to fetch me from my rooms. At the Queen's orders."

"The Queen is long since abed" the old man said, seating himself at the desk and gesturing Matthew to sit opposite. "in St James' Palace". Matthew deposited himself on the large and ornately carved chair. "As indeed I would be myself, were I not having to talk to you Master Prior." the old man added. There was a pause before the voice confirmed, "You will have to make do with me for the moment."

"Might I ask whom I am addressing?" Matthew wanted to know, after another protracted silence.

"The man looked Matthew full in the face. He was probably well in excess of sixty years, though his eyes were bright and alert. They drove arrows into Matthew's soul.

"You 'may' ask a great many things," the old man told him, picking up a piece of the parchment from before him. "For example, this note is from Sir John Cranton, presently residing with us here at the Tower. He 'asks' if I will offer him some leniency on account of past services." He picked up a pen, dipped it into the ink and scratched the word 'Refused', across the bottom of Sir John's epistle. "You see" he said, holding up the parchment, the better for Matthew to see it. "He asked – that's his right as a free born Englishmen. But it won't keep his head familiar with his neck tomorrow."

Matthew gulped.

"On the other hand I suppose we can learn nothing without asking," the old man mused. "So, for what it's worth to you, my name, Master Prior, is John Cecil, though if you have heard of me at all, and I am vain enough to believe that I may have been mentioned in your company, you doubtless know me as Lord Burghley."

Oh Christ!, thought Matthew, so loud that the sound echoed several times like a great church bell around the echoing recesses of his head.

"Oh my Lord", he spluttered. "I had no idea. I thought you to be some sort of secretary, or servant?"

Burghley was the shadowy First Minister of the Queen. It was said that she never even passed wind without him weighing the political and international implications of it. The man standing before the writer was, in every sense of the word, the most powerful man in the realm.

"Then your assumptions were correct Master Prior", he confirmed, almost smiling. "I am most definitely a secretary to Her Majesty the Queen, and also her willing servant. These positions I hold by the Grace of God and the generosity of Her Majesty. I undertake them with the utmost diligence, because she is my monarch and I love her right well." His eyes narrowed as they caught Matthew's once more. "Do you love your Queen Master Prior?"

Matthew had recently loved, or rather lusted after Frances Earnshaw, a Chandler's daughter from Greenwich, though she wouldn't entertain him until he became rich. He knew he should love his God, though their acquaintance had not been extensive over the years. He supposed he loved his parents - though both were long since dead. But his Queen? Perhaps the supposition of love for one's monarch was worth considering, and in any case he knew full well as a writer that the words available to the English language concerning this complicated emotion made few distinctions between 'types' of love.........

His musings were shattered as the voice boomed out again.

"I asked you Matthew Prior. Do you love your Queen?"

Matthew jumped in his seat and admitted that his affection for his monarch knew no bounds and that he would, of course, prove loyal and true to her Britannic Majesty, no matter what the cost to himself.

The old man's voice became calmer.

"Good." He looked down on the desk and picked up another piece of parchment. After scanning it for a moment he said. "And so to business. You are from Yorkshire Master Prior?"

"Why yes sir," confirmed Matthew, "from Stanton Prior. It's only a small village - and dull at this time of year I shouldn't wonder. I recall......"

His nervous babbling was cut short.

"When I want a history of the provinces I shall come to your lodgings and order one," Burghley intoned. "Now listen to me very carefully Matthew Prior, because I am an old man, I have the gout and the ague, both of which make me rather bad tempered. It is not in my nature to suffer fools and I do not care to repeat myself. Do you follow my direction henceforth?"

Matthew dare not speak, but he nodded as graciously as he could.

"Then you must do exactly what I say. Nor more and no less. Tomorrow at noon you will go to the shop of Bartholomew Thrace. He is a seller of wine and has his premises in the Vintner's Row. There you will be given instructions as to what is expected of you. In the meantime you will talk to nobody concerning this interview. You will ask no questions of me and you will go straight home to your lodgings and your bed. Good night Master Prior."

Matthew sat for a moment, despite himself, but the voice was insistent.

"I said Good Night Master Prior."

Matthew was puzzled, but he rose and turned for the door. He did not consider himself to be a handsome man, and his frame had seen better, slimmer and more agile days. All the same his head and his body were accustomed to their imperfections and he dearly wished them to remain attached, one to the other.

As he reached for the handle and pulled the door towards him the ageing voice spoke again.

"Wait".

Matthew froze in his tracks.

"Come back to the table and pick up the purse ".

Matthew did as he was bid and there, sure enough, to one side of the parchments was a leather purse, tied with red strings.

"This is for you Master Prior." Burghley told him. "As an indication of the generosity of Her Majesty to those of her subjects who know how best to serve her. Take it and go."

For the first time during the interview Matthew was fully in tune with the sentiments of the voice - he was too poor to be inquisitive where cash was concerned. The voice continued.

"There is more where this came from. Simply follow the instructions you are given, and you will not be the poorer. Now go home Matthew!"

The guards muttered as they were forced from the warmth of their garrison out into the cold April night once more, and despite the obviously important nature of his business within the Tower, even the grey gelding showed him no more respect than had been the case on the outward journey. But he managed to make it back to Wyatt's Yard without vomiting again, and he still had his head - at least for the moment.

Matthew dismounted and turned to talk to the soldiers, but they were already trotting off into the mist that was swelling up from the river. In less than a moment they were gone, and Matthew was alone. The Moon was high above the low mist and its silver beams enhanced the gleam of the gold that tumbled out of the purse and into his hand. Ten sovereigns - Full ten sovereigns. He bit into one, half ashamed of thinking that the Queen of England might deal in dubious coin. It tasted better than the mutton and mead - travelling in either direction.!

At six the next morning the Watch cried from the street beyond Wyatt's Yard and Matthew stirred. Dawn had broken and a pale sun stole into his consciousness. Well at least he could make some money from the dream, he consoled himself, his mouth tasting like bitter aloes and his head throbbing from the ale. There may be a story here worth a few pennies to someone.

Rising from his cupboard bed Matthew stared blearily around the room, and almost immediately his gaze alighted on the gleaming pile of coins on his work table. It hadn't been a dream after all. Suddenly, and for reasons he could barely guess at, he was rich beyond belief. But he wasn't to be left in peace. The invisible familiar who sat on his left shoulder at times like these, and which was always certain to wring misery from any twist of fortune had not deserted him.

"What use is all this money", the familiar wanted to

know, "if you are to become a pawn in the machinations of the Royal Court? Queens don't bestow this sort of cash on the likes of you unless there is danger somewhere along the road."

Matthew shrugged. Was he not the writer of 'A Gentleman of Etruria', the hero of which had undergone a hundred perils to win the love of his maid and his true inheritance? If he wrote it, could be not be it?

"Oh yes," agreed the familiar, "but it wasn't even a very good play was it? What a foolish fellow you are Master Prior. A play is simply a fabrication.. And as your father continually told you: 'There's always a price to pay!'".

Matthew wasn't listening. He was already wondering where he could go to get change for a sovereign without attracting too much attention. He decided to walk across the City and buy himself a new doublet and cloak in some district where he wasn't known. If he was going to come face to face with adversity and perhaps even danger before the end of this day, he might at least meet both looking tidy.

Chapter 2
The Dead Vintner.

It soon occurred to Matthew that the smart new doublet made his dark breeches and hose look even shabbier than they had appeared before, whilst the new breeches only demonstrated how patched and dirty his boots had become. His aged hat did not match the new ensemble at all and the finished look simply demanded a new, starched ruff.

The man at Salter's, in Paternoster Row, had commented that no gentleman these days would think of walking out in the street without a silver topped stick - "purely as ornament you understand", and the tiny, neat stitches on a pair of the finest kid gloves he had ever seen made them impossible to refuse, particularly at the modest price demanded.

Matthew had chosen a scarlet cloak. Well.... a playwright was expected to cut a dash. It would be good for business.

With his change in fortune it appeared that even the weather had improved its mood and the spring sun shone brightly on the busy city. Now, for the first time in many months he found his old accustomed stride as he paced up Grace Street, between cream and black gables. He had breakfasted on oysters and cold mutton, and while he was eating he had spent a good half hour concocting a tale of dead uncles and family wills, in order to explain his sudden rise in the world. It was the essence of Matthew's nature to make the best of good fortune, no matter from what direction it came. He looked above his head, to where the sun penetrated between the overhanging gables of the shops and houses. It carried with it the first, full promise of spring and as it rose, high over the city, the shadows of bitter winter shortened. Surely nothing could go amiss on such a beautiful morning?

On the cobbles of The Shambles, butcher's boys were hoisting buckets of water from the well, to wash away the blood of the animals slaughtered that morning. The smell of fresh baked bread taunted his nostrils, mixed with the more pungent odours emanating from many a grubby alley. Matthew peered into every nook and cranny. No matron sitting on her doorstep, mending in hand was safe from his penetrating gaze and no child chased an errant piglet up the dusty byways but he noted the event. Here was all the noise, bustle, bluster and mayhem that made up the City and he relished it all far more than the green valleys and rolling hills of his birthplace.

The premises of Bartholomew Thrace were behind a prosperous looking tavern, in the Vintner's Row. The shop front was tidy enough, the wooded shutters protecting the front of the building from the night and its denizens were put away, and the premises stood open to the street and the morning.

It was a large room, filled with bottles and barrels. Pots and jars of every imaginable kind cluttered each recess, or which there were many; but there was no sign of customers, despite the comings and goings in the street; and there was no shop keeper or proprietor in evidence. Matthew wandered about, reading the words on labels adorning large earthenware jugs. He took in the scent of bunches of lavender and thyme in a large open, wooden boxes, obviously a sideline of Master Thrace and he looked longingly at bottles of fine French spirits, before realising with some unexpected pleasure that they could now be his - should he so desire.

MATTHEW PRIOR – THE QUEEN'S PAWN

Minutes passed, and though Matthew called out, first quietly, and then much louder, nobody appeared. Eventually boredom set him to wandering. At the back of the shop he spied an open doorway, doubtless leading into a storeroom or perhaps living accommodation. It was dark in the entrance, and something crunched under the stout heel of his new boots as he stepped into the shaded gloom of the entrance.

Matthew looked down and as his eyes became more accustomed to the gloom he could see the broken glass and the red of the wine, running away at an angle to a dimly lit doorway beyond. Several bottles had been broken, and by the smell that wafted up they had been filled with some heavy, sweet wine. But then he realised that it wasn't wine at all, at least not all of it. On the far side of the doorway, slumped across a pile of wooden wine crates was the grim and bloodied body of a man.

The writer stepped back with a gasp, the lifeless eyes were wide open and stared at the ceiling. The man seemed to have been about Matthew's own age, but obviously smaller in stature and stocky, with dark hair, grizzled to grey at the temples. His once white shirt was redder that Matthew's new cloak and even now blood dripped from the hideous gash in his throat, down onto the floor, there to mix with the wine that ran in rivulets towards some unseen corner.

The writer bent lower, to examine the body. The wound to the right of the dead man's throat was deep – it had obviously cut right through the main artery. The hideous gash tailed off towards the left side of the neck, where it petered out to an angry scratch. The man had the most piercing blue eyes Matthew had ever seen: they looked straight ahead, and carried no sense of horror – more a look of utter surprise.

Matthew would have closed the eyelids, had he been offered a moment to do so.

From the far side of the dark doorway came a shuffling, causing Matthew to straighten and to call out, involuntarily,

"Who is it? Who's there?"

There was a rush of air as someone approached at speed through the casement from the blackness beyond, probably trying to gain the street door, a path blocked by the not insubstantial frame of the writer. A sort of wrestling match ensued, with Matthew struggling to subdue - he knew not who. His new broad-brimmed hat fell over his eyes, making it even more difficult to ascertain who his assailant might be. His hands flailed as he tried to gain a grip on his attacker and alighted on what could only have been a firm breast. The attacker was no man, but a slender woman! He had a split second to gain the impression of a slim, medium framed figure, before the bottle crashed down on his skull and he slumped to the floor, where a mixture of Madeira and blood soaked into his new clothes as he lay senseless amongst the broken glass.

As he regained his senses he could see chinks of light breaking into the near blackness and he found himself laid on his back on a wooden bed. The walls of the room in which he lay were of rough stone and somehow appeared familiar. A stern looking man of fifty years or more with a pale complexion stooped over him. Despite the gloom of the place Matthew could make out the impassive features, above what looked like a clerical collar. The man spoke, obviously to someone who was out of Matthew's line of sight.

"He'll be right enough. He took a good crack to the head, though it's far from serious. I would be very surprised if it's done him any permanent damage."

The man was a Scot and Matthew took him for a doctor, a species of which he was inordinately mistrustful. Memories of childhood bleedings and leeches always entered his mind whenever he came across a doctor in any social situation, which wasn't often. Professionally he avoided them altogether and doctored himself on the rare occasions that necessity demanded.

Another face came into view. This one was younger but far more hideous. The man had a square set jaw, a large, full lipped mouth and a nose that was misshapen and distinctly bent to the left. He had cold dark eyes, one of which was partly closed by an old but obviously vicious scar, running down from his forehead to his eyelid. It was a face known to Matthew, and belonged to a squat but muscular brute of a fellow called Timmins.

Ned Timmins was a member of the London Watch, a group of men employed by the city to enforce law and order, and who chose their own methods of doing so. Matthew had once or twice encountered Timmins at gatherings in particularly rowdy inns, or whilst attempting to unlock the door of his lodgings after a boozy end to one of his rare successful days. Neither was there any wonder that he recognised the room where he lay. It was a cell where he had slept off more than one binge. Timmins peered down at Matthew, coming so close that the rancour of his breath sent shudders of revulsion through the still prostrate figure. Recognition showed in the ugly man's face.

"You know me," he growled, staring hard at Matthew, whose head was sore and bleeding. "We're old friends 'aint we?" he went on. "You're Matthew

Prior, one of those infernal writers".

Matthew tried to speak and attempted to sit up. For the moment it seemed as though both were impossible. His head began to swim and he slumped back onto the wooden bed, closing his eyes once more.

"Don't you worry Master Prior," Timmins assured him. "We can talk soon enough, and I don't doubt that the Sheriff's men will be along to ask you a question or two as well. He turned away from the stricken writer to talk to the doctor, but Matthew could plainly hear the conversation.

"Oh yes," he informed the other man. "I know him well enough. It'll be no mystery. All those writers are the same you know, forever drinking - and most of 'em as poor as church mice. He was probably trying to get spirit from the wine merchant, and when he couldn't pay for it, he fought with the man, who came off worst."

"Aye!" the doctor replied, "but not before he'd given our friend here a hefty crack with a bottle. Nothing a day or two won't put right though."

"Well", the Watchman observed, "He can't have been that badly injured. He had enough left in him to cut the Vintner's throat."

The doctor murmured something that Matthew couldn't make out and then said, in a louder voice.

"If you need me again you know where I'll be."

"I do right enough", replied Timmins. "But I doubt we'll need your services for this one again, unless you deal with the dead. He'll hang for sure."

"If he does," answered the doctor jauntily, I know a medical school that would pay well for the body. You let me know."

With a shudder of horror Matthew Prior slipped back into semi-consciousness and when he awoke again the two men had left the cell.

He lay in the dark, wondering who had attacked him, and why. It appeared that his familiar had been right for once and his hand instinctively went to his belt, but the purse, containing a small proportion of the money he had been given the previous evening was in place, so he clearly hadn't been robbed. The bulk of his new fortune was hidden beneath a loose board in the floor of his lodgings. His new clothes were sticky, hopefully with wine, but his hair was clearly matted with his own blood. He took in this fact, though the pain was diminishing somewhat.

A vision of his father floated before his eyes as he stared up towards the pin-point of light that filtered through the high, grilled window.

Walter Prior had been a kindly man but always ready to hand out pearls of wisdom to his renegade son.

"London is a place of vice." he had told Matthew repeatedly. "You will find naught there but misery Matthew."

Once grown he had never listened to his Father's advice as a point of principle. The mild mannered Squire, though genial enough and no tyrant as a parent, was always a little too ready with his Northern homespun philosophy. By the time Matthew was growing to manhood, as the last in a series of eight children, Walter Prior had more or less retired from his local and regional responsibilities. As a result he had plenty of time to bombard the always rebellious Matthew with a tirade of 'truisms', none of which seemed remotely appropriate or relevant.

As Matthew lay on the hard boards, his head aching and contemplating the gory details of the fate that awaited a commoner convicted of murder, Walter's observations regarding London suddenly seemed more apposite.

ALAN BUTLER

From birth Matthew had been destined to enter the Church, and this may have been yet another reason why the pious Walter had wished to inculcate a sense of morality and, failing that at least a modicum of common sense into the boy. Despite the fact that anyone could see the attainment of a clerical career for the always wayward Matthew was ever going to be an uphill struggle, there appeared to be no logical alternative. Five of Matthew's siblings were boys, and each older than he. His mother, the ever resourceful Eleanor, had managed to keep all her children alive, but the tiny manor of Stanton Prior, hard by the Moors in the Valley of the River Aire, baked a small pie for so many mouths. Two of his brothers were already clerics, albeit of the English Church, but nothing that they could offer in the way of influence or encouragement had the slightest influence on Matthew, who resolutely failed to apply himself to 'the cloth.'

Although quick enough to absorb that portion of his studies that suited the prospective profession of writer, Matthew had appeared to singularly fail every attempt at improving his Latin, and everyone who ever taught him pronounced that his knowledge of the Scriptures was appalling. In reality his Latin was excellent but he had been wise, or foolish, enough to hide this fact from his tutors; despite blows raining down on him over miserable years in a freezing cold classroom as punishment for his stupidity.

By the time he was eighteen years of age the whole business seemed, for a while, to be of little importance, for Matthew fell in love, and was loved by, Celeste Arden, the eldest daughter and heir of Sir Archibald Arden of Kirk Standing, in the lush valley of the River Wharfe. She was of an age to be wed, and although the suit was not what her parents might expect in terms of Matthew's status, they had an abiding love for the wayward young man and a deep respect for his family. As a result they would gladly have accepted him as their son-in-law. No sooner had the betrothal been announced however than poor Celeste succumbed to the plague. Matthew was heart-broken and though the Arden's kindly and tactfully, pointed to Celeste's younger sister Rosemary, Matthew would have none of the match and soon estranged from his family he had run away and joined a band of travelling players.

After a couple of years trudging the byways of Britain he had found his way to London, and there, with the exception of a protracted visit to Italy and France, he had been ever since. At first the life had been exciting. Matthew had a ready wit and was never short of company. His nimble and inventive mind found a ready market amongst the moneyed rakes of the City. He penned trifles for them, and earned himself some sort of living in return. Oftentimes he would act small parts in one or other of the plays that were constantly being staged outside the city and south of the river and though he was no Greek tragedian, he shifted well enough.

Latterly life had been more difficult. The certain moment when one or other of his plays would achieve the success that all his friends declared they deserved was constantly moving forward with the years on the calendar. On the occasions that fortune did smile on him Matthew would temporarily, live the life of a gentleman, treating his friends and drinking until all hours of the night. His life was a somewhat bumpy road, each sleepy hollow of which seemed more low than the last. But despite his lack of success Matthew was generally bright of spirit and ever given to an optimism that, from childhood, his family had declared to be generally misplaced in consideration of the risks he was inclined to take.

He had no comprehension of the time, or even the day come to that. The mystery of his female assailant occupied his mind, for an errant star in the ascendancy at the time of his birth had bestowed upon him a curiosity that had proved a danger in infancy, and a distraction with adulthood. Green velvet - he distinctly remembered a gown made of green velvet. So whoever tried to divest him of his brains, and the person who presumably cut the throat of Bartholomew Thrace had been very well to do. No commoner could contemplate wearing a garment made from a material which cost in excess of a sovereign a yard.

He stared into thin air through narrowed eyes, the better to focus his wits on the events of a few fleeting moments.

He smiled to himself. The breast had been firm, and the bodice of the gown cool and curvaceous to his touch. He had always preferred women of spirit, but gently feeling the matted patch of hair, which was very tender to the touch, he had to admit that here was too much feminine fire - even for his tastes.

Some hours seemed to pass and Matthew was aware that pangs of hunger were beginning to gnaw at his stomach. He was busily sorting out the framework of a new series of sonnets, based on the identity and exploits of a mysterious 'Woman in Green', when the door of the cell burst open, and Timmins blustered in.

"Well you're a fine fellow and no mistake!" Timmins grimaced as he stooped over Matthew, his putrid breath once again assailing the writer's nostrils. He leered and a series of rotting black stumps betrayed what had once been two rows of large teeth. "It seems as though you have friends in high places." He snorted contemptuously and then added grumpily, "You're free to go! That is after you've spoken to the Sheriff's Officer."

A tall blond man entered the room. He was an individual of about Matthew's own age, carrying a lamp and writing implements. For the first time light filtered through the cell and Matthew noticed a small table near to his bed. Timmins brought in a chair and the man seated himself. There was nothing remotely threatening about his behaviour, and he instantly treated Matthew as if he were a victim and a witness to a crime rather than the perpetrator of one. His questions were measured, civil and perhaps even deferential.

Matthew described the state of the shop on his arrival, the first view he had of Thrace's body and then related what he had gleaned about his attacker. The Sheriff's Officer, who had announced himself as Jonas Kaye scribbled down a few notes and then said.

"Well Master Prior. I'll report your story back to the Sheriff himself and no doubt he will want to pursue the matter. After all we can't have honest citizens murdered in their own places of work – or anywhere else for that matter. We've been to look at the Vintner's shop," he went on, "And as far as we can ascertain there's nothing missing, so it's unlikely that the motive for the murder could have been theft. So for now, I'll bid you a good day and hope that your head soon recovers."

Matthew thanked Jonas Kaye and got shakily to his feet. Timmins had been lingering in the doorway and as Kaye left he walked forward and said, with a distinct tone of venom in his voice.

"You might think you've got away with this 'Mr' Writer, just because you've got influence somewhere at court. But I know you killed that Vintner. So take care 'Master' Prior. I'll be watching you like a hawk."

The writer steadied himself for a moment with his hand on the bed. Timmins hovered close to the door.

"Well come on then," he bellowed after a moment or two, "I haven't got all day. Surely you don't like this place so much that you want to stay here?"

Matthew managed to make it to the door, and walked out into a dingy, foul room. A further door led into another chamber, slightly less obnoxious than the first, and thence to a door that opened into the street. Matthew leant against the door frame for a moment, before launching himself into the night, for it was dark again by now.

Timmins looked up at Matthew, from two full hand spans lower and yet such was the girth of his solid body he may have been a third again as heavy as the writer.

"We'll meet again I've no doubt Master Prior. Someone with a title might not take you for a villain - but I do." He snarled and took on the aspect of a rabid wolf. Without any further comment Matthew pushed himself through the door and was soon walking up Grace Street, towards the River and his lodgings.

His new clothes were a disgrace, and would have to be cleaned carefully by someone who knew exactly what they were doing. So it was the old and somewhat shabby Matthew Prior who wandered into the White Goose, a Southwark tavern beloved of his fellow writer and actor friends. He had bathed his head but decided not to remove his hat whilst at the inn, for fear of too many questions being asked. Although apprehensive, every instinct in his body told him that, for now at least, he was not in imminent danger. He was sure that his injury was received only because he had been in the wrong place - at a time that was distinctly inconvenient for the murderer of the Vintner. After all - someone had made very sure that Thrace would never see the light of day again. If the mysterious woman had been deliberately waiting in the shadows for Matthew she would have left him with very much more than a sore head!

The tavern was busy with ribald seamen of indeterminate nationality, but they seemed jovial enough, gabbling away in tongues that Matthew could barely guess at. The atmosphere was warm and welcoming, if somewhat fuggy, after the chill of the cell, which in turn had been only slightly worse than the damp of his own room. The inns by the River, those at Holborn and the crowded, narrow streets amongst the 'stews' of Southwark were his real business address. A writer must see life to reflect it, and that meant going abroad - which inevitably cost money. As a result his lodgings were modest, but then devoid of life and laughter the finest palace would be poor fare to a mind that constantly demanded stimulation.

Close to the spluttering fire Matthew could see John Acres, the small, mouse of a man who had become one of his dearest friends and perhaps the one person in London who genuinely believed in the writer's true talent. He was deep in conversation with Richard Culpepper, a red-faced Lancastrian, who had vacated a prosperous family seat in favour of the delights of the capital. Culpepper clutched half a chicken, which he waved to and fro, in order to reinforce whatever point he was trying to make to the ever affable John Acres. As Matthew approached John looked up, and smiled warmly.

"Mattie!", he declared, rising from his seat and beckoning. He nudged a sleepy sailor on a stool next to his own and taking a small coin from his purse thrust it into the dusty man's hand. The matelot smiled a toothy grin and vacated his seat willingly. John reached up and clapped his friend on the back. He gestured,

"Here man, sit yourself down. I was just saying to Dick here that I thought we might see you before the night was out."

Matthew lowered himself into the seat. He caught the attention of a shawled, middle aged woman who was attending the tables close by. Ordering food and drink he then turned his attention to the two men who were once more deep in animated conversation.

"And I tell you John," remonstrated Culpepper, his half chicken cutting tight circles in the air, "that these Spaniards won't be content until they've murdered every man and violated every woman in the kingdom."

He took a hefty bite of the chicken, and whilst striving to drive home his point at the same time almost choked. Coughing and spluttering he turned an even deeper shade of crimson than his normal hue, until a huge sailor, full six feet and a half in size and with a girth to match, slapped him so hard on the back that his nose almost made contact with the rough, oak table. The offending morsel dislodged and recovering himself, Culpepper swivelled round in his seat, preparing to remonstrate with his saviour for almost breaking his back. Staring up towards the ceiling, which was where the sailor's head seemed to be, he had second thoughts and simply uttered his thanks before turning back to John and Matthew.

John smiled affably.

"Richard is very frightened by the Spaniards Matty. He thinks that we will all be Papists again before the year is out."

"More likely dead," came the reply and then, "Better dead than a Catholic in any case."

The last remark had been uttered in a louder voice than Richard Culpepper had intended, and he glanced around the room to ensure that nobody had registered his outburst, for though his contemplation of the delights of the Catholic faith were clearly not pleasant, he did not particularly want to greet death either - for the moment.

Matthew Prior and John Acres had both been in London long enough to know that religion was not a good topic of conversation, at least not in public places. It seemed for the moment that England was in secure Protestant hands, but the spiritual comings and goings of successive monarchs prior to the arrival of Queen Elizabeth had left people nervous, never knowing from one moment to the next where their religious loyalties should be seen to rest. To Matthew it was all academic. His two cleric brothers enthusiastically embraced the Church of England, though his late father had never relinquished his hold on what he had believed to be the 'true church' and towards the end of his life had suffered financially on that account. But Matthew was not a deep believer, or at least held steadfastly to the adage that 'God helps those who shift for themselves'. He did have a faith of sorts once upon a time but the death of Celeste Arden, no matter how sincere his prayers, had more or less put paid to any expectation that a remote and disinterested creator might have his needs at heart.

"So what have you been up to today Mattie?", John wanted to know, perhaps as a diplomatic change of subject. His small black eyes twinkled like those of an inquisitive shrew in the light of innumerable smoky, tallow candles. "I thought you would have been at the Pile, this afternoon. Graham's play is quite good, though the audience wouldn't let it be heard of course."

The Pile was a new theatre, on the south bank of the Thames, not far from London Bridge. It's real name was 'The Lexicon' but it was a wooden structure and like most theatres around London at that time hastily constructed from wood. Hard by the jetties with their disused and rotting hulks, the theatre looked immediately at home, and so the Pile it became, almost from the moment of its first performance.

Graham, of whom John Acres spoke was Sidney Graham, the son of a clergyman from Surrey, with a penchant for comedy and powerful friends to back his work. Was Matthew jealous of the man's success? Of course he was, but he couldn't fail to admire the quality of Graham's writing, even though it was sometimes hard to distinguish amongst the clamour and ribald behaviour of the afternoon audiences at The Pile.

"Oh," said Matthew dismissively, "I've been here and there." He dared not make a whisper of the events of the last day, particularly within the hearing of Richard Culpepper, who found it hard enough to hold his own water at the best of times. But the writer's mind had not been at rest since the morning and its surprising events. John Acres was astute, and close to the machinations of the Court, for he had a cousin who served a highly placed Minister, and John had been an actor and part-time theatre manager long enough to have literary friends from some of the best families in the land. John knew much about the workings of the monarchy and would have told what he knew - but any sort of conversation on the topic was bound to be difficult.

Matthew sat, pensive for a moment, wondering on the events of the day and musing as to the identity or motive of the murderous woman in green. But his thoughts were cut short by the arrival of his food and drink. "First things first," he thought, suddenly realising that he had eaten and drunk nothing since breakfast.

"A man can't think straight on an empty stomach", whispered his invisible familiar, ever willing to remind

Matthew of his late father's inimitable wisdom. For the second time in a single day he was forced to agree and greedily set about the business of feeding his body – his mind could wait.

Chapter 3
The Problems of a Queen.

The room grew hotter and Matthew's head began to ache again. The conversation passed this way and that, generally concerned with literary matters, and the many plays that were presently being presented in a number of new theatres springing up beyond the City. No playhouse presently existed within London itself on account of the religious views of the authorities.

All in all things looked grim for the writers and actors of London. The officiating authorities that held sway over the City represented a body replete with Puritans – killjoys all and opposed to any sort of entertainment. The Lord Mayor had, only days before, put out a proclamation lamenting the number of hours lost amongst the apprentices and journeymen of the City, while they idled their afternoons away at one of the new theatres. Matthew knew that the real reason for trying to ban the theatre was because it offered sites where possible disaffection could ferment – with the aid of drink into unruly behaviour. Just a week or two previously a large group of London's apprentices had rioted on the grounds of a perceived injustice meted out to one of their number. They had assembled at one of the theatres south of the Thames and had then marched back into the City, where they did a good deal of damage. It had been predominantly this occurrence that had spurred the Lord Mayor into penning his edict.

It was inevitable that Richard Culpepper would tire of the discourse and wander off to find more stimulating company eventually - he invariably did. Richard was born of a wealthy family but he was no intellectual. His childhood and adolescence had not been 'bookish', for the Culpeppers of Lancashire were in the main dynamic - but dull. Richard Culpepper fancied himself as a patron of the arts and wanted to be considered a 'cultured' man, but the minutia of the writer's art was of little interest. Finally the lure of a trim waist and a pretty smile was enough to draw him forth into the London night, leaving Matthew and John alone at the gnarled oak table.

"You're not fully present tonight", the ever astute John Acres commented. Pale of complexion and never seeming remotely robust or healthy John Acres was, nevertheless intuitive, with an enquiring, active mind. When animated by conversation that interested him, which was almost always, he was razor sharp and was invariably admirable company. Far beyond this, John Acres was a sterling friend and, Matthew considered, a man of true integrity.

"No", replied Matthew, bringing himself back from the land of deep contemplation, a resort that he often visited if he had something particular on his mind.

In the main Matthew Prior was as genial and bright as his smaller and more fragile friend, but he was given to prolonged, silent periods which occasionally puzzled those who had come to know his more sociable tendencies. Friends who knew him well had often said that Matthew did not have interests, only obsessions, and this was somewhat true. Perhaps this aspect of his nature stemmed from the possession of an insatiable curiosity regarding the position of every warp and woof of life. In addition to his interest in writing Matthew was a keen astrologer, had read works of alchemy, was fascinated by architecture and had an abiding interest in numbers, which he considered to be the building blocks of everything in the observed world.

He stirred in his chair. The room had emptied somewhat, most of the foreign sailors having stumbled forth into the night. Now only a few boatmen and dockside workers sat here and there, talking amiably. Matthew liked it that way and found it comfortable to swim in the ebb and flow of low-spoken trivia. But he was too puzzled, too confused to remain silent as Lord Burghley, the old man at the Tower – that bastion of Elizabethan national and foreign policy had warned him to do.

"John", he said, after a moment's contemplation, "I want to show you something".

He removed his hat. Though he had bathed the wound as best he could it had not yet begun to heal, as he knew it would given time. His dark hair was matted with dried blood and the injury obvious, even in the dull light of the low beamed, dark tavern room.

"Becket's bones!," exclaimed John Acres, and gave a long, low whistle. He stood and examined Matthew's dented skull. "Have you had a doctor look at this - how did you come by it?"

"You know my opinions regarding the medical profession," retorted the writer, waiting for his friend to retire to his seat before replacing his hat. "It will knit together soon enough, and as to how I came to have a hole in my head," He stopped and looked around. There was nobody in earshot, as long as he kept his voice low. "I shall inform you now - though only upon receiving your solemnest oath that what I have to tell you will go no further.

John Acres looked genuinely hurt. After a moment he leaned over the table.

"Master Prior, I have known you now for more than ten years, and I trust that during that period you have never found me wanting when it came to keeping my word - or my council. And now, whatever new adventure has befallen you, I urge you to relate the details quickly, before I contrive to offer you a matching dent on the other side of your thick skull."

The two men laughed amiably. Without further ado Matthew related the events that had taken place since the arrival of the palace guards the previous evening. As he spoke, each detail came full and fresh into his mind again; the discomfort of his ride to the Tower, the low crack of Burghley's voice, the surprised look in the dead Thrace's eyes and the memory of the foul breath of his temporary gaoler.

John clapped Matthew on the shoulder.

"Well here's the stuff of adventure" he exclaimed when Matthew finished his story, his busy little eyes reflecting the light of each taper as they darted back and forth. "And you have no idea at all why you were told to contact this Bartholomew Thrace?"

"None", admitted the other. "As you know well", he continued, "I stay deliberately away from the workings of the State. It is dangerous enough being a pensman in this city at the moment."

"Do you have any family contacts at Court?" John wanted to know.

Matthew shuffled in his chair. "John", he insisted. "The Priors have been sitting in their dull manor since Adam was a boy - or at least found their seat there shortly after the Normans arrived. In all that time the only way the family has distinguished itself has been for its insistence on ineffectuality." He grunted "Through all the misery and mayhem of the Wars of the Roses, which raged about the North Country on all sides of Stanton Prior, my family refused to take sides - even to the point that our neutrality became a danger in itself. No", he insisted, "For all his faults my father knew, as did his before - and as I do now, that monarchs make dangerous friends." He took a large pull on the ale that stood in the goblet before him. "I've often thought that our family motto should have been 'We Revel in Obscurity".

John Acres laughed.

"Well then", he commented, "we must look for other reasons to explain your sudden rise to wealth and the desire on someone's part to divest you of your head." He fell silent for a brief span. The room was growing increasingly warm and stuffy. Someone opened a creaking door and allowed the chill of the early spring night to enter. "I saw my cousin Walter only a day or two ago", John commented after a few moments. "He says that life at Court is particularly interesting at the moment."

"How so?", Matthew wanted to know.

"Oh it appears that her Majesty is in mortal danger."

The writer took another swig of his ale. "Well there's nothing extraordinary in that." For as long as anyone could remember there had been any number of plots, or supposed plots being hatched by one faction or another to rob Elizabeth Tudor of her throne, and even her life.

Elizabeth sat high in state, but low in the estimation of many men.. And perhaps here lay the crux of the matter. How, many had wanted to know from the outset, could a woman hope to manage the reigns of the racing horse that England had become? In fact she had ridden the steed more than tolerably well. But the situation, the suspicion and the intrigue had been multiplied simply because, from the time of her accession, Queen Elizabeth had adamantly refused to marry.

It was far too late now of course, everyone knew that. She had been on the throne of England for thirty four years. Even allowing for the fact that she was only twenty five when she had been crowned, that meant she was now an old woman of fifty nine years. No matter how elevated she was in the minds of so many people who could remember no other monarch, even the 'Virgin Queen', Gloriana herself was not going to produce an heir now.

Only about a decade previously she had finally stopped proclaiming to Parliament and her people that it was her intention to secure a husband and ultimately a successor to the Tudor dynasty. But the truth was, and all thinking men knew it, that there had been nobody available and probably not a man born who would have made a suitable husband for the Queen. Those who had the standing might have wanted more than a bedded wife, and those who would have been content to sail in the wake of the 'Good Ship Bess', hadn't the breeding.

Elizabeth had fought hard to climb the steep steps that led to England's throne. Declared a bastard at the execution of her mother Anne Boleyn, the unfortunate girl had remained a nonentity during the latter part of her father's reign and a virtual prisoner whilst her half sister, the suspicious and spiteful Mary Tudor had forced a bloody path back to Popish ways. But Elizabeth was a survivor and it was well known that she had a tenacity and a natural strength that no person, male or female, could better. As more than one broken-headed retainer had been forced to comment, after feeling the full eight of the Queen's displeasure, "She doesn't need a man - she is one!"

Here were sown the seeds of so many threatened overthrows - the lack of a viable heir for the English throne, which after several centuries of bitter feuding amongst the English nobility, back before the reign of Henry VII was seen as a threat to both religious and political stability.

John was adamant.

"I think we should take these threats to the throne very seriously," he vouchsafed. "It seems that there is a pretender to the throne lurking somewhere in the background who is even more determined than Scottish Mary was."

The little man was alluding to Mary Stewart, erstwhile holder of the Scottish throne. She had been deposed by her own Lords many years previously, in favour of her young son James. Running to her English cousin Mary had thrown herself upon the dubious mercy of Elizabeth, who found she had gained a guest she could well have done without. Mary was a Catholic, and though in the early days of her stay in England Elizabeth had seen no real harm in her cousin's chosen religion, successive problems in the administration of the Church had hardened the English monarch's attitude towards Catholics. But of far more import was the fact that a certain section of disaffected English Catholics firmly believed that Mary Queen of Scots had a better claim to the English throne than did Elizabeth herself. As a result the unfortunate woman had been locked up in one safe keep or another from the moment she had set foot on English soil.

In the end Elizabeth had been left with little real choice. Despite numerous warnings Mary Queen of Scots continued to allow herself to stand at the centre of intrigue after intrigue, each one more dangerous to Elizabeth's crown and to her life's blood. Reluctantly, and, everyone supposed, with tears of genuine sorrow, Elizabeth had given instructions for Mary to be executed five years ago in 1587. Not that her death had eased the religious or dynastic problems surrounding the throne, if only because Queen Elizabeth could not live forever.

"It's all rumour and counter-rumour at the moment," John said, lifting a hand to call the serving maid and order more drink. "... but rumours tend to be taken to the bosom of our Virgin Queen." He leaned closer once the serving wench had trotted off to get his order. "There'll be hell to pay if it's true, and since it's a certain fact that the Pope has even offered 'incentives' for the Queen's assassination, the latest turn of events means there will be no Catholic safe in the country."

"Who is the danger from now then?" Matthew wanted to know. "Is it as Dick fears - The Spanish?" He laughed. Only four years previously the finest fleet that Spain could amass had been smashed to pieces by the English navy, and by the British weather, practically before any Spanish soldier could put a foot on land.

"No, not the Spanish Mattie," replied John, leaning forward in his seat, the better to avoid being overheard. "But the threat is real, Walter says that the guard around Queen Elizabeth herself has been tripled in the last few weeks, and with good cause. England is being positively flooded with Jesuits – they're coming out of the woodwork all over the place. And as you know only too well there are plenty of people around who would relish a return to the bosom of the Pope.

The Jesuits were a Catholic order of Priests, full of religious zeal and indignation, intent on overthrowing Protestantism and restoring the 'old ways' everywhere.

For all his professed disinterest in matters ecclesiastical, a shiver ran down Matthew's spine.

"What!?" he exclaimed. "John you can't be serious. It would be the best way to disaster for England." He gesticulated. "Tolerance," he said," it's the only way. I don't care what God the next man chooses to follow and I'm damned sure that the same would be said by practically all sensible Englishmen." He realised that his voice was carrying and fell silent.

"I suppose it's all a matter of options," John commented quietly. "If any of these Catholic plots were to succeed and we ended up with a Catholic monarch, do you think that the Papists would graciously allow us to continue in the way we have for the last half century?"

Matthew was dismissive. "It's too late John. We've come too far."

England had lurched backwards and forwards from Rome to Canterbury in the years since Elizabeth's father, Henry VIII, had first cut all ties with the Roman Catholic Church. His Protestant son, Edward had managed only a short reign, too brief a period to fully consolidate what was still seen by many loyal Catholics as a schism. Edward was succeeded by Mary, the daughter of the staunchly Roman Catholic Katherine of Aragon and she had ruthlessly destroyed all vestiges of the Protestant retainers surrounding her father and stepbrother. It had been a bad time for England and, as far as Matthew could tell, not a period that anyone, not even the remaining Roman Catholics would relish returning. From the start Elizabeth had preached as great a degree tolerance in religious matters as she dared, whilst remaining publicly definite in her Protestant leanings. Matthew had often conjectured to himself that in all probability the Queen was actually no more religious than he himself was.

"Aye! Right enough", the smaller man agreed, himself born of a family that owed its rise to the old Archbishop Thomas Cranmer, a Protestant elevated by Henry and destroyed by Mary. Like most of the writers and actors in London John preferred to steer a careful path in his own religious observances, for audiences were the meat and drink of his profession, and might be of any denomination. For certain, whilst it was the business of the playwright to entertain and inform, it was criminally dangerous, even in these more enlightened times, to preach.

"But for all that", he continued. "It isn't merely hearsay Mattie. "My cousin is assistant to the Queen's private secretary and he himself has penned some of the documents that have been passing to and fro. There are now three seminaries on the Continent turning out Jesuit Priests at a fantastic rate. There's no way of stopping them." He leaned forward again. "Trade is bad at the moment, and many people are saying that we need better contacts overseas – and that our Protestant ways are preventing that."

Matthew looked dubious.

"It's just Her Majesty posturing John. You know what she's like for playing one off against t'other." Amongst the royal watchers of the Capital, Elizabeth was well known for spinning a web of intrigue that none could penetrate. It made her feel secure to have each at the other's throat. It was part of the merry dance that kept the Court, and the kingdom, on its toes.

"I would have thought so too", said John, "but that's not all." He looked around again. "There was a genuine attempt on her life a few days ago, whilst she was down in Surrey. They say the man was a Roman Priest, almost certainly a Jesuit. He tried to stab her whilst she was out walking. Fortunately the guards were close by and disarmed the man. Walter says that the man is quite mad, and that he would probably have tried to murder Saint Peter himself if he'd been ordered to do so. " He shrugged his shoulders. "But it isn't what you or I think that counts Mattie."

Matthew straightened for a moment, and then relaxed back into his seat again.

"Monarchs are constantly in danger. Worse than this has taken place before, and rumour has it that the Queen just shrugged it off - sometimes with a laugh."

"Mattie, this is no joke, I'm serious. It's causing disaffection at Court and there are conversations taking place in corridors. Important people muttering in corners - and that's dangerous. If the Queen doesn't take positive action soon - well," He threw his head back and sat back heavily in his chair, "it could be the worse for us all."

For once the ever affable John Acres looked in deep earnest. Probably not surprising, Matthew thought, for John's family, and many like it, would have the most to lose if the pendulum of religion swung back to the Vatican. But this contemplation was ungracious, he knew it and repented the thought. After a moment he said.

"Be that as it may, I can't see that the affairs you talk of, real or imagined, could be related to the happenings of my life this long day past."

The little man looked thoughtful.

"Perhaps not. But all the same, if you want to pursue the matter any further, it might not be a bad idea to find out more about the Vintner. Most importers of wine have close contacts with France and Spain. People there are more likely to do business with a fellow Catholic, so plenty in the wine trade hold to the old ways, if only for the sake of their businesses."

"Do you think your cousin may be able to fathom why Lord Burghley, of all people, summoned me to the Tower"? Matthew wanted to know.

"I doubt it", admitted his friend. "The Cecil's are a law unto themselves." He smiled. "But you can be sure of one thing Matthew, it wasn't him who had a bottle broken over your head. When Burghley wishes someone dead – they stay dead."

Matthew was pensive. "And it also seems that Lord Burghley doesn't suspect me of cutting the throat of Master Thrace either. Someone got me out of jail, and presumably Lord Burghley would have no problem doing that. But that still leaves one big problem John."

"And what is that?" his friend wanted to know.

"What on earth should I do with the money? Whatever the Vintner was supposed to tell me has gone with him to the grave. I can hardly walk up to the front door of the Tower of London and offer to give back the gold." He thought about the new clothes. "Besides, I've spent some of it already."

John agreed that it was a difficult problem. He considered the dilemma.

"I know it seems a great deal of money to you or me," he admitted, "but to Lord Burghley it's corn for the chickens. And if you can't fulfil your obligation to whoever summoned you - well", he said with a sweeping gesture of his short arms, "it's hardly your fault."

Matthew wasn't entirely reassured, but he had to admit to himself that there was little he could do except hold onto the coins and wait to see if anyone contacted him again. He furrowed his brow.

"But it can't be over yet John because as I said, someone arranged to get me out of gaol, when it would have been simple to have me hanged for killing the Vintner. I was covered in the man's blood and found literally red-handed at the place of his murder." Matthew reached down and rattled his purse. "All the same John, there's no point in looking a gift horse in the mouth." He gestured to the serving woman to bring more drink.

As Matthew made his way home some hour or so later, he walked close in the wake of the lamp boy who led him through streets and alleys back to his lodgings. This was a precaution that the playwright would normally not consider, but on this night every doorway seemed to contain watching eyes and he felt a hot gaze on his back from each casement. Not that the small lad picking his way between the rubbish and the cobbles ahead of him would have afforded the slightest protection if he had been attacked. Like as not the youngster would have taken to his heels at the first sign of trouble. But for all, the warm glow of the lantern on a night when the rising moon was often obscured by dark clouds was somehow welcome.

North of the river Matthew was somewhat puzzled by the tortuous route chosen by the lamp boy. It was not in the least difficult to keep pace with the emaciated form in front of him, who looked so slight that a breath of wind might carry him aloft. Matthew looked at the lad and wondered if Bartholomew Thrace might have had a son, or at the very least a wife to mourn his passing. True, he hadn't known the man, and perhaps the Vintner might well have been involved in some nefarious business that had led to his untimely end. All the same Matthew couldn't get the thought of those open, staring eyes out of his mind.

"Mind your own business," said Matthew's familiar. "Why create problems for yourself? For all you know your usefulness in this business is over. You might never hear another word about it. But that means staying quiet and not putting yourself deliberately in the way of harm."

For once he couldn't fault the advice, but neither could he deny the memory of that lifeless stare. Someone had murdered Bartholomew Thrace, and had done their best to damage his own health too. Could these events somehow be associated with the latest, dangerous, rumours from the Royal Court? It didn't seem at all likely, and yet his one and only instruction had come specifically from that self same high place.

He was so preoccupied with his own thoughts that the lamp boy, and his cheerful light, had disappeared before he realised. Matthew hadn't particularly worried about the unaccustomed route because these lads knew every pathway and alley of the City but now he stood in an unfamiliar setting, under the dark body and tower of a church that he only half recognised. Close to his right was a graveyard, where spectral, spiky yews stood gaunt in the night, drawing the essence of those buried below and passing it back to the darkness of eternity.

Drunken gravestones lurched this way and that in their frozen intoxication and for the first time since leaving the tavern Matthew was aware of a chill breeze blowing up from the river, now away to his right. An owl hooted from somewhere away beyond the limits of the crowded city streets and far from the dark oasis of the churchyard. And then he heard the voice - the same voice that that he had first heard at the Tower.

"Master Prior," the voice rasped, obviously from somewhere in the immediate black recesses of the church yard. Instinctively Matthew began to walk towards the sound.

"No!" the voice insisted. "Stay exactly where you are and no harm will befall you."

Imagining any number of bright blades illuminated by the face of the moon, which even now was probing the heavy clouds above, Matthew remained transfixed. There was no point in running, and in any case he didn't know in which direction to flee. It was unlikely that the owner of the voice, the old man Lord Burghley, was alone. Matthew was unarmed, and in any case no match for trained soldiers. He consoled himself with the thought that if anyone had meant him harm he would have been dead in the gutter already.

"Your Grace", Matthew managed at last, "the man you told me to contact is dead – murdered as like as not." His words fell like lead to the place where the metalled street gave way to a low wall and the tousled grass beyond.

"The realm is in danger Master Prior," Burghley told him, remaining in the shadows. "And you have the chance to serve your country and your Queen."

Despite his fear Matthew was curious, which since he was a child had always tended to make him reckless. He stared into the silver world, as the near full moon now broke fully through to paint the shadows and sharpen the angles of the granite slabs.

"But I don't know what you expect of me" he admitted. "I have no power to help anyone. You must know that I am a copyist and a playwright, I know nothing of matters of State - or anyone of consequence come to that."

"Aye," the understanding voice confirmed, "but you do have connections with a family bearing the name of 'Arden', do you not?"

This allusion could only be to the family of Sir Archibald Arden, whose daughter, Celeste, Matthew had long since hoped to marry, before his hopes were shattered by the summer pestilence that had taken not only his dear Celeste but a good third of the population of her village. But it seemed to Matthew that the Arden family were as safe and remote behind their own ancestral walls as his own family had always been - in fact more so. It was true that Matthew was abroad in London, and that his two brothers were clergymen, one in Yorkshire and the other in Oxford but as far as he knew none of the Priors or the Ardens ever set foot out of the North, except on the most rare occasions.

"You know of whom I speak?", Burghley wanted to know.

"Yes", Matthew confirmed," though I don't see ..."

The voice cut him short again.

"It isn't your business to see Master Prior, but rather it is your task - to do!"

Matthew wanted to shout, 'to do what?" But Burghley's was not the voice of a man who was used to being questioned, that much was certain. Discretion being the better part of valour Matthew relented.

"Tell me what you require of me My Lord and I will endeavour to undertake the task - if it be lawful".

"That's better Master Prior," came the reply, the voice almost cooing. "Now then, to business. You are to discover who murdered Bartholomew Thrace."

"The Vintner?" asked Matthew.

"Oh Master Prior," the voice was at pains to point out. "Bartholomew Thrace was far more than a humble seller of wine. But no matter. This is the first of your tasks."

"Can you offer me any possible motive for the murder of Thrace, My Lord," Matthew almost pleaded, realising full well that he knew nothing at all about the man, which might make apprehending his killer somewhat difficult.

Burghley replied immediately.

"You will discover at least a portion of what you need to know about Bartholomew Thrace when you have undertaken your second task Master Prior."

"Then pray My Lord, what is the second task" Matthew asked respectfully.

"A much easier and more pleasant command, I do assure you. Tomorrow, at noon you must present yourself at the river gate of Hampton Court. You will wear a sprig of rosemary pinned to your doublet, so that those there can recognise you. They will direct you to a meeting with..." the voice hesitated but then came again, "...with someone who can explain a little of what befalls you at this present time."

Matthew stood for a moment, now again in blackness as the Moon rode the edge of a new scudding cloud before being wholly engulfed. It seemed like an age.

"That is all." Burghley confirmed, though still without showing himself. "Now walk straight ahead of you, turn left at the end of the churchyard and your lamp boy will be waiting there for you."

Matthew hesitated for a moment and then thought better of it. He walked on slowly, until the merest streak of light showed him the way around the far edge of the church yard, and there, sure enough, was the same emaciated form that had accompanied him from the tavern.

No amount of questioning would elicit anything but the most perfunctory response from the urchin. He had been dragged into the darkness, bundled round the corner and told to wait where he was. At the same time he had been given a hand full of small coins. Undoubtedly here was a waif who had spent his whole life being instructed by others. He exhibited not the slightest trace of either surprise or curiosity and it was obvious that he knew no more than he was saying.

There was plenty to keep the writer's mind busy as he lay awake and thoughtful in the blackness of his little room, Sleep would not come, and when finally it was forced upon him by fatigue, it arrived with a riot of bending, merging images. In the recess beneath the floor boards, under his old writing table the money given to him the previous evening remained safe and secure, except for the fact that the leather pouch had seemingly spawned a mate, for when he had checked his hiding place there were now two matching pouches, the second of which also contained 10 golden sovereigns. Apart from his now yet greater wealth everything appeared to be undisturbed - except for one other addition to his shabby room. Hidden beneath his rough blanket, and on the flax ticking of his feather pillow, was a sprig of fresh rosemary. He presumed it a gift from some unknown person who had saved him the problem of finding such a token on the morrow. He was in bed and almost asleep before he remembered that today had been the anniversary of his birth, probably the most eventful birthday of his thirty-five years on earth.

Chapter 4
A Vision from the Past

The crowded confines of the City soon slipped behind Matthew as he sat reasonably comfortably in the prow of the small boat, surveying the dots of colour that indicated wild April flowers along the edge of the sparkling Thames. He had been up bright and early that morning, breakfasted by eight and away by nine to buy yet more new clothes, and to commit the soiled items to the care of a capable old crone who lived in Pecket Row, hard by the Fleet.. Half fearing that, in some undeniable way, his ostentatious choice of garb had contributed to his sore head and not knowing what the day held in store for him Matthew settled for slightly less gaudy attire, choosing a russet doublet, with matching trunk hose, slightly brighter stockings and German style hat of dark gold, with a handsome feather from some exotic bird.

There had been little choice regarding the mode of transport he should use to travel the few miles to Hampton Court, a large royal palace upstream of London in the heart of the countryside. A few days earlier he would have counted the hiring of a boatman as prohibitively expensive, unless he had recently been on the receiving end of a commission. Now the few pennies demanded by the oarsman seemed as nothing and the sudden feeling of opulence that overtook him did something to allay the dull though still present ache in his head and the feelings of apprehension that caused his breakfast to stir before it settled.

Matthew was not a total stranger to dangerous experiences. Queen Elizabeth had been on the throne of England since 1558, so the youngest of the Prior sons had known no other monarch. During most of her reign England had been generally quiet, as least as far as foreign wars were concerned and so Matthew had not served in the Army, as his father had once done. However there had always been a degree of disaffection to Tudor rule, together with the fact that ruthless bandits, petty criminals and simple n'er do wells still roamed the more desolate parts of the country, and especially the North.

At 15 years of age Matthew had been sworn into the local militia of which his father was the nominal commander. It was a raggle-taggle soldiery and it was well for England that its like was not expected to beat off the French or the Spanish, both of which had threatened to invade England at one time or another during Matthew's life. There were sorties into the hills high in the Yorkshire Dales and in the Pennines to face off raids by the Scots. In reality the term Scot in this connection was rather misleading. The real border was far to the North, but some of the bands of criminals to be found amongst the crags were certainly Scottish in origin. On two occasions between his sixteenth and eighteenth year Matthew had been present when such bands of desperadoes had been found and surrounded. In those frightening moments he had seen men fight and die, had drawn a sword blade in anger and tasted the iron saliva of raw fear.

But that time was far behind him now, and he had never yearned for the life of the warrior once his flight to freedom and the theatre had torn him from the Northern hills.

Beyond his own casement he had discovered a sweet late April morning, with all the promise of impending summer ahead. The street markets were filled with bright produce, brought in by pack-mule and cart from the surrounding countryside and by ships from the Continent. Flocks of half grown lambs bleated and gambolled their way to the butcher's quarter, fat pigs, bullied and prodded by their elfin masters followed on, searching here and there for fallen scraps and nosing vigorously at the accumulated debris of the street.

Matthew had stopped to survey the scene and taken a moment to retrieve the sprig of rosemary from the leather pouch at his belt. He pinned it to his new doublet and then sauntered down the street, taking in the noise and commotion of a city he had come to love for it vivacity, and even its stench, for after so many years both spelled home.

The day was still young enough and since Matthew was in the vicinity of Vintner's Row, he had thought he would begin to address the first of Burghley's tasks for him, namely discovering the identity of Thrace's murderer.

The shop had been barred and shuttered. Perhaps Thrace had not enjoyed the comfort of a family after all, for even the living quarters around the back of the shop appeared to be deserted. A wicker fence divided the back of Thrace's shop from the premises next door. Peering over it Matthew spied a youngish man, fresh faced, blond and tousle-headed, moving barrels about.

"Good Morrow", Matthew had called. The young man looked up at him.

"And the same to you Sir," the youth answered. "But if you seek Master Thrace I doubt you'll have a long wait, for he was foully done to death yesterday."

"That I know," the scrivener had confirmed. "What's your name young'un?"

The lad walked toward the fence. "It's Abe Sir – Abraham Jennit. He'd looked Matthew up and down, taking in his new attire. "Be you from the Sheriff?" the young man had enquired. "I spoke to one of the Sheriff's men yesterday." He displayed a downcast look. "But I couldn't be of much help. I didn't hear nothing – on my honour I didn't!"

Matthew had thought it might be best not to tell young Master Jennit that he had no legal standing whatsoever.

"I believe you Abe, and I'm sure the Sheriff does too. But tell me, did you know Master Thrace well?

"Not powerful well Sir," was the reply. "In fact hardly at all. He only came here two years ago, and even then his shop was more often closed than open." The lad pondered again for a while." It ain't decent to speak ill of the dead Sir but he was a hard man to get to know.. My Father…." The lad gesticulated to the shop, "he has the business here. My Father and Master Thrace never actually had words, but they weren't friends. But for all that," he'd continued "We'd not wish that sort of end on anyone – not even a Papist."

Matthew looked the lad straight in the eyes.

"You're telling me that it was common knowledge that Bartholomew Thrace was a Catholic?"

"As common as maybe," Abe had replied. "Oh he didn't shout it from the shop front of a market day, but for all he made no bones about the fact." The lad looked surprised. "I'm sure I don't know how he remained in business, what with him never a'going to Church of a Sunday and all."

This was a puzzle because Matthew knew that though there were many people around with Catholic leanings, anyone who wished to stay out of trouble and to keep his personal fortune intact would be tardy about admitting the fact. Heavy fines could be imposed on those who refused to attend their local Anglican Church at least once a month.

"Just one more question Abe," Matthew had assured the lad, who was looking a little worried, facing what he must have considered to be an authority figure, and mentioning matters religious into the bargain. "Did you see a woman around Master Thrace's shop yesterday morning. You'd remember her right well if you did, because she was a real lady. She was wearing a fine green gown?"

The young man had pondered for a moment.

"No Sir I did not" But then I was busy in our own shop. The first we knew about the murder was when the City Watch arrived and carried someone out of Master Thrace's shop on a plank. He'd looked at Matthew closely. "He would have been a man not unlike yourself in looks and stature," he had confirmed.

Matthew had thanked Master Jennit. The story remained the same, no matter to whom he talked in the Vintner's Row. Thrace was a spasmodic tradesman – not over friendly but at least civil – and everyone knew for certain that he was a Catholic. It wasn't much help, but it must surely have meant that 'someone' was protecting Thrace, for nobody was aware of him ever being fined for pointedly refusing to attend church. Matthew decided he could do little else for the moment, and in any case the sun was climbing fast and he had a journey to make.

At the jetty, just a little to the west of London Bridge, Matthew had found a little knot of boatmen playing dice on a flat rock, above the tide line and in the rapidly drying mud. They were a rough looking bunch, all rags and tatters. Theirs was a hard life. The charges they were allowed to levy were fixed by law, their wages were not high, and sometimes customers were hard to come by. Matthew had approached one of the men, a massive brick of a swain who looked as though he had the strength to get to Hampton Court in the blink of an eye.

"Can you take me up river?" Matthew wanted to know.

"Not I", replied the giant.

"Are you not one of the boatmen then?" enquired the writer.

"That I am sir," had come the instant reply, "but you'll want to speak to Josh, that's him over there." He had gesticulated to where a small, weasel of a man with long grey whiskers was painting some foul smelling substance onto the keel of an upturned boat.

Matthew had shrugged.

"He looks occupied. Why can't you take me?"

'T'aint my turn. We does our work by turns, and now is Josh's turn."

The older man had turned as Matthew approached and a bargain was soon struck, the asking price, plus an extra half penny if the ride was smooth and Matthew arrived without being soaked.

The bright river was low, but rising as Josh deftly pushed away from the jetty. He was a man of few words and so Matthew had plenty of time to take in the scenery as the City of London slipped behind them and the country beyond beckoned. The old boatman took deep, deft strokes, coaxing the water past his oars and never seeming to wake it from its dreaming loveliness in the shimmering haze of the morning.

The river gate of Hampton Court enjoyed its own jetty, but no personage of note was in residence and so there were but a few small craft moored there, and no sign of a sentry in the little hut that guarded the path between the river and the great house.

Hampton Court had once been the property of Cardinal Wolsey, who, in the time of Henry VIII had been the most powerful and richest man in England, some said richer by far than the King himself. Queen Elizabeth's father's relations with his erstwhile statesman and advisor had soured when Wolsey had floundered over the necessary arrangements concerning the King's divorce from Katherine of Aragon. In a vain attempt to save his prestige and ultimately his life, Wolsey had given the splendid new house at Hampton Court to King Henry, and from that day it became one of the more favoured of the Royal Palaces. Imposing and broad timbered it looked as impressive and new as the day on which it had been completed.

Stepping ashore Matthew paid the boatman and then dismissed him, having no idea concerning the duration of his business at the Palace. He supposed that there were locals who would be glad to earn a few pennies to row him down river again - failing which he would simply have to walk.

The day was growing warm, and the writer fanned himself with his hat as he watched a portly, surcoated man, more steward than soldier, puffing his way down the path some minutes after his arrival. The man was amiable enough and soon caught sight of the rosemary on Matthew's doublet. Its pungent, aromatic smell had assaulted his nostrils on the journey up river and he had puzzled frequently at the strange choice of the token.

"Ah Master," blustered the uniformed man as he clattered along the wooden jetty, "Good day to you." He gestured towards the cloudless arch of the sky, "Tis a fine morning and kind to my old bones after the chill of such a winter."

Matthew returned the greeting and, the portly man going before him, now walking backwards and gesturing him to follow, now turning face on to the path to avoid stumbling, they made their peculiar way towards the Palace. He'd never seen the place close up before and had only caught glimpses of it from the safe distance of the road or the river. The steward panting all the way, but keeping up a constant stream of pleasantries, they came by degree to the edge of a formal garden. Box hedges skirted a geometrical pattern of flower beds, where spring blossoms smiled at the sun, by now close to its zenith. At length they drew level with a sort of bower, where tall shrubs protected a rustic seat, which turned its back on the imposing splendour of the Palace, away across to the sparkling river.

"I have been told to ask you if you would kindly occupy this seat", wheezed the servant, taking a cloth from somewhere beneath his clothing and dusting the bench, gesturing deliberately but politely for Matthew to do his bidding. Matthew took some farthings from his purse and pressed them on the old retainer, who reluctantly accepted the gift before bowing and waving as he made his way, like a broken pack horse, up the path towards the Palace itself. Soon he was out of sight, leaving Matthew to smile at the performance and to wonder what awaited him in the quiet of such a lovely setting.

He didn't have long to consider, for though his gaze took in the broad sweep of the water, with the dense trees and rolling pastures that lay beyond, it seemed only minutes before the sound of rustling material caused him to turn sideways in his seat, back in the direction of Hampton Court itself. Swirling towards him, resplendent in a Dutch style gown of deep red, was the stately form of an attractive woman. He judged her to be some years younger than himself, clearly a gentlewoman. Her swept-back hair, under a tight fitting and stylish bonnet was as dark as the wings of a raven that had been walking around the borders but which took to wing at her approach.

She had dark eyes, large and wide, set in a fine complexion, lacking in artificial embellishment but lustrous and healthy. There was something altogether familiar about her looks, the roundness of the chin and a certain slight but attractive cast in the left eye. He couldn't help looking at her curiously as she advanced.

Then, in an instant, the years rolled back. He was standing close to another river, far away to the north, in a rich, green water meadow, down below the sloping grounds of Kirk Standing Church. He had been a much younger Matthew Prior then, full of vigour and deeply in love, locked in an embrace that should have spanned a life, but which was pared down to a few short months by the keen knife of a pestilence that ripped his young life asunder. And the woman who advanced towards him now, a half smile on that serene face, seemed to be none other than an older version of Celeste, whose caresses on that day by the River Wharfe had fixed in his heart the one, enduring love of his life.

He must have been mesmerised at the recollection, for even when she spoke, and in the instant that he instinctively rose at her arrival he could find no immediate way of responding to what must surely be a spectre.

"Well met Master Prior", she said, with a confidence that betrayed instantly that this was not his beloved Celeste, who had ever spoken in the merest whisper, with downcast, maidenly manners. The figure before him was tall of stature, as Celeste had been, but more confident.

She smiled kindly, but the look betrayed an impish enjoyment of the moment. "What? Stuck for a word Master Prior, that's not the man I remember at all?"

Her voice was cultured, but with the slightest trace of the North about it, and now the mists of time were burned off by the light of recollection. He caught the merest scent of the rosemary pinned to his doublet and smiled at the obvious pun. This could only be that same Rosemary, whom the Arden family had offered to him as compensation for his lost Celeste; the younger sister whose hand he had pointedly refused sixteen years ago.

"Mistress Arden," he managed to say, recovering himself and taking the proffered hand for a moment in his own. Even as he said the words he noticed the broad band of gold on her left hand and remembered that he had been informed of her marriage, years ago, to Lord Armscliffe, a man whose position and fortune had eclipsed that of her own family, and certainly Matthew's. "I'm sorry," he said, bowing slightly. "Lady Armscliffe."

She smiled and said,

"I'm glad you recognise me Matthew, it's been a long time. But you are correct. It isn't Mistress Arden these many years gone, for though you were not disposed to accept my hand, Lord John Armscliffe, from Farnsworth was not so tardy." She sighed, "and though he is now laid to rest for nearly a decade, it's his name I bear."

Matthew surveyed the still lovely face and across the chasm of the years wondered even now at his folly for not at least considering the proffered match. He searched his memory but try as he may he found it difficult to recollect anything more than scanty images - for both before and after their enforced parting, his eyes had been ever for Celeste alone. The younger sister had been only fourteen when Celeste had died. Although she had been ever the joker, hiding behind this bush or that wall to tease his moments of intimacy with Celeste, Rosemary had seemed an inconsequential slip of a girl and she had remained that way in his mind for the full span of the intervening years.

His new hat was in his left hand, for he had instinctively removed it when he rose to greet the lady.

"Oh!" she said, in a tone that could have betrayed either genuine concern, or recognition, or both, "your poor head."

"I have it still," he commented, and then added with a smile, "though as to its shape I must confess that it is now somewhat less regular than two days ago."

She motioned him to sit, and with a rustle settled herself by his side. She was truly beautiful this young woman - but of course, he assured himself, not so young after all, though the searing winds of time that had dulled even the image of Celeste in his mind had failed to make an impression on her sister, except in so far as the pale sun of autumn ripens an already beautiful damson. And so he gazed at her for a moment, and in the family likeness a thousand thoughts of moments that might have been fluttered around him in the warmth of the grown day.

"So Master Prior," she said after a moment. "How best can you be punished for your faithlessness, not only to your own family - but to mine too?"

"Madam," he responded instinctively "I do not know..."

"Do not know?" she cut him short, though with no discernible venom in her steady voice. "Do not know Master Prior? A man who runs away to London, ignoring the pleas of his own dear family: a cur who spurns the adoring glances of one who would have been ready with her heart." She moved a hand to her breast. "Fie on you sir!"

Matthew smiled. The Ardens might have been a family that rarely strayed into the South but they had a reputation of their own at home. For some generations it had been a boast of the Ardens that their daughters were as educated, forthright, and as much as society would allow as emancipated as their sons. It appeared that this generation was no different. And so, recovering from the shock of so unconventional an introduction, Matthew answered in kind.

"Madam you toy with me. You were but a child, and as for my family... Well, I dare say they manage all the better for my absence." He stoked up the fire of his own pretended indignation. "In any case," he went on, "I wrote to them last Christmas!"

The woman laughed, and though they had not cast eyes on each other for sixteen years, he knew instantly that they would be friends. They looked at each other and for the briefest moment, a mere second in which the aching, yawning absence of Celeste did not pervade what he knew had become a stony heart, he could not understand why Rosemary would have been so much less of a fortune than Celeste to a poor Squire's son.

They walked amongst the box hedges and beyond to a woodland path that skirted the formality of the ordered gardens. For nearly an hour they spoke only of the beautiful valley where they had both grown, of the little town of Otley and of the market by the church. They remembered childhood games on the sides of the steep hills and spoke of the sweet nature of Mistress Arden the elder. Rosemary told him of her father's near madness, of his grief and rage at the loss of such a beautiful flower, but that how, as time proves a healer to all, he collected himself and took solace in his other children, all thankfully brought to healthy adulthood.

Matthew was prevailed upon to offer a summary of his adventurous life, and of his days in France and Italy. She beseeched him to relate something, though only an acceptable part, of the life of a playwright in the great City of London. And in all this time Matthew made not one enquiry concerning this meeting, nor wondered for a moment why the younger sister of his dead sweetheart should come to be walking the grounds of one of the most important houses in the Land. For away from the noise, bustle, smell and squalor of the city, it seemed enough for the moment to be in this place, where the thrushes and blackbirds sought to sell the day to the highest bidder and all care floated down stream on the silver Thames.

All too soon a cloud, one of many billowing up from the south, obscured the sun and brought a chill to the air and a halt to the holiday. By now they were seated amongst the branches of a fallen oak and, with a short pause after the laughter engendered by another common remembrance, Rosemary grew more composed, and the playwright knew that he was about to learn the price of this unexpected interlude.

"Matthew", she began, all pretence at formality now impossible between two people who had grown on the same grass and whose uniqueness was all the more tangible in this 'other country' of the south, "I told you that I am a widow." He made to offer his condolences, but she pulled him up. "No Matthew. It's a long time gone and in any case, though he was as good to me as any husband thirty or more years my senior could have been, it was not a match made in heaven. But," she continued, stooping to pick a broad stalk of grass and dissecting it as she spoke, "his was a powerful family." For a moment she smiled again, "Not at all like ours".

There was a moment's silence but Matthew said nothing. "In truth", she offered, "And despite the fact that our renewed acquaintance is so recent, I must tell you Matthew that the match was none of my or my family's wish. Lord Armscliffe was close to the throne and though his lands bordered ours in Yorkshire he was at Court as much as in the North." She sighed deeply. "He saw me, and using the influence he had with the Queen, well – he had me." She looked into the middle distance. "None can gainsay the Queen of England."

He wanted to find some word, anything to lift the veil that had descended across her face like the dark cloud obscuring the sun above, but what was to be said?

"Well", she continued, sounding almost rueful, "Lord Armscliffe was powerful. Power brings responsibilities - and widow or not, I have mine." She fell silent again and even looked a little downcast. And now he felt it necessary to speak.

"Lady Armscliffe - Rosemary. If what you are trying to say has anything to do with the recent events in my own life, which is likely since I am here talking to you now at the behest of the most powerful courtier in the land, then tell me I pray." He looked at her for a moment, at the way the small breeze had forced wisps of dark hair to fall from their fastening, to frame her oval face and then he continued. "If there is any way that I can be of assistance to you, then you merely have to tell me. And perhaps on the way, as was suggested to me last evening, you might be able to answer one or two questions for me."

She looked at him with sincerity and touched the back of his hand where it lay in his lap.

"You always were a charmer Mattie, even as a boy." She removed her hand from his. "I have nothing but potential danger to offer you Matthew. In fact you have already been injured on my account." Suddenly she looked genuinely concerned. "Though I would not have wished it so."

A heron swooped low over a far tree, on its way to find its midday meal in the water beyond and Matthew's gaze followed it until it disappeared from view.

"Whatever has happened," he said in a low tone, "is done and finished." But not being a man of grave tendencies he was constrained to add, pointing to his new apparel, "In any case, I was paid well for the privilege of a new ordered skull and who knows but that it might have served to reorder my errant wits."

The moment of tension was gone and she smiled again.

"Come", she rose and beckoned him to follow. "We'll go to the house and eat, and while you avail yourself of the Queen's finest victuals, I'll tell you all I can of this strange business."

Chapter 5
Rosemary's Tale

Inside the great house all was deference and attention. Despite the quietness of the river mooring the place seemed to be in a frenzy of activity, with servants running this way and that, here carrying great piles of linen, and there taking prodigious quantities of meat and fruit to the kitchens. Rosemary had told Matthew that the Queen would be arriving at Hampton Court that very afternoon. As the pair passed through the broad entrance hall Matthew became aware of the smell of herbage, where servants were spreading fresh rushes and greenery at the edges of rooms. They had hardly set foot inside the house proper when a virtual bevy of serving women and liveried men bustled about them. One old woman in particular paid special attention to Rosemary. She had a face that resembled crumpled calico, with her hair secured beneath a starched white cap, under a dark wimple.

"Why Lady Armscliffe", she extolled. "How long have you been out there. It 'aint Summer yet my girl." This strange mixture of etiquette and scolding amused Matthew but he stifled a grin.

"Oh Agnes", his companion sighed. "I'm a full grown woman. How long will it be before you stop treating me like a child?"

The old woman smiled warmly and showed no sign of considering herself chided by her better. "Good Lord my dear," she exclaimed. "You'll always be a child to me."

They were ushered into a small banqueting hall, and Rosemary explained that old Agnes had been a servant of her late husband's family. Her position had always been that of a nurse for the children of the family. Rosemary said with a sigh "And since I have no children of my own, it seems as though I'm fated to put up with Agnes forever."

"At what age did you marry?" Matthew wanted to know, as a stout black chair of enormous ornamentation was lifted out from under a wide oak table for him to be seated.

His companion sighed again.

"I was just fifteen, so I suppose to Agnes, and to everyone else come to that, I was barely more than a child." She seated herself opposite and a series of servants arrived carrying all manner of cold dishes, which were set between the pair. Matthew wasn't in the least hungry, a sure sign that his curiosity was aroused. When the servants had departed, shutting the stout oak door behind them, Rosemary spoke.

"The reason you find me in this great palace Matthew," she began, "is because at the time my husband died we were residing here at his house in London."

"Then how long have you lived in the Capital," he wanted to know.

"Over thirteen years; a good proportion of the time you have been here."

He was surprised and it must have shown in his face.

Oh don't worry Master Prior, she assured him. "I would have contrived the means to seek you out and renew our acquaintance, for life was dull enough both before and after my husband passed on. But my life and my time were not my own."

"How so?"

"Because," she explained, "my husband, Sir John, was Master of the Queen's Horse. After his passing, of a fever brought on by a simple winter chill, Her Majesty was inclined to take me under her wing. I have to admit," she said, colouring a little, "it wasn't attention that I either sought or relished. But," she sighed. "Here I am still, a Lady in Waiting to the Queen of England."

"Then you don't live here, at Hampton Court?" Matthew wanted to know.

"I live where the Queen lives Matthew, and that can be almost anywhere that takes her royal fancy. Of course I still have my house in London, on the Strand. But I enjoy it rarely these days." She leaned towards him and said, conspiratorially, "As the Queen grows older it takes longer each day to prepare her to meet her subjects. She is not so agile as she once was, or as she would have those around her believe. There are a whole bevy of we Ladies in Waiting, and none of us short of a task to perform..." she sighed, "Day or night!."

"You don't care for your position then?" he asked.

There was the slightest trace of emotion in her voice as she replied. "I was born of the minor nobility and married into a position further up the tree of state. It is not my business to 'care for' anything Matthew. I am grown wise enough in the ways of the world to realise that our purpose here below is 'to serve'." The cloud across her visage lifted, almost as soon as it had arrived, and her face became like the sun again. "But for all it is not so bad a life Mattie. I have all I need, and more than might be expected by many a widow in this land."

She looked across at him.

"I tell you these things Matthew, not because I seek your sympathy, for in truth I can tell you that I am, or rather have been, tolerably content in the service of Her Majesty. But rather I rehearse this tale so you may understand why our paths have crossed again in this way. So do not pity my condition Master Prior," she scolded his expression, "for Queen or no, Elizabeth Tudor is grown old and will not live forever. I, on the other hand, have lived only thirty summers. Who knows", she added. "I may yet shift independently at last."

"So tell me then Lady Armscliffe...." He was uncomfortable with the title, but knew that a familiarity passed easily down stairs was not comfortable ascending them, and she was higher above him than the spire of St Pauls since her marriage into the Armscliffe clan. Her beetle-browed expression forced him to boldness. "So tell me Rosemary, why has my Lord Burghley sent me here to see you today?"

"Now therein lies a tale," she told him, lifting a heavy wine jug to pour him a drink. "But in principle the reason is simple enough. It is because I was born an Arden."

"An honour no doubt, but why should that fact be of interest to Lord Burghley." He inclined his head in deference, "For though I doubt not – nay, I know, that yours is an illustrious heritage, the Arden's are hardly dukes or earls."

"They are not," she admitted. "And thank the Lord for it. But we are blood tied to a family of much greater station. My mother, as you may remember, carried the maiden name of Stanley."

Matthew might have known once, but it would have meant little to him. Of course everyone knew that the Stanleys were amongst the greatest land owners in England. They held vast areas of Lancashire, as well as the Isle of Man and many manors in Derbyshire.

"The Stanleys?" he questioned.

"Yes Matthew, the Stanleys. My Mother, who yet lives at home in Wharfedale, is a cousin of John Stanley, the Earl of Derby."

Matthew lifted his flagon. "Then I revel in her good fortune," he toasted, "for the Earl of Derby is loved and respected across the length and breadth of the land."

She looked at him reproachfully.

"You know full well Master Prior that he is not. He's a blustering old fool. And since you are something of a student of English history," she continued; "you also know that he springs from a line of virtual warlords who have changed sides so many times across the last century that even monarchs were dizzied by the speed of their comings and goings."

Matthew wondered at her candour.

"Well", he said after a moment. "Our relatives are God given. I dare say He knows best."

They both laughed. And then she continued.

"But the Earl of Derby's eldest son, Ferdinando Stanley, who as you no doubt are aware carries the title Lord Strange, is at least partly the reason for our so long overdue reunion Matthew." She lifted her own flagon, "so we might at least manage a toast to him."

"Right willingly," he said, and then drank deeply. "And for more reasons that you know Rosemary. For Lord Strange may yet prove to be the making of me."

"Ah," she responded, a look of comprehension passing across her face. "You speak of Lord Strange's Men."

He nodded.

"And how might that illustrious group of players assist Master Prior?" She enquired, though the look on her face indicated that she already knew the answer. Her expression bespoke a knowledge of his hopes.

"Because Rosemary, I live in hope that they, and the other companies in London may one day be regularly performing my plays each afternoon at Southwark and perhaps elsewhere in the country when they are on tour."

"I trust it will be so," She assured him. "And it is opportune that Lord Strange's men figure in your thinking already Matthew because it is about them I want to speak. But first you must know the background. However," she told him in a cautionary tone, "You are now in the employment of Lord Burghley. He has bought your time, your loyalty and your discretion Matthew, so what I have to say to you must go no further. If it does," she continued, "it could easily threaten not only your own life, but mine also."

"I hope Madam," Matthew replied, "that I would be considered gallant enough to protect your secrets, merely on the strength of ensuring your safety." He smiled. "But in truth Rosemary it is only fair to confide to you that I am not entirely happy about meeting my maker yet either."

"Well then Matthew, here it is." She sat back in her chair. "My Lord Burghley is convinced that Lord Strange believes himself to be a natural successor to the crown of England."

"And is he?" Matthew wanted to know, not being versed or even particularly interested in genealogy.

"Possibly," she confirmed. "There may be better claims about, but Lord Strange 'is' the great grandson of Henry VII, Queen Elizabeth's grandfather.

Lord Strange, Ferdinando Stanley is blood related to the crown on both sides of his family. In any case, " she added. "there are so many claimants to a vacant English throne that at the end of the day it would probably come down to politics – and sheer force of arms if necessary."

"As far as I am aware, though she is not young the Queen is hale and hearty," observed Matthew, "so does all of this matter for the moment?"

Rosemary pushed back her chair and rose. Her dark hair, partly captured beneath a Flanders style bonnet, shone blue from the light that streamed in through the large casements. She strode to an adjoining table, where a number of documents were had been placed.

"These documents relate to statements taken from a Jesuit Priest, who was captured trying to enter England at Southampton some weeks ago. His name was George Sale, and he was a native of Lancashire. His orders were to travel to his own home region, and there to spread the Catholic faith."

Matthew knew that probably wouldn't be too difficult. The North West was a hotbed of Papist sentiment.

"This foolish man," Rosemary went on, "carried certain letters, which my Lord Burghley's experts have looked at carefully. One of the letters appears to be from a merchant by the name of Rich. But my Lord Burghley believes that it is actually from the pen of a secretary to the Pope, a man called Cardinal Ruchio. Its content is innocuous enough. It is ostensibly addressed to a baker, in Formby, Lancashire; a man by the name of John. The letter says that 'the sender' is aware that 'the old baker' is past his time. It tells John that if he will not quit of his own accord, this old baker must be replaced, for the good of the town. It goes on to suggest that when the moment is right Rich will supply the corn that John needs to bake his bread."

Matthew looked puzzled so Rosemary continued.

"If the letter came from the Pope's secretary, then undoubtedly it refers to the succession. You know of course Matthew that there is a price on the head of Her Majesty?"

He nodded. It was common knowledge. It was now nearly twenty years since the Vatican had excommunicated Queen Elizabeth. Some years later a remarkable Papal Bull had actually suggested that anyone assassinating Elizabeth would be well within their religious and legal rights to do so. Not only Protestants and Catholics alike in England had been outraged at the Pope's Bull but foreign princes, even those opposed to England, had openly distanced themselves from its content. But there were fanatics enough about and several attempts had been made on the Queen's life already.

"My Lord Burghley takes it that the 'old baker' is meant to be Queen Elizabeth, and that the mysterious John is someone the Vatican would wish to be her successor. It appears that the offer of corn either refers to money, which might be used to fund an insurrection, or perhaps even to a Catholic army."

"Ingenious," remarked Matthew. "But who is John?"

She looked back at him.

"A very interesting question Matthew, and one that is at present taxing Lord Burghley. The Priest in question would say nothing, even under the most extreme torture. But since the letter was intended for a region that falls under the sway of the Stanley family, the most likely recipient of such a letter would be Ferdinando Stanley – Lord Strange."

"Is this tenable?" Matthew wanted to know. "And even if it is, what has this to do with you or me?"

She left the papers and returned to the table at which she seated herself once more. She lay her slender hands in her lap.

"My involvement comes about partly because I am close to the Queen, but also because I am related to, and therefore, as Lord Burghley sees it, trusted by the Stanley family."

"And me?"

She drew in a breath.

"I am sorry to say Matthew that you are here at my

suggestion."

He could no pretend to understand what she meant and it must have shown on his face because she continued.

"Lord Strange is young and handsome – a veritable 'peerless knight', or at least he is in the estimation of the Queen. She will have nothing said against him, not even by Lord Burghley, whom she trusts more than any living individual. If Lord Strange is to be shown to be masterminding a plot to kill the Queen, and then to try and seize the throne, Lord Burghley will need irrefutable evidence to lay before Her Majesty. The Queen has Lord Strange at Court as much as possible, and he is her champion at the jousts. She is," assured Rosemary, "not to put too fine a point on it, in love with the man."

Matthew wasn't particularly surprised by this revelation. It was well rumoured that the only consideration that troubled the Queen was her advancing age. She was known to be inordinately vain, and perhaps felt that the attention of younger noblemen might somehow stave off the ravages of the passing years. At any rate she relished their company.

"Well even if this is all true," offered Matthew, "I hardly see how I can be of service. I've never even met Lord Strange."

She sighed again. "One of the few pieces of information the Queen's inquisitors were able to wring from the wretched George Sale was that on his way North he would be calling at London, and that specifically he would visit the Rose Theatre, in order to see a play entitled 'King Henry VI'."

"It's a good play," confirmed Matthew. "I don't blame him." And then there was a moment of realisation before he said. "The play is being performed by Lord Strange's Men."

"Quite," Rosemary answered.

"Perhaps there's a connection, " Matthew admitted. "But you must know Rosemary, that the company uses Lord Strange's name, with his permission of course, simply to avoid charges of vagrancy. Besides, I know the owner of the company personally. His name is James Burbage and I'd wager the twenty sovereigns I have from the royal purse that he's as loyal a subject as ever took breath in England. "

She smiled. "I don't doubt it Matthew, and neither does my Lord Burghley. But there are many other actors in the company, including, and most especially, the writer of the play George Sale was interested in viewing."

"You mean Will Shakespeare?"

"The very same," she confirmed. "And it might interest you to know Matthew that Will Shakespeare is also related to me – a second cousin."

Matthew looked confused.

"You seem to have a great many relatives Lady Armscliffe?"

"Indeed I have Matthew, and Will Shakespeare is one of them. His mother's maiden name was Arden and she came from a branch of the family not too far divorced from my own."

The writer thought for a few moments. "I'm afraid I don't fully comprehend the flow of this river Rosemary," he admitted.

"William Shakespeare comes from a small town in Warwickshire, a place called Stratford - upon - Avon. His father, John Shakespeare, who has held various positions in the town, and who was once the Mayor, was, in the past fined on several occasions for refusing to attend Church."

"Well that's common enough," interjected Matthew.

"Yes it is," Rosemary agreed, "But according to Lord

Burghley's intelligence John Shakespeare was as slippery as an eel. He always claimed to be penniless, yet at the same time he was also prosecuted on several occasions for dealing in wool."

"There's nothing peculiar in that either. Of course it's illegal to trade in wool without a licence but you know as well as I do Rosemary, that small-time wool selling goes on in all country areas." He smiled. "I would be amazed if your family and mine had not been involved in it back in Yorkshire."

She returned the smile.

"So would I Matthew, but the last time John Shakespeare was caught selling wool, the amount involved was over two hundred pounds."

Matthew let out a long, low whistle. This was a colossal amount of money.

"It follows," Rosemary continued, "that if I am related to Anne Shakespeare and also to Lord Strange, then there is also a family connection between the Shakespeare's and Lord Strange. So, let me ask you this Matthew; when did James' Burbage's company become 'Lord Strange's men?"

"Why, when the Earl of Leicester died a few years back, in 1588 it must have been. They went under his patronage before that."

"And are you aware that this took place at exactly the time Master William Shakespeare joined the company?" she wanted to know.

"I don't suppose I'd ever stopped to think about it. Are you suggesting that it was Will Shakespeare who prevailed upon Lord Strange to become patron to the company?"

"It seems very likely," she replied. "So Matthew, this is what we have." She stirred in her seat. "A Jesuit Priest is caught at Southampton, with a letter that could easily suggest that Ferdinando Stanley, Lord Strange, has designs on the throne of England, and that the Pope knows he has and approves of the situation. The Jesuit priest in question is prevailed upon to admit that there is some sort of link with Burbage's players, which just happen to be Lord Strange's Men. One of the actors in that company, and an up and coming writer into the bargain, is Will Shakespeare, who is also related to Lord Strange."

Matthew shrugged. "This is all very interesting Rosemary, but it hardly seems to prove anything substantial."

"Substantial proof is not Lord Burghley's pottage Matthew. He's quite prepared to see Jesuits and conspiracies under any bed. But think on this. A short time ago an uprising took place amongst the apprentices of London. It wasn't much but it took some quelling. The ringleaders said it had been inspired by some minor penalty the City authorities had meted out to one of their number. But none of them knew who the wronged man was, or even what his supposed transgression might have been."

Matthew had been present in the City when the riot took place. It was ugly, and some damage was done to property close to London Bridge. "Young men are hot headed Rosemary," he suggested. "Apprentices are always getting themselves into trouble."

"That is exactly what I said Matty, until my Lord Burghley offered me a few other morsels of information."

"Such as?" he queried.

"The fact that the assembly of apprentices began outside a theatre in Southwark. That theatre was the Rose. A fair proportion of the apprentices involved had been inside the Rose, watching a play. The play was 'Henry VI, part iii', the story of a weak, old and ineffectual monarch who is overthrown by a young, vigorous and handsome knight."

"Edward Plantagenet? " he suggested.

"The very same," she confirmed.

"And now you are going to tell me Rosemary that another piece of this puzzle locks into place when it is realised that the play in question was written by Will Shakespeare? But is this all credible, and what does it mean? A few dozen drunken apprentices are hardly likely to shake the kingdom to its foundation."

"I agree," she told him. "But it may go further than that Matthew – much further. And so we come to the way you can serve your Queen, and earn your sovereigns into the bargain."

"By doing what Rosemary?"

"By becoming a member of Lord Strange's Men and then by discovering if the company is sheltering a Jesuit conspiracy to assassinate the Queen and replace her with Ferdinando Stanley. And most especially by discovering whether Will Shakespeare is part of such a notion."

"Well," he said. "It's a good plan, except for the fact that James Burbage doesn't exactly relish my company. Apart from anything else I'm not the greatest actor in the world and to the best of my knowledge the company has all the men it needs at present."

"You won't be joining the company as an actor Matthew – well not simply an actor. You'll be a copyist, working with William Shakespeare. You might have to help out with the box at performances and run a few errands; and you could have to take on the odd small role; but you'll be in the company, and that's where Lord Burghley wants you to be."

"It sounds suspiciously as if you have already arranged this," Matthew observed, looking at Rosemary through slightly narrowed eyes.

"As a matter of fact I have Matthew. I made it my

business to pull a few strings with Master Burbage."

"Exactly How?"

"Well," she said. "Every theatre company is desirous of performing before the Queen – what could be better for prestige, or business? I simply told him that I knew your family well and that they feared you were starving to death in London. Burbage obviously already knew you and said of you....." She searched her mind. "What was it he said? Oh yes. He said you had a neat copying hand, that you could rhyme tolerably well and that in hid opinion some of your plays 'stank worse than the Fleet in August.'"

Matthew wasn't used to this sort of candour, at least not from a woman. He wondered if the Arden's may not have taken matters a little too far in the liberal education of their daughters.

"Well I suppose that was at least honest," he finally admitted.

"Yes," Rosemary replied. And on the promise of some performances, in a month or two at St James' Palace, before the Court, Master Burbage promised to give you a position with the company – most specifically working with Master William Shakespeare."

He eyed her suspiciously, though he could not avoid applauding both her enterprise and her organisational skills.

"And what exactly am I expected to do when I become one of Lord Strange's Men?" he wanted to know.

"Lord Burghley wants you to discover if there are any closet Catholics in the company, and specifically any Jesuit connections. He is certain from information he has obtained elsewhere that you will find something if you dig deep enough. And he is especially convinced that you will find Master Shakespeare to be the chief ingredient in this recipe."

He was silent for a while and Rosemary could see that there was something specific going through his mind. After a while she said

"I can see a question in your face Matthew?"

He stirred uncomfortably.

"I was merely wondering Rosemary. Why do you allow yourself to become involved in these matters? Surely such intrigue is not the expected lot of a Lady in Waiting?"

She smiled again, a perfect smile; a smile of such warmth and beauty that it eclipsed the bright sunshine streaming in from beyond the windows.

"The motto of my husband's family is 'Monarch and Country'. In any case Matthew, you have met Lord Burghley yourself. Would you have refused his proffered opportunity for you to serve the Queen?"

"I take your point," the writer admitted. "So," he said, looking into the deep hazel eyes and realising that it would be difficult to refuse this woman any service, whether the imposing figure of Lord Burghley was present in the scenario or not. "You had better acquaint me with the details of my new role Lady Armscliffe."

Chapter Six
All the Lord's Men

London Bridge was full of life on the following morning. It was the only route in and out of the city for people, carts, animals and even spies passing between the City and the south, particularly to the villages on the far bank that were rapidly becoming part of London itself. The bridge had become an extension of the vast array of buildings that proliferated north and south of the Thames. Indeed, the many shops, dwelling houses and even stables that were actually built onto the bridge were expensive and desirable properties. For one thing they were cleaner that the crowded allies and yards beyond the mighty river in both directions. Refuse of all kinds could be despatched into the water on the seaward side, and water for every domestic and commercial purpose drawn up from the landward parapet.

Matthew strolled south, taking in the vast array of wood gabled properties and the more robust ones of brick or stone. They seemed to fight for position, jostling to gain more space and a steadier hold to their foundations. So crowded did the bridge appear that it seemed to all that it was a wonder the edifice could survive and did not crumble with the weight and crash into the water below.

He had an appointment with James Burbage, who, he had been informed, could be found at this time at the Rose Theatre, in Southwark. Matthew had found the presence of Burbage at the Rose slightly surprising because the owners of this particular theatre had not formerly been on good terms with Lord Strange's Men.

Burbage had his own theatre, north of the river. However, such had been the success of his new selection of plays, particularly those penned by the up and coming Will Shakespeare that only the Rose was large enough amongst the City's theatres to accommodate the vast numbers of customers who were flocking in every afternoon of the week. The only days the actors could take their ease were for Sundays and religious holidays. Even bearing in mind its already grand size, the theatre had undergone extensive enlargement on the strength of the success being enjoyed by Burbage and his company. It was said that the Rose could accommodate over 2,000 patrons for any given performance.

Gaining the south bank of the river Matthew strolled through narrow alleys, mainly comprising a ramshackle assortment of houses, commercial properties, inns and 'stews' all of which benefited greatly from the new importance that Southwark was enjoying. Turning back on himself, to face the river once more, with the spires of London's many churches in the distance, Matthew was confronted by the spectacle of the Rose, circular and solid, rising above the squalid streets, it's oak timbered girth ship-like and reassuring.

Through the entrance, which was open at this hour for players, general workers on the fabric and visitors such as himself to pass through, Matthew stared up at the stage, which was roughly at eye-level for those standing in the cockpit below. To either side ranged the galleries, where richer patrons could purchase a seat for the duration of any given performance. There was a uniform price of one penny to enter the Rose for any play. Once inside, the production of a further penny would obtain a seat in the gallery, where another penny would enable the richest patrons to procure a cushion.

There was a workman in the gallery, repairing seats, but he seemed to be the only person present.

"Ahoy my good fellow", shouted Matthew. "Could you tell me if Master Burbage is present?"

"Aye," said the other, looking up from his work. "Last time I saw him he was in the tiring house."

Matthew climbed the steep steps onto the stage; the platform of dreams that he loved so well, and strode across to the curtained area to the rear. This was the tiring house, which in addition to being the dressing room for the actors, served as a properties store, office and a dozen other purposes. Matthew drew the heavy curtain to one side and saw Burbage, sitting on his own at an oak table. He was counting coins.

"Ah, Master Prior", he said, with half a smile. "I've been expecting you."

Matthew hesitated in the gap, unsure how to proceed. "Don't stand there man," Burbage told him. "Come away in."

Matthew strode in and seated himself where Burbage indicated, on a bench opposite his own stool. Matthew was no stranger to the bluff, often domineering and generally showy James Burbage. He was a man in his middle fifties, respected, if not universally liked, throughout the theatre community for his fair dealing, good business sense and his excellent nose for a new play. There was a time when Burbage had staged one or two of Matthew's creations, so the opinion he had passed to Rosemary regarding the writer's acumen as a playwright Matthew knew to be simply typical of Burbage's idiosyncratic sense of humour.

Burbage was a man of medium height, with a shock of dark brown hair that showed not the slightest trace of grey, despite his years. He had a critical gaze and a regal bearing, probably acquired from so many years playing leading roles. When Matthew was seated James Burbage said:

"Well Matthew. It seems you have some important people looking out for you?" He broke into a broader smile. "But none of us are the worse for that I'll be bound. So" he went on, dropping some coins on the table. "Here's the offer. Five pence each day," he laughed, "and all the hazel nuts you choose to eat. You'll copy for Master Shakespeare, and assist with the box each afternoon. You can also help with quick changes and do whatever is necessary to keep the tiring house tidy during and between performances. We might even expect you to do a small role now and again. And to top it off," he exclaimed. "Here's my hand to say we'll let bygones be bygones. No point in bearing a grudge eh Mattie?"

Matthew took the proffered hand. The cause of the quarrel between the two men had been Burbage's lack of sensitivity regarding the sensibilities of the writer. Matthew had written a play entitled 'Cupid and Venus'. It wasn't brilliant, but funny and clever, which even Burbage had admitted. Matthew had offered Burbage the play, back in the days when his company was still 'Lord Leicester's Men'. The playwright himself was occupied elsewhere and hadn't seen the finished piece until the afternoon of its opening. He had been staggered to realise that Burbage had completely rewritten large parts of the story, missing out two whole scenes from the third act and replacing them with something of his own concoction, which in Matthew's' comprehension took the play from the realms of the amusing into that of the farcical. He had not been happy and had told James Burbage so.

Things were not going well at the time for Lord Leicester's Men, or for James Burbage himself. Business was poor because plague was hovering on the edge of the city and many of the would-be patrons were out of town. A sharp exchange had followed during which Matthew had told Burbage he was a third-rate bit player, not fit to kill a calf at country fairs, and Burbage had informed Matthew that he could take his play and throw it in the nearest midden, adding that the day he produced another of Prior's plays would be the same day on which he could expect hell to freeze over.

Now it appeared all was forgiven and forgotten, as indeed it would have been by Matthew soon after the event, for although he had a temper that could blow up like a July storm, he was just as quick to calm down and regret his words.

"You can start today if you've a mind Mattie," James said. "There's parchment and quills on that table over there. And you'll find the parts I want copying out. It might he rather difficult for you to decipher some of them, they're in such a bad state, but do your best. We're reintroducing 'Father Ignatius", by Sam Hardcraft. We're going to do it on days we know will be quiet in any case but it might earn a few pence." He laughed. "And there's another bonus. We won't have to pay the author because, as you know, he's been dead these four years gone.

Sam Hardcraft had been a thoroughly decent schoolmaster from Oxfordshire, who had achieved some small success with his writing in the provinces and who had eventually moved himself and his family to London, the better to exploit his talent. Like so many writers he had not fared particularly well and as was the case with more than a few people who moved to London from the country his health had been affected by the heavy, noxious air of the crowded city streets. After a very moderate success Sam had suddenly died of unknown causes one winter's day, whilst bringing home fuel for the family fire. His wife and children still lived in Holborn and were often in want. Now his plays were being staged again and his loved ones would receive not a crust from the performance of Hardcraft's work. It was hard, but everyone knew that this was the way life was.

"Will should be here soon. Have you met him yet Mattie?" Burbidge asked. "He's quite a playwright, and a pretty good actor to boot?"

"Oh yes, I've seen him on the stage on several occasions Matthew confirmed, but I haven't met him. I have no idea why not. Just one of those things I suppose."

A few minutes later Burbage announced that he had business north of the river and that he could be expected back about an hour before the performance. "There's no rehearsals today," he'd told Matthew. "We're doing Henry VI part i tonight, and the company know it so well I've told them not to come in until they're due for the performance."

Matthew was already working and acknowledged Burbage's departure, but as soon as James had left the copyist looked around for some document that might tell him who was working with the company at present. He was in luck, for hanging on the wall was a Plot, a document to remind the actors of the running order of the play they were to be performing that afternoon. There was a long list of names and it looked as though most if not all the actors in the company were taking part in the production.

Some of the players were famous already. Burbage's own name was at the top of the list and, with his experience and standing he was playing a major role. The title 'Mr' denoted those players who were senior in the company. Amongst these were George Bryan, Thomas Pope, Richard Cowley and Anthony Roper. Matthew had known all these men, almost from the time had been living and working in London. He would have been surprised indeed if any of them had allowed themselves to become involved in any sort of political or religious plot. Two of them, Bryan and Cowley, were married men with children, and although actors, were staunch churchmen of the established Protestant faith. Thomas Pope, despite his surname, almost certainly had no Popish leanings. He was steady and quiet off stage, one of the mildest and least controversial characters Matthew had ever known and a good personal friend. Anthony Roper was a strange individual, close, often dark and brooding, a man with whom Matthew had never been able to establish a rapport. Matthew had literally no idea of the nature of this man's beliefs.

Further down the list came John Duke, an actor Matthew also knew little about, and then Richard Tarlton, who in addition to being one of the best comedy actors on the London stage, was also something of a playwright, with several popular comedies to his name. Matthew knew him well and often saw him in this or that drinking house. 'Rich' as he was generally known, was charitable, jovial and naturally funny. Next came Robert Pallant, a man who had been notorious as a brawler when young, but who was now calmer and more settled. A little further on was John Sinclair, who had worked his way up from playing women's parts as a young man, to taking larger roles. He was of Scottish extract; a good 'stock' actor and another man of seeming integrity.

Only nearer the bottom of the parchment did Matthew find himself in totally uncharted waters. He had heard of Nicholas Tooley, one of the best young actors in the business and famed for his portrayal of female roles. With the lack of 'Mr' in front of their names the remaining players were probably also young, hence not known to Matthew. Companies needed young men of some talent to play the young women's roles, but the majority of them did not endure to develop into seasoned professionals and so fell by the wayside. Matthew made a mental note of the names Alexander Cooks, Robert Gough and Tom Campion. The only remaining actor on the list was William Shakespeare himself, whose name also appeared as author of the play.

Matthew was standing and considering the list when a man of medium height, with shoulder length sandy hair, shorter on top and beginning to recede, walked into the tiring house. The two writers faced each other for a moment; the one a virtual nonentity from Yorkshire, the other already a time-served playwright and a well established actor from Warwickshire. This surely was Matthew's most likely candidate for any plot against the Queen. The man's plays were pithy, adroit, often political and, to Matthew's practised eye, appeared to contain dozens of references that could be interpreted in a number of different ways. This was William Shakespeare.

Before he had left Hampton Court on the previous day Rosemary had acquainted Matthew with all she knew of her second-cousin, whom she had personally met on only three or four occasions, two of which had been within the last month. By reputation he was a self-made man of some genius. Indeed he had risen like a star in the last two years. However, regarding his life between the ages of eighteen and twenty-seven virtually nothing was known, nor was the man inclined to illuminate any interested party.

Will Shakespeare had been educated in a grammar school in his own home town of Stratford upon Avon, and at a time when his father was still a man of some standing in the community. By all accounts he had done well enough, though any pretension he may have had for furthering his education at university were dashed for two reasons. Firstly, by the time Will had finished at the grammar school, where he had apparently been an usher and so had remained for a year beyond the normal span, his father was beginning to fall foul of the local authorities and appeared to have suffered financial setbacks. Whether this situation was genuine – or feigned, Rosemary could not be certain. Local authorities chasing those who were unwilling to attend the established church at least once a month would naturally tend to go for those people who quite clearly had money and who could therefore afford the hefty fine that would be levied. Wise Catholics found somse way of hiding their wealth and if successful might cause local law enforcement officers to pass them by as not worthy of official attention.

In addition to his father's falling standing in the community, Will Shakespeare had married at the tender age of eighteen years. It seemed that he had dallied with the affections of an older woman, Anne Hathaway, herself a person of some gentility from a village close to Stratford. Anne had become pregnant and William had done the right thing by her.

It was possible that these facts had effectively put paid to any thoughts he may have had of a more protracted education but they had not kept him in Stratford. For reasons which seemed to be clouded by some uncertainty Shakespeare had disappeared from his home town for long periods, though he did return once or twice a year. Doubtless his skill on the stage indicated that he had served his time in the profession. North Wales or Chester had cropped up as possible resorts in Lord Burghley's investigation but there was no confirmation of what company Shakespeare had joined – if any. The whole situation was very strange and it wasn't until four years previously, at the age of twenty-five, that Will Shakespeare had arrived in London. He had quickly secured a place in Burbage's company, which at the time was seeking a new patron. Within days of Will Shakespeare joining the players they became known as Lord Strange's Men. It seemed likely that Will had somehow persuaded Lord Strange to act as new patron for the company, but of his actual association with the Stanley heir nothing was known. Rosemary had told Matthew that on two different occasions she had broached the subject of the 'missing years' with Shakespeare. The nearest she could come to pinning him down was when he told her he had spent the intervening years participating in various business interests that had served to support himself, his wife and his now growing family.

It was clear that Will knew how to perform on stage and almost from the moment he had joined the renamed company he had also begun to write. His earliest attempts, Titus Andronicus, and Romeo and Juliet had been popular from the moment they were first staged. Now, with the three histories relating to Henry VI also under his belt, and a further one relating to the earlier King Richard II, any new production bearing Shakespeare's name could be guaranteed to have a steady stream of patrons walking south from the City to whichever theatre Lord Strange's Men were playing at the time.

Shakespeare was an enigma. The accusations of Popery that had been levelled at his father had to be born in mind, together with his apparent links with the Stanleys, a family which, in itself was suspected of having remained true to the old faith. These facts, together with the puzzle of the man's unwillingness to talk about his 'silent' years, made it certain that Will

Shakespeare was the individual Matthew would have to watch most closely if he was going to discover any genuine plot to assassinate the Queen and to restore the Catholic faith to the crown and the country.

Now the two men looked at each other. Matthew took in a determined but kind looking face, with large thoughtful blue eyes and a short, neat ginger beard. Will Shakespeare was on the slim side of average and not tall. He wore dark, respectable clothes and though he was smart, there was nothing in the least pretentious about his looks or his bearing.

"Good day," said the Yorkshireman. "My name is Matthew Prior. You need no introduction for I have seen you act on several occasions. You, I am certain, are Master William Shakespeare."

Will smiled kindly.

"And I have seen you act too Master Prior," he said, his voice low and measured and carrying the faintest trace of a Warwickshire dialect. "Not only that but I have seen and read some of your plays. When James told me that you were joining the company I did not know if I should feel sorry that a man of some talent should be forced to earn a crust as a copyist, or be all the more grateful that I would have the company of someone of obvious wit and cleverness."

It was a pretty speech and yet the man appeared, from the first, to be totally sincere. Will Shakespeare's reputation preceded him and he was famous for his friendliness and fair dealing. From the very second that the two men shook hands warmly it would have been difficult for Matthew to feel that he was in the presence of a person who would be capable of plotting to murder anyone. However, Matthew had lived enough and suffered sufficiently from youthful naivety to know that first impressions could be very deceptive. He had a task to perform, and he would undertake it to the best of his ability.

"Why thank you Master Shakespeare," Matthew responded, though I think you do my work and my talents more service than is due to either."

"Not at all," Shakespeare replied. "But no 'masters' here please. My friends call me 'Will' and I 'will' be very happy to count you amongst them if I may be so bold Matthew?"

It was a fine start. Soon Shakespeare was telling Matthew that now the company had secured performances for the Court, only a few weeks hence, he was desirous of preparing a new play. It would follow on from the third part of Henry VI and would be a tragedy, the story of usurper Yorkist king, Richard III. Matthew knew himself that the writing of a new, full length, play was no mean undertaking and Will explained that his way of working was to produce a new work in stages, so that parts could be copied and handed to the actors as soon as possible. That way the players had more time to learn the lines. Obviously this would mean copying the various parts a number of times and it was for this task that he would be grateful to have a neat, observant and accurate assistant.

"I believe you are a friend of my cousin, Lady Rosemary Armscliffe?" Will asked, as he unloaded parchment and quills from the leather satchel he had carried with him into the tiring house."

"I think the term 'friend' would be rather more than my present station allows or deserves, considering her position at Court," Matthew confessed. "Though it is true that our families were and are close, both in terms of geographical location and mutual respect."

"Yes," came the reply. "We must all be careful regarding our stations. But all the same the lady speaks well of you Matthew and she vouchsafed to me that had you not been possessed of a curiosity to see the world and a determination to suffer the vicissitudes that attend the life of a writer, you may even have taken her to wife?"

Perhaps Matthew's eyes dropped, for Rosemary had been much on his mind since he had parted company with her at the river gate of Hampton Court Palace. In truth he could not avoid somewhat regretting his rash behaviour after the death of his dear Celeste.

"She is too kind Will, but that was many years ago, and I doubt not that she got a better deal when she married Lord Armscliffe, for though she is now sadly a widow, she tells me that the man treated her tolerably well." He smiled, "And left her well provided for, which is more than I doubt I could ever have done. In short," he admitted, "I fear I would have made a poor husband."

"Be that as it may," Shakespeare said. "She has a significant respect for you, and since I have a great regard for her, you will forgive me for counting you as a friend."

Matthew made it plain that he found no difficulty in such a proposal. They talked for a few minutes, by which time other actors from the company were beginning to arrive, in order to prepare themselves for the forthcoming afternoon's performance. The majority of the older players Matthew greeted cordially. One or two of them, Richard Tarlton and Thomas Pope especially, were surprised but pleased to see him associated with the company. Only Anthony Roper ignored his proffered hand, but Matthew merely assumed this was because Roper was preoccupied rather than rude. Perhaps he was nervous about the forthcoming performance?

Matthew had previously met young Nick Tooley. He was a precocious young man of about seventeen years, an ex-chorister who had possessed such a natural bearing when playing young female roles on stage that it had been extremely hard to view him as anything else. Nick was not especially likeable and Matthew would soon find him to be 'difficult' and possessed of a sense of his own importance that could be annoying in the extreme. Tooley was coming to the end of his career as far as young female parts were concerned and was beginning to develop a more robust and masculine figure. Tom Campion, a boy who was perhaps a year younger than Tooley, was a different kettle of fish altogether. He was what older actors tended to call 'a pretty boy'. He had dark, flowing locks and a slim, androgynous figure. He was certainly 'pretty', rather than handsome, with fine features. His limpid dark eyes carried lashes so long that that even the fairest milking cow would have given a ransom to possess them.

James Burbage soon returned and as the actors began to don their costumes and to prepare for the performance Matthew assisted where he could but kept a careful eye on the company as a whole. This wasn't difficult since he was an inveterate people watcher in any case. One or two facts soon became obvious.

All the actors of the company, including Burbage himself, showed a distinct 'deference' in their dealings with Shakespeare. Despite his affability the younger members of the cast always called him 'Master William', or 'Master Shakespeare'. Although Shakespeare didn't own any part of the company as far as Matthew was aware, he was obviously held in a degree of awe by the youngsters and was feted, even by the time-served veterans.

The young actor, Tom Campion, was playing the part of Joan of Arc in the performance. His costume was elaborate and difficult to manage, so Matthew stepped forward to help in the tying of laces and cords. Once or twice he looked over to where Anthony Roper was fastening his doublet or donning his boots. The older man stared at young Tom Campion with such a look of disdain that Matthew wondered at it. Perhaps it was natural, Matthew told himself. The boy actors like all youngsters, tended to be pranksters and were constantly up to mischief. It was possible that Tom Campion had angered Roper in some way. But the dislike didn't appear to pass in both directions, since the lad was forever smiling at Anthony Roper, complimenting him on one thing or another, or asking after the health of his family.

Matthew noticed all of this. He was watching carefully, for any sign that might lead him to forming conclusions about Lord Strange's Men so nothing was beneath his scrutiny. Not that he was particularly surprised. He'd been associated with the theatre for long enough to appreciate that all manner of relationships developed between the actors, many of whom were temperamental and sometimes even wholly unpredictable by nature. .

The patrons were starting to arrive and Matthew was despatched to the theatre entrance, to help with the box. The audience was composed of both men and women, though women would never have come to a theatre alone, for fear of being taken as prostitutes. The cross-section of society that passed through into the cockpit and galleries of London's theatres was fascinating and varied. Over the last decade interest in drama had proliferated. As a result a new breed of playwright, like Will Shakespeare, was beginning to emerge. These writers had the skill to entertain the rank and file, most of whom were illiterate and knew no Latin or Greek. But at the same time there were elements to the new plays that did appeal to the more educated audience members, mostly those seated in the galleries.

Within a short space of time the Rose became crowded with journeymen, artisans, gentleman and aristocrats. Like all men of business James Burbage wished to derive as much cash from each production as possible so he had employees selling hazel nuts and oranges, others providing drinks of many different sorts and even one employee selling printed sheets for the more literate amongst the audience, carrying a cast list and detailing background, as well as the settings of the various scenes. The place was a veritable hive of activity. The gaudy colours of some of the more flamboyant theatre goers contrasted sharply with the dull greys and blacks that represented more formal Elizabethan apparel. Flags and bunting fluttered gaily around the edges of the galleries and a small group of musicians on the stage entertained the audience as they talked and chattered, ahead of the performance.

Two or three minutes before the commencement of the play, Matthew returned to the tiring house, where all was activity of a different sort. Last minute adjustments were made to costumes and short spats broke out between various cast members – which Matthew was aware was an integral part of the business of theatre. Other players were seated quietly in corners, whilst the ever business-like Burbage who had seen the whole thing so many times was ignoring the hubbub and quietly attending to his accounts at the central table.

Meanwhile Will Shakespeare had seated himself at another table. He had a lesser part in the play but he was already in costume. Matthew could see that he was writing furiously. Periodically he would lift his gaze from the parchment, stare blankly ahead of himself for a few moments and then pick up the quill and begin again. Without any prompting he would rise from his seat, pass through the curtain onto the stage and deliver his lines, before returning to his writing as if no interruption had taken place.

Matthew looked across at the first sheet Will had written. It carried the title 'The Tragedie of King Richard III'. Whenever Shakespeare returned to his seat he wrote at a phenomenal speed, rarely corrected anything and he even joined in snippets of conversation that happened to catch his attention. No distraction seemed to shake his concentration, so that it appeared as if there were two distinctly different Will Shakespeares' – one who went about the everyday business of being a colleague and an actor and another who was totally and irrevocably focussed on the new dramatic production.

Matthew observed Shakespeare's way of working with increasing incredulity and then shrugged, assuming that the man must be merely copying down his ideas – the skeleton of a play that he would have to actually pen later, when circumstances were more conducive to concentration. And then, whilst Will was once again on stage and the tiring room was quiet, Matthew picked up the first sheet of the four or five that already existed and read.

"Now is the winter of our discontent
Made glorious summer by this son of York:
And all the clouds that lour'd upon our house
In the deep bosom of the ocean buried……..

It went on, line after line, a soliloquy of stunning perfection, profound sentiment and undoubted wit.

Transfixed he read on sheet after sheet, and didn't notice that Will had returned to the tiring house and was standing, smiling at his shoulder. He felt the breath of the other man on his collar and turned to look into those large eyes. The critics were correct, he decided. This man was an undoubted genius – but was he also a Jesuit spy and a would-be regicide? Matthew smiled back and replaced the parchments on the table.

Chapter Seven
The Watching Game

As the play drew to a close the actors assembled in the tiring house. The Rose had enjoyed another virtually full house and James Burbage was clearly in a jovial frame of mind as he totalled up the takings and assessed what each actor's share would be. Each participant in the play was paid a proportion of the proceeds from the audience in the pit, two shares for every time-served performer and one for the boys. Proceeds from the galleries were split between James Burbage and his silent, non-acting partners, and also went to pay for the hire of the theatre.

When the last members of the audience had left and the theatre was emptied of patrons the curtain to the tiring house was opened. Burbage gathered the various vendors around him and took the money they had collected, paying them the previously arranged share before they left. But one young woman, who had been selling hazelnuts hung back once she'd had her due. Matthew didn't recognise her. She was an earnest girl, probably no more than about fifteen or sixteen years, but well developed for her age and neater than most of her vending colleagues. She was dark in complexion with large eyes; pretty enough except for the fact that she bore a troubled look and tended to gaze about in a haunted sort of manner. When the actors were back in their everyday attire and had been paid the girl moved towards Anthony Roper.

"Come father", she said, taking him by the arm. "It's time for us to go home."

Matthew knew that Anthony Roper was a widower and that he did have a child, a girl by the name of Jane, though he had not met her previously. This must surely be her. Matthew was busying himself putting away costumes and the pair apparently did not realise that he was eavesdropping on their conversation.

"In a few moments my dear," Anthony Roper said, looking at the girl affectionately and giving her hand a squeeze, "but first I must have words with Master Campion."

The girl scowled and began to protest but Roper had already signalled to Tom Campion, who walked over to where they were standing.

"Hello Jane," he said, smiling sweetly at her. "How pretty you look this evening."

It was a simple and friendly enough greeting but it precipitated an odd response from Anthony Roper. Jane smiled at the young man, somewhat awkwardly though almost warmly Matthew thought, but the moment she did so her father snapped.

"Jane, go and wait for me in the cockpit. I needs must have words with Master Campion."

"But Father!" she said pleadingly.

He looked about to become angry but Tom Campion took the heat out of the situation by saying quietly.

"It would be best to do as your Father bids Jane."

With a look of resignation the young woman turned away.

The two men moved to the back of the tiring house, out of earshot of anyone. Campion looked diminutive in stature when compared with the larger and generally more robust Anthony Roper. It was impossible for Matthew to hear their words, though it was obvious that what was passing between them certainly was not friendly banter. Anthony Roper was glowering down at the smaller, young man, who in turn seemed to be

ALAN BUTLER

gesticulating towards Jane, who was now talking at the opposite side of the stage to some of the other theatre staff.

It was self evident from their gestures that harsh words were being exchanged, certainly from Anthony Roper's direction, though what with the noise and clatter on all sides it was impossible to ascertain what was being said. Roper was shaking his head vigorously as Tom Campion continued to gesticulate towards the girl. After some moments Roper turned, red faced and obviously furious and strode off to join his daughter. In a moment they were across the cockpit and out into the early evening of Southwark.

Matthew shrugged and turned his attention to the main focus of his interest – Will Shakespeare. He too had donned his everyday clothes and was once again sitting at his table, oblivious to the clamour taking place on all sides and busy scratching more words hurriedly onto the parchment.

Matthew interrupted the busy scribe saying. "Do you require me any further today Will?"

Shakespeare looked up from his work, though showed not the slightest trace of annoyance at being disturbed.

"No Matthew", he replied. "By tomorrow I should have enough for you to begin copying the parts and then we can hand them to the players I have in mind for each character. I will remain here and work a while, though in an hour or so I must be on my way as I have business elsewhere." Returning his gaze to the parchment Will Shakespeare once again began to write almost frantically, without any apparent pause to consider the speeches that flowed from the quill as if the speeches were already dissolved in the very ink itself.

Taking his leave of Burbage Matthew strolled out of the entrance of the Rose theatre and into the noise and clamour of the early Southwark evening. All manner of people came and went in the approaching gloom of the evening and already lanterns and braziers burned on the corners of the crowded streets and alleys. Almost immediately beyond the entrance to the theatre Matthew was approached by a young woman with whom he was not familiar.

"You look a handsome gentleman," she told him, in a voice that betrayed her East Anglian origins. "If you have a couple of pennies in your purse I could show you a performance better than anything you would see in there." She gestured towards the theatre.

Being accosted by prostitutes was almost a regular occurrence in the streets south of the river. Matthew bore them no ill will; just like himself they had their living to earn. The young woman in question was presentable enough, and probably had not been in the Capital for long. She appeared healthy and strong, which was more than could be said for many of the wretched young creatures who had served the denizens of the city for a protracted period. All the same, and despite the money in his purse, Matthew declined the offer gracefully. The girls shrugged and moved off to find a more likely target for her wares.

A little further on, though still within sight of the only entrance to the Rose, was an open piece of ground, formerly the site of a warehouse that had burned down some year or two previously. The space afforded appeared like a clearing in a dense forest as the dwellings of the rapidly swelling Southwark pushed in from all sides. But the site of the warehouse had been put to good use because upon it, on most afternoons and evenings, a multitude of market traders gathered to service the daily needs of those living in the houses, inns, tenements and stews of the riverside.

Matthew decided to linger amongst the assembled stalls, waiting for Will Shakespeare to leave the theatre. He had determined to follow the playwright, who, by his own admission, had business of some sort that evening. Shakespeare was the main focus of Lord Burghley's interest and Rosemary had told Matthew that it had been difficult, if not impossible, to gain any evidence regarding the man. Burghley's spies knew that Will Shakespeare often kept to his own lodgings in Hog Lane, Shoreditch but they had been singularly unsuccessful in establishing his whereabouts when he was not either at home, or at any of the venues Lord Strange's men played. If Matthew was to discover the existence, if any, of a Jesuit plot within the ranks of Lord Strange's Men, Shakespeare's movements when away from the theatre might yield a clue.

Fatted geese looked mournfully out of wooden cages at Matthew's feet and ragged urchins ran this way and that, some on lawful business for the stallholders, others no doubt up to some mischief or other, for Southwark was a relatively lawless place, particularly after dark. Fruit and vegetables brought to London by boat from across the Channel adorned some stalls, whilst others sported ribbons and brocades. One enterprising soul had set up a brazier, with a huge iron pot suspended from a tripod above it. From this came the unmistakable aroma of mutton broth. In the relative warmth of the evening old men sat at trestle tables by the wall of an inn. The building, though relatively new, seemed to lean at a precarious angle above the makeshift market place and a painted harlot at a first floor casement hurled a selection of invitations and insults at the passers-by.

Matthew moved amongst the stalls, investigating an assortment of used clothes, no doubt formerly the property of plague victims from the previous autumn, when the pestilence had once again visited the poorer parts of London.

Almost absently Matthew brushed aside a young lad who was hanging too close to his purse and smiled kindly but dismissively at two more ladies of the night who were hopeful of early custom. He knew both the City and Southwark well. Within both lay the meat and drink of his inventiveness and though a threatening and even dangerous place to those who arrived daily from the country, London and its environs represented little threat to a time-served city dweller such as he had become. The place had grown to one and a half times its former size in the time he had lived there and Southwark in particular had tripled its dimensions becoming in recent years, the fleshpot for those living north of the river, where puritan zeal reigned supreme and the nights were very much quieter, but not a portion as interesting.

Purchasing a tankard of ale from the inn Matthew seated himself behind a knot of noisy revellers, yet still within view of the Rose, and he contentedly downed the rough brew in solid mouthfuls until he saw the slightly diminutive figure of Will Shakespeare pass through the entrance.

Will walked up through the maze of alleys until he came to the river and then strode northwards across London Bridge, towards the City. Matthew followed at a respectable distance. Will's lodgings, in Shoreditch, lay about a mile hence, to the north, and that indeed was the direction that the playwright took. Matthew kept to the shadows but was in little fear of being detected since Shakespeare kept a brisk pace and never looked back. On they went, up Grace Street, past Matthew's own lodgings in the little yard off Eastcheap. This part of London was especially crowded in recent years.

Former gardens and burgage plots had given way to new buildings, commercial and domestic and no organised street plan was discernible away from the main thoroughfares that had existed since time out of hand.

The spire of St Clements loomed over the buildings to the left, then St Edmund the King and St Michael's, as they crossed the Leadengate Street and on into Bishopsgate. Gradually the hotchpotch of buildings gave way to more graceful dwelling houses, for the area around St Helen's, Bishopsgate, was the preferred domicile of some of London's most successful businesspeople. Matthew wondered if Will would keep his step north, for past the North Folgate, Bishopsgate gave way to the former village of Shoreditch, now absorbed into the growing London, where Will Shakespeare had his lodgings.

Night was now drawing in, though away to the west across the crowded rooftops the sun, reluctant to retire, painted a vivid red pallet, edging a few menacing grey clouds with gold. In the shadow of the old church of St Helen's, Bishopsgate, Shakespeare eased his pace. Just beyond the churchyard lay four or five large dwelling houses, all with extensive plots of land to their front. It was by one of these, a relatively new looking building, large, four-square and grand, that Will brought himself to a halt. Matthew hung back, dodging into the lichgate of the church, where only a week or two before he had stood as the coffin of a friend, James Piper had paused, before the pall bearers bore it solemnly on, into the body of the Church.

'In the midst of life we are in death'. The words echoed through Matthew's mind and he shuddered slightly. But someone was approaching from behind. A tall man in a dark cloak. He bore himself well and was dressed like a gentleman, his fine cloak pulled about him as the chill of the evening penetrated the streets; creeping up from the river like cold fingers and promising an air frost once the sun was finally abed. The man would not see Matthew, who withdrew further into the shadows, standing between the church gate and the large stone monument of some local family. Daylight made one last effort to exert its influence as a slight breeze, blowing from the west lifted the clouds momentarily free from the waning glow, illuminating the face of the man. He sported a stylish beard. If not handsome the individual was striking and everything about his bearing made him a gentleman for certain.

A few steps further on Will Shakespeare was standing, watching the approaching man with obvious recognition. The distance between Matthew and the two was great enough to obscure any words that passed between them but he could clearly see the firm handshake that took place and thought he heard the word 'brother', filter down the dusty lane. The pair were joined by a third man, who was walking down from the direction of Shoreditch and another strolled out from the maze of streets to the left, which led back into the old City itself. It was impossible to determine anything about these individuals, save for the fact that one was a great deal taller than the other, and that both seemed well dressed and self-assured. Mutual greetings and handshakes took place and then the four walked between the tall pillars that guarded the gate of a large house.

Matthew quitted his shelter and walked back through the lichgate and out into Bishopsgate. The small huddle of men disappeared into the shadows between the large gateposts of the house and were gone. Matthew made a note of the location. The house was the first dwelling beyond the churchyard, in a northerly direction. It was larger than any of its companions, with a sort of ornamental tower at each of its four corners. The arms of the family was set proudly in gilded metal about the gate posts – an insect, which looked like a grasshopper.

He shivered a little as the sun finally sank irrevocably into the west and the city settled into the night. There seemed little point in staying and he decided to walk back towards London Bridge. A gnawing in his stomach reminded him that it was some hours since he had last eaten, and the warm glow of the crowded inn beckoned. Looking once again at the fine house he turned and soon quickened his pace, retracing his steps back in the direction of the river and the White Goose, where the mutton pasties were delicious and John Acres might provide some information.

The diminutive form, sitting at one of the tables just inside the door of the inn dismissed the giggling young woman who was sitting on his knee with a playful tap on the rump and then rose slightly as Matthew entered.

"Well met Mattie," John said jovially. "You seem jaunty enough this evening. I would hazard that nobody else has tried to reorder your wits since we last met?"

Matthew confirmed that he was in good health and that the wound on his skull appeared to be healing rapidly enough.

"So," said John, "sit you down Master Prior and tell me how goes the life of a government agent." He realised what he'd said, and looked around, apologetically and a little furtively, but nobody was in earshot, or if they were showed no interest.

The taller man sank into the proffered chair and ordered food and drink. He remembered, with a sudden flash, that he was, for now at least, a man of means. He called the girl back and changed his order from one of ale to that of the deep, blood red French wine that he relished so much. The wine came quickly, together with Matthew's own drinking vessel, which resided at the inn – a battered pewter tankard, a gift from Walter, the least puritanical of his elder brothers, when the man had checked up on the would-be writer soon after he had settled in London.

Matthew gulped down the liquid greedily. It hit his slightly chilled stomach and since he had an empty stomach it almost immediately caused him to flush. He thought of the hot vineyards of central France, of distant vistas and picturesque villages and wondered, just for a moment, why he had stayed so long from his travels, in this frosty city.

John was smiling.

"Well," he said. "I've been waiting with baited breath to hear what has been happening to you since we last met. Life's dull at present." He shrugged. "At least it has been for me."

Matthew returned the smile. "I'm sorry for that John, but I'll try to lift your flagging spirits, though I warn you, I'm in need of your knowledge again."

It didn't take long for Matthew to rehearse the events of the previous days. He told John about Rosemary, and his visit to Hampton Court – of his new position as copyist to Lord Strange's Men and of the supposed Jesuit plot he had been set to uncover.

"And what of Master Thrace the Vintner?" John wanted to know. "Has anyone been apprehended for his murder?"

Matthew frowned.

"Alas no John. And I have to admit that it's a matter I've barely addressed. He seems to have been a strange man right enough; close and brooding if his neighbours are to be believed. His shop looked prosperous enough, but from what I was told he was rarely there.

John thought for a moment.

"I've made what enquiries I could," he told Matthew, "though I haven't gleaned much more about him than you seem to know yourself. He was a Catholic right enough, though how he managed to survive without losing his fortune and his business in fines might be something of a puzzle." He drew closer to Matthew. "But I can tell you one thing about Thrace that might be worth a drop of that wine. He was a friend of Christopher Marlowe."

This was slightly surprising news. Marlowe was one of the most talented poets and playwrights in the Capital. Matthew could understand how a relationship might have existed between Marlowe and Thrace, though only at a professional level, for Christopher Marlowe was a notorious drinker – and a dangerous man when in his cups. But all the same, Marlowe was also a university man, with a razor sharp wit, a genius for word play and an inveterate hatred of the merchant classes. On any night of the week Marlowe might be found sharing a flask with a peer of the realm or perhaps a common boatman from the dockside, but he abhorred the rising tradespeople of the city, insulted their guilds and contributed to pamphlets that were so inflammatory he was shunned by almost anyone who had an eye to preferment.

"Why would Marlowe have any truck with a man like Thrace?" Matthew wanted to know.

John raised an eyebrow.

"Why does Kit Marlowe do anything? You know he's a law unto himself Mattie. But in any case, if my contacts at Court are to believed there's a lot more to Master Marlowe than meets the eye. If you've a mind and you catch him in the right state," he took a sharp intake of breath, "which these days might be no more than an hour each day; perhaps he can furnish you with more information about your dead Vintner."

"I hope so," Matthew admitted. "Because if I fall short of the expectations of my Lord Burghley I could yet find myself turned inside out on the gibbet for murdering Thrace myself. I must admit I would feel rather more comfortable if I could discover who did cut his throat, and why."

In his spare moments Matthew had mulled over the situation. Had Thrace been known as a lady's man it might have been partly understandable. However this did not seem at all likely. If the accounts Matthew had elicited from Thrace's neighbours were anything to go by the Vintner had rarely kept company with anyone. He certainly wasn't married, and though he clearly dealt in strong drink, if he'd quaffed and whored his way though boozy nights in any of the City's inns and brothels, he'd left precious little evidence of the fact. In any case the green gown worn by the woman who crowned Matthew so effectively indicated a person of some standing and was certainly not the attire that would be worn by any common prostitute, nor yet by the wronged wife of a merchant. Matthew certainly didn't relish the prospect of seeking Marlowe's assistance in any matter; he was a dangerous man to know, though it seemed likely that on this occasion he would have to make an exception.

In between mouthfuls of the mutton pasties Matthew told John of Burghley's and Rosemary's suspicions regarding Will Shakespeare. John looked dismissive.

"I'd be surprised Mattie," he offered. "Shakespeare has a reputation as white as snow. As far as I know he lives a notably sober life and rarely does anything to rock his own boat, or anyone else's come to that."

Matthew agreed, and confirmed that he had found the Warwickshire man both affable and straight-dealing, at least as far as their limited relationship had been concerned.

"But there's something afoot John; else why would Will Shakespeare be meeting with gentlemen of rank in Bishopsgate?" He thought of the clothes of the tall man – of his fine boots and fashionable hat. People of rank and standing might be found in some of the most disreputable establishments across London: one might see them at the bear or bull baiting; at a gaming house, or out of the city at hare coursing. All the same this sort of person would rarely have any social contact with a mere unlettered playwright like Shakespeare, unless it was to receive a dedication for a new work or to be sought out for patronage.

John wanted to know the details and Matthew described the house, its position adjacent to St Helen's Church, and of the gilded insect above the gate. John let out a long, low whistle, as he was wont to do when struck by any sort of revelation.

"So!" Matthew wanted to know. "Whose house is it, Master know-it-all Acres?"

John remained silent for a moment, no doubt to increase the tension. He was that sort of fellow, but nonetheless likeable for it. "Master Shakespeare must move in high circles indeed, though I'd be astonished if you found a Jesuit plot behind the walls of that grand house."

Matthew nudged him playfully.

"Well don't just sit there smirking John. Who lives there?"

"The motif over the gate is indeed an insect - a grasshopper to be precise Mattie, and that means that the house is that of Sir Thomas Gresham. At least it would be if the man were not sleeping next door, in St

Helen's Church. But his wife, Dame Jane, still bides there."

"And who might I ask my ever so well informed friend, is, or rather was, Sir Thomas Gresham?"

John scoffed.

"It's plain to see that you don't often lift your head from those wretched parchments of yours Mattie. Until his death, probably fifteen years ago or more, Sir Thomas Gresham was one of the richest men in London; aye and most likely for many a mile beyond it. He was a mercer and a financier. Do you know the Royal Exchange in Cornhill?"

It was an ill-considered question Matthew thought. The Royal Exchange, with its money houses, shops and meeting rooms, was one of the grandest buildings anywhere in the City.

"Of course I know it you dolt. Everyone does."

"Yes," admitted John, his little, dark eyes gleaming, making him appear more mouse-like than ever. "Though few know how it came into being."

Matthew considered for a short while. He'd never stopped to wonder. It was called 'The Royal Exchange', so he took it that the Crown has some hand in its construction.

"No doubt you'll tell me," he suggested.

"The Royal Exchange my friend was built by none other than Sir Thomas Gresham. And I can tell you this Mattie, that though it must have cost a fair king's ransom to create, it didn't make so much as a dent in the Gresham coffers.

Matthew sat back in his seat and picked an errant strand of mutton from between his teeth with a fingernail. This was going to take some thinking over. He signalled the serving girl and ordered another flagon of wine. Taking from his pocket a piece of parchment he placed it before his friend.

"Very well," he said. Let us dismiss Master Shakespeare from our minds for the moment, though you may be in a position to do me another favour."

"Just say the word Mattie," John Acres smiled.

"These are the names of all the members of Lord Strange's men at present. If you have the time I wonder if you could run them by some of your contacts at Court, just to see what turns up."

"I would be glad to Mattie," the small man assured him. "But don't expect too much of me. I may know one or two people of note, but I certainly do not move in the elevated circles of some of my friends — Master Matthew Prior for example."

Chapter Eight
At a Lady's Pleasure

Matthew was fond of Saturdays as a general rule. There was something particularly fascinating about the City's preparations for the Lord's Day. The streets were more than usually alive and some of the more prosperous citizens took the afternoon to promenade when the weather was good. It afforded a welcome distraction and sometimes a commission or two from a patron with money, and a lady to woo. However, this Saturday he liked even better than most.

When he had returned from the Inn the previous evening, late and a little worse for the drink, Matthew had found a note pushed under the door of his lodgings. It was written on the best vellum, folded neatly and it smelled of lily-of-the-valley. Scrabbling around in the semi-darkness Matthew had searched for the heel of a candle and struggled with his tinder box, the better to see the contents of the note. After a few fuddled moments he unfolded the vellum and saw the few words, written in small, neat handwriting.

'There's breakfast to be had at my home in the Strand.' And it was signed simply 'R'.

Rosemary had avoided arranging any future meeting with Matthew when he had seen her at Hampton Court. The Queen had been travelling up river later the same day, to entertain foreign emissaries at the palace in the evening. Rosemary had said that on the following day or at the very latest the next it was the intention of the Queen to be out of London, passing north with her entourage to Northamptonshire. She had no idea whether or not she was to accompany the Queen, for the monarch was fickle regarding such details and rarely made up her mind about who would act as servants of the royal person, until the last moment. But the arrival of the note indicated that Rosemary had not gone north with the Queen.

It was another bright and sunny day. The cobbles outside Matthew's lodgings were wet, and he had been awoken on several occasions during the night by the sound of heavy rain running down from the roof to splash onto the ground below. The promised frost had come to nothing as the sky had clouded. Now the rain had passed and there was azure blue from horizon to horizon. The river, often dirty, foaming and angry in the preceding months, was wearing its most sequinned spring attire as it dappled in the early morning sun.

The London house of the late Lord Armscliffe was not actually in the City at all, but it lay to the west, in a fashionable suburb to the south of Covent Garden, near a thoroughfare that overlooked the river and which was known as 'The Strand'. It would have taken Matthew an hour or more to walk through the City to the house, skirting The Temple and then following the great river. Since he didn't possess a horse of his own and was still feeling affluent, instead of travelling on foot he passed upstream by boat, from the wharf hard by London Bridge.

There was a good vista of the spires and towers of London from the river. All along the north bank of the Thames were wharves and warehouses. Craft from destinations throughout Europe and beyond lay tied up and even though the hour was early, groups of men were coming and going – bringing to dry land the produce of a dozen different nations and replacing them with English merchandise – mainly bales of wool.

Armscliffe House sat conveniently, with its front facing towards the Strand and its gardens to the rear overlooking the river. Matthew found it easily from the description Rosemary had offered at their last meeting. The high gates were flanked on one side by a small lodge and at Matthew's shout a liveried servant walked from the door. It was obvious that he was expected because before he had the opportunity to utter a word the man smiled and pulled open one of the large wrought iron gates. Beyond lay a series of box hedges laid out in a complex geometric pattern, and some hundred yards beyond lay the house itself. It was built of in-filled timbers and utilised bricks of differing shades, forming herringbone patterns with diamond motifs and other pleasing designs. Armscliffe House was an imposing structure and not for the first time since he had been reintroduced to the younger sister of his erstwhile love Matthew felt somewhat inadequate.

The large door at the top of a short flight of wide steps gave way before the push from the servant, who had led Matthew along the path, between the low hedges. He found himself in an oak panelled hall which was high and imposing. Tapestries adorned the walls but light blazed in from un-shuttered casements and the place smelled dry and sweet. Around him lay an array of doors, and a grand flight of stairs that led to an upper floor. The servant tapped gently on a door close to where he was standing. He then opened the door and walked in, beckoning Matthew to follow.

Rosemary was sitting by the window. It was a comfortable chamber, though not ornate. Carved oak furniture filled some of the space, with a trunk or two and a very imposing sideboard, which carried biblical designs picked out in light veneers on the dark wood of its many doors. Beneath one of the large, leaded light windows was a table, groaning under the weight of an array of food that could have breakfasted a regiment. There was ale and wine, great loaves of bread, shining and crusty, and wound into braided patterns. Pewter platters sported a mountain of oysters, a poached salmon and some young trout; there was half a haunch of venison, and a brace of water fowl. In addition Matthew's eyes fell on fruits, dried and fresh, and sumptuous whipped syllabubs in tall, crystal glasses.

As Matthew entered the room she rose with a smile, every inch the lady that fate had made of her but dressed simply for a day at home, wearing a gown far less ostentatious than the one that had adorned her at Hampton Court. Gone were the farthingale and fashionable pointed bodice, replaced by an outfit of more simple, almost country style. The bodice, the front of which was picked out in fine needlepoint, retained the low, square neck fashionable in and around London, and it emphasised her slim waist. Below this she wore a full skirt, light in colour but of a heavy weave and not made from the satins or silks generally to be found at Court.

Rosemary's complexion was also more natural than the one achieved at great expense and effort by most ladies of fashion. Though certainly not granted a pale skin, she appeared to shun the face whitening preparations that were now even worn by the wives of merchants. Her eyebrows, instead of being plucked away completely and replaced with false, dark, high-arched brows were her own and they complimented her large eyes admirably. She had a delicate and well shaped nose and lips a little fuller than courtly women would have considered desirable. Her teeth, which showed often, as a smile seemed to be commonplace upon her face, were white and even. At her neck hung a single amber pendant on a silver chain and her hands were bare of ornamentation save for one large, jewelled ring on her left hand.

Matthew took in the picture in a moment. He removed his hat and bowed low.

"Good day Lady Armscliffe", he offered; looking at her carefully, the years rolling away and stunned by the similarity between the vision that stood before him and his memory portrait of Celeste, his long-dead love.

"Let's have none of the 'Lady Armscliffe' Matthew", she responded, as the servant retreated and pulled the door closed behind him. In this place at least I am at home, and when I am, I'm Rosemary to my friends." She smiled. "Especially to my old friends." She resumed her former seat and bade Matthew to sit himself opposite. "So," she continued. "You were not abed too late to take breakfast with me?"

"Madam," he responded. "You wrong me much, for I am a man of sober habits and I am rarely abed later than the Night Watch calls nine."

She knew he was lying, and had she not, the smile on his face would have given the game away immediately. "Well I'm pleased to see you here all the same. And how prosperous you look."

The new clothes Matthew had purchased on the morning he had been attacked in Vintner's Row had now been cleaned and though Matthew possessed no looking glass he had viewed his reflection in the river when he had disembarked from the boat and thought he looked well enough. For all that, he was not a vain man and though when money permitted he flirted with fashion, it was, in truth, of transitory interest to him.

"If I do Rosemary," he told her, "it is thanks to the generosity of my latest patron, Lord Burghley." His face dropped a little. "Though I doubt not he'll see me in beggars' clothes again soon enough for all I've discovered on his behalf."

"Come, come Matthew", she almost ordered. "Rome wasn't built in a day, I am certain you are doing all you can for your Queen and your country. But there's enough time for matters of state presently. You came here to breakfast with me, and I dare say the journey has sharpened your appetite?"

Indeed it had and Matthew ate heartily, whilst Rosemary mainly watched, only partaking of the meal sparingly herself. The oysters were especially delicious, with a tang of the sea still on them – as fresh as the morning. Matthew never drank wine early in the day, so he quaffed a flagon of ale – bitter with the taste of hops, a new trend in English beer making and a crop regularly to be seen these days when in season, being brought into the city in great cartloads from Kent. Matthew commented on its quality and Rosemary told him that she had a small brew house attached to the kitchen garden, where Sol, one of her menservants, happily practised his brewing skills for the household.

As they dined they talked about this and that, sharing reminiscences about Yorkshire and the childhood they had in common. Rosemary told him that she rarely travelled to the North, since her duties at Court were somewhat onerous and demanded most of her time. She smiled as he reminded her of days stealing rosy apples from the orchard of the Priest in her own village, and of the time she had been spying on Celeste and himself and had tumbled into the mill pond with a great scream. Matthew had waded in and pulled her out, stinking and covered in weed. She'd spluttered for a while but had suffered no ill effect.

"Ah Matthew," she commented. "I'd almost forgotten that I owed you my life."

"Hardly," he retorted. "The water was only a foot or two deep. And in any case," he laughed, "I'm certain you were in greater danger from Celeste's rage than from the miller's pond."

"And I was sent straight to bed with foul smelling goose-grease on my chest and no dinner."

He put down an oyster shell, looking across into the soft hazel eyes that creased slightly at the corners when she laughed. Her black hair was pulled up and back, showing only slightly under a simple but attractive bonnet. She was relaxed and assured; beautiful enough he thought to be painted by some great artist, exactly as she was now; framed by the light from the window behind her and glowing with vitality.

Their eyes met for a moment but then he lowered his gaze quickly. The table between them was not so large, but the chasm in station yawned deep and impenetrable. It didn't do to harbour ridiculous false speculations; he'd been a poor man and a writer long enough to realise that fact.

When the meal was over and the reminiscences shared they retired from the table. Rosemary, who it seemed was ever happiest when out of doors, invited Matthew to walk with her in the extensive gardens behind her house. She told him that in those moments she had been able to call her own she'd taken a great delight in re-ordering the lawns, meadowland and formal gardens that swept down from the house with a fine vista of the river in the distance across water meadows where the tender shoots of green corn were already showing above the water's margin.

Atop a central path was a small temple or shelter. It mirrored the design of the house and faced south, its open front approached by five or six steps. Within the structure was a carved wooden seat and the two settled there for a while, to discuss Matthew's most recent discoveries out of earshot of the servants.

"So how do you find Will Shakespeare?" Rosemary wanted to know. "Does he carry the marks of a Papist devil as my Lord Burghley seems to assume?" She smiled.

"Not at all," Matthew had to admit, "though I doubt I'd recognise the fact even if he did. On first impression I'd have to say that he is an immensely likeable person. He's obviously hard working, and such a good instinctive writer that a few hours spent in his company has made me realise I should have become an Osler."

"Stuff and nonsense Mattie," she scolded. "Some of your work is very fine and well you know it."

He didn't pursue the point by enquiring how she could know anything about his writing. It would hardly have been modest. Instead he rehearsed his conversations with Will Shakespeare and explained to Rosemary how he had chosen to follow the playwright to Bishopsgate, and the house of the late Sir Thomas Gresham.

Rosemary pursed her lips, thinking for a moment.

"I never knew Sir Thomas Gresham," she told him. "He was dead before I came to London, but I have met his widow, Dame Jane, on a number of occasions. She's old now and perhaps a little failing in her wits. All the same she has moments of startling lucidity and seems to have been an astute and intelligent woman."

"Has she any leanings towards the Church of Rome as far as you are aware?" Matthew wanted to know.

"I would doubt it very much," Rosemary replied. "Sir Thomas was one of the Queen's most trusted financial advisers. He died an extremely wealthy man and bestowed a great percentage of his fortune upon various charities – some of which are definitely Anglican in origin and nature. As far as I am aware neither Sir Thomas nor his wife showed the slightest tendency towards Catholicism. Of course," she added,

"Sir Thomas Gresham was already a man of some influence at Court when Queen Mary was still alive. That means that the family must have shown Catholic leanings at that time."

"There's nothing too strange about that," Matthew observed. He knew full well that a large percentage of people would adopt any form of worship if it offered them preferment, or even security come to that.

Matthew was too young to remember any monarch apart from the present Queen. However, he had learned from the words of his elders just how dangerous the different religious adherences had been after the death of King Henry VIII.

Henry's son, Edward VII, being in his minority had, all the same, shown distinct and quite fanatical Protestant tendencies. When he had died before reaching adulthood the throne had passed to his half-sister, Mary, daughter of Henry's first wife, Katherine of Aragon. Mary had been a staunch Catholic, ready to burn anyone who refused to embrace her own form of Christianity. Protestant England had shuddered during her reign. She had died of cancer and her younger half-sister, Elizabeth, daughter of the deposed and executed Protestant Anne Boleyn, had been the only logical candidate for the vacant throne. Now it was the turn of the Catholics to shudder, though in truth, at least early in her reign, Elizabeth had shown tremendous tolerance. Only with the passing of time and the proliferation of religiously inspired plots and threats to the stability of England had Elizabeth's regime hardened its attitude towards the Church of Rome.

Rosemary said

"All I really know of Sir Thomas Gresham is that he cared more for learning than religion. I remember hearing from my late husband that Sir Thomas bestowed a college, with professors in a number of subjects who lecture several times each year to anyone with the desire to learn – no matter what their rank or station.

"Then perhaps Will only travelled to Bishopsgate to improve his mind?" Matthew suggested.

"Perhaps," she responded. "But it isn't likely. If memory serves lectures are given on specific saint's days. They take place on the festival of Mary the Virgin and St Michael the Archangel. Neither of those fall this month. And in any case the lectures are given in rooms at the Royal Exchange, in the Cornhill." She concentrated for a while, as if trying to rake up memories from the past. "My late husband was a small beneficiary of Sir Thomas' will. I read a copy of it at the time. I remember thinking it to be an extraordinary document. When Dame Jane passes to grace almost all of the remainder of the family fortune will fund the further efforts of the college. The couple had no children who survived."

"Then Master Shakespeare must have had other business in Bishopsgate. It might have thrown some light on the matter if I had been familiar with the men he met there; and particularly one. He was a tall man with a very regal bearing. An aristocrat I shouldn't wonder. If not then certainly a gentleman."

"Can you describe him?" Rosemary wanted to know. "If he is a man of rank there is a good possibility that I will know him."

"Hardly," Matthew admitted. "It was turning dark. Though I'm sure I'd recognise him again if I came across him."

He sighed.

"It would help somewhat if I fully understood what it is I am supposed to discover." He looked at her with tenderness. "Of course had I not been summoned to serve by Lord Burghley I would not have met you again, but aside from that blessing I don't fare well and appear to be lacking an ability for solving mysteries. For example," he continued, "I'm no nearer discovering who killed Bartholomew Thrace; and to be quite honest with you I don't really know where to begin. It might be easier if I knew what Thrace was to Lord Burghley but that information wasn't vouchsafed to me." He looked at her. "Do you have any knowledge of his role Rosemary?" he asked, chancing his arm.

"Mattie", she admitted. "I'm as much in the dark about that as you are."

"Then how does Lord Burghley expect me to discover anything?", he asked in a slightly frustrated tone of voice. "Wouldn't it be natural for him to confide what he knows to us? At least that way we would be as wise as he is."

Rosemary shook her head.

"You don't know Lord Burghley Mattie. I doubt that he even trusts his own reflection. He's worked so long for the Queen, seeking out intrigues of one sort or another that he trusts nobody. Everyone is given half a tale and expected to discover the rest for himself." She patted Matthew on the hand. "But he's nobody's fool and if he took you on for a purpose it was because he believed that you were equal to the task."

The morning was passing more quickly than Matthew had wished. He had to be at the Rose by an hour after noon, and that would mean departing very soon. Whatever he had or hadn't gleaned about the murder of Thrace his primary objective was to discover some sort of plot within Lord Strange's Company and he could hardly do that if he turned up late for his appointment on only his second day of employment.

She had bidden him a warm, and even an affectionate goodbye, walking with him to the gates of the house, and beseeching him to keep in regular touch. Since the Queen would be out of London for some days it would be possible for Matthew to find her at home at almost any time. As the boat gently pulled downstream, with the ebbing tide, Matthew could still see her face in his mind's eye. It was a face that was rapidly growing dearer to him than was probably wise. The situation was made worse by the fact that Rosemary appeared to take a special delight in his company too.

Ordinarily, if the woman had been of Matthew's own station, he might have presumed to probe a little deeper as to her possible feelings, but Lady Rosemary Armscliffe was higher than heaven to a man who made his living in the dusty streets of London – and someone who was an untitled pensman to boot. No, he told himself, he must keep his mind on the task in hand and recognise that in a world of appointed stations some things were possible, and others were not.

It turned out that there was little for Matthew to do at The Rose. The company was performing another of Will Shakespeare's plays, this one a tragedy, entitled 'Romeo and Juliet'. Matthew had seen the play before and particularly loved its language. It allowed the lads in the company a greater part in proceedings than the history plays did, since there were several young female parts. Matthew picked up some possible animosity, directed by Nicholas Tooley, at the younger actor Tom Campion. Nick was obviously now too old to be considered for the role of Juliet, who was indicated by the script to be no more than fourteen years of age. As a result he had been given the role of Juliet's mother, Madam Capulet. There were several vitriolic scenes within the play between Juliet and her mother and Matthew noticed how much Nicholas Tooley seemed to relish the opportunity to play his role to the full, pulling Tom Campion around the stage and to Matthew's comprehension overplaying the part allotted to him.

The play passed well enough. Shakespeare was not present himself, since he had no role in the production, so Matthew had chance to watch the company carefully, freed from the restrictions of his copying duties, at least for the moment. He couldn't actually see the performances from behind the tiring house curtain, but he could hear them, and monitored the various cast members in their offstage moments.

Romeo and Juliet could not be considered in any way to be a contentious play, dealing as it did with the feuding between two families in Verona. It was obvious from the quality of the production that Lord Strange's Men were not in the least 'strangers' to this particular play. Only Anthony Roper, who took the part of the Prince of Verona turned in a less than sterling performance. His movements, such as Matthew could glimpse them, were wooden and his speeches, some of the most powerful in the play, lacked real conviction. This was surprising because Roper was well known as an almost inspirational actor. However, in this production he appeared to be constantly distracted. When off stage he was irritable and touchy, snapping at Matthew a couple of times regarding costumes or properties, and in particular scowling regularly at Tom Campion, who never responded, except with apparent patience and a nervous smile.

When the performance was over, and the crowded theatre cleared of patrons, Matthew lingered in the tiring house, listening to the conversations of the actors. But all seemed routine and if anyone within the company was party to a plan to murder the Queen of England they certainly did not give the game away within his earshot. In fact things only began to become interesting just after the company had been paid and were readying themselves to leave. Several burly men appeared at the entrance to the theatre, all of them armed and wearing the livery of the Sheriff of London. One of them strode forward, across the cockpit and onto the stage. Matthew recognised him immediately, it was Jonas Kaye, the Sheriff's officer who had questioned him about the death of Bartholomew Thrace.

Kaye walked across to James Burbage, who was paying the vendors. Burbage had his back to Kaye, and so did not register his approach. But Jane Roper, who was standing with left hand outstretched, waiting for her pennies withdrew her hand as Burbage was accosted by the officer. Burbage turned quickly at Kaye's words.

"James Burbage," he said sternly. "You are the proprietor of this theatrical company?"

Burbage wasn't over impressed with the Sheriff's officer and had doubtless crossed swords with him on several occasions previously.

"You know fine well that I am Master Kaye," he responded.

"In that case you will kindly instruct every man jack of them to remain in the theatre until we are done here?"

"Done with what?" Burbage wanted to know.

Kaye didn't reply, but he called forward two of his men. He spoke to them quietly and they walked across the stage and into the tiring house. Kaye then turned his attention to Matthew, who was folding a flag nearby.

"Master Prior; a word please," he said, most politely. He led Matthew to one side of the stage, out of earshot of the assembled players and other theatre staff. Matthew was puzzled.

"Master Prior," Kaye began, keeping his tone of voice low. "When I spoke to you about the death of the Vintner, Bartholomew Thrace you told me that you were attacked and injured by a woman wearing a green velvet gown. Is that correct?"

"Why yes," Matthew confirmed.

"And do you think you would recognise this person again, if they were to stand before you?"

"I doubt it," said Matthew immediately. "I could tell you, as indeed I did, roughly how tall the woman was, but I didn't see her face at all because my hat had fallen over my eyes and she had hit me with the bottle before I had the chance to rectify the situation."

Whilst Matthew had been talking one of Kaye's men had come forward from the tiring house, bearing in his arms a sumptuous gown of green velvet. Kaye's face bore a look of triumph. He pointed to the gown.

"Would this be the apparel that was worn by your attacker Master Prior."

Matthew looked at it carefully.

"It certainly could be. It's the right hue and material."

The Sheriff's Officer turned his attention to James Burbage once again.

"Master Burbage. Does this gown belong to your company?"

"Of course it does man," Burbage commented dismissively. "Your men have just removed it from one of the trunks in the tiring house."

"And who generally wears this gown in your 'theatrical productions'?" he wanted to know, uttering the words with an obvious level of disdain. "It obviously wouldn't fit any of your full grown actors?"

"Well generally speaking at the moment that particular gown is worn by Tom Campion." James Burbage pointed to the lad, who suddenly went very pale and looked extremely nervous. "In fact," Burbage went on, looking around the company, "I daresay he's the only one who could get into it now that Nic Tooley is growing so fast."

Kaye inspected the gown. Matthew was standing close beside him and could clearly see dark marks on the front of the garment, and especially around the hem.

The Sheriff's Officer looked at them carefully. Then he seemed to make up his mind. He threw the gown over one arm and walked across to Tom Campion. He put a hand on the lad's shoulder and the young man seemed to diminish in stature.

"Thomas Campion," he said in a stern tone of voice. In the name of the Sheriff of London I am arresting you for the assault of Master Matthew Prior and on suspicion of the murder of Bartholomew Thrace, a Vintner of London. You must come with me now for further questioning.

The boy looked astounded.

"I didn't attack Master Prior. And I certainly didn't kill Bartholomew Thrace. Why would I do such a thing? The man was my father!"

This last remark came as an obvious revelation to Matthew, and judging by the sharp intake of breath, to one or two other people too.

"Take him back to the city and put him in a cell," Kaye said to his fellow officers. I don't doubt the Sheriff will want to speak to him personally.

In a few moments, protesting and struggling, Tom Campion was led from The Rose.

There was a stunned silence for a moment before a buzz of conversation broke out amongst those still assembled in the theatre. Well, thought Matthew. That's one of my problems solved at least. Perhaps, he concluded, as he wandered back to his lodgings in Eastcheap later that night, the fact that Thrace had some connection with Lord Burghley and that he had come to be murdered were not related at all. The events may have been nothing more than a simple coincidence.

"And I'm the Prince of the Indies", said his familiar. He ignored it.

It had been a long time since he had risen from his bed and Matthew decided to retire early. The following day was Sunday. There would be no production at The Rose so Matthew would have the day to himself and he was determined to root out Christopher Marlowe in order to try and gain some information from the man. He knew from past experience that this task was not likely to be easy.

Chapter Nine
The Machiavellian

The sing-song bells of St Clement the Dane with their distinctive 'Oranges and Lemons' awoke Matthew, perspiring and deeply uncomfortable from an extremely disturbed night's sleep. One so accustomed as Matthew to downing whatever alcohol was available before retiring was bound to find it difficult to sleep peacefully without recourse to his usual 'night-cap', and he had enjoyed, or rather endured an entire night of dreams – some confused, others lurid, cruel and disturbing.

Time and again, in his mind, he had come across the horrible spectacle of the body of Bartholomew Thrace, lying in that great pool of blood, a surprised look in his still open, staring eyes. Countless times during the dark hours he had struggled with the mysterious woman in green before finding himself, once again, outside the Vintner's shop, ready to view the whole spectacle once more. In each visitation his recollection of the events of that extraordinary morning seemed to revisit his mind with ever- greater clarity.

The visions of the killing of Bartholomew Thrace remained with him as he struggled from his bed-cupboard and donned his clothes. Once out from between his thick blankets he became aware that it was somewhat chilly in his rooms. He'd been too busy to buy coals and in any case there would be no time to remain in his chamber and write on this day.

The sky outside his dirty window was grey and leaden, though it did not appear to be raining. Matthew relieved himself in the large pot, kept for the purpose in one corner of his small lodgings and then, after ensuring that nobody was actually walking underneath his casement, he opened the window and tipped the contents into the yard below.

There was some stale bread on his desk, and a half-full bottle of wine. Normally he shunned anything but ale before the middle of the day but 'needs must when the Devil drives.' He poured some of the wine into a goblet and dunked the bread in it until it became soft enough to swallow. It was difficult to tell which tasted worse; the almost mouldy bread or the vinegary wine. One thing was certain, both were a far cry from his breakfast of the previous day.

At least, Matthew assured himself, even his meagre breakfast was likely to have been more substantial and more palatable than that enjoyed by Tom Campion. Almost certainly the boy would be lodged in the Sheriff's cells near the Guildhall. Matthew had personal experience of the place, having been kept there one night several years before when involved in a brawl at an inn close to Cheapside. Too many people had been involved in the disturbance for the City Watch to cope and the overflow had been carted off to the cells near the Guildhall. These were located in a dank cellar, with light filtering in from the tiniest aperture, rat infested bedding and water dripping from the roof.

Matthew thought back to the previous evening. As Tom Campion had been dragged away by the Sheriff's men he had clearly intimated that the murdered Vintner, Bartholomew Thrace had been his father. Bearing in mind the task Matthew had been assigned by Burghley, the situation might be nothing more than a bizarre coincidence. Nevertheless the revelation intrigued Matthew and he determined to try and establish more about the situation.

Hurriedly finishing dressing he left his lodgings and went straight to Pudding Lane, one of the few places he would bo would be able to obtain fresh food and drink on a Sunday morning. There was a small Jewish community in the vicinity and people of that persuasion were not restricted by the draconian Puritan laws of London to remain closed on the Christian Sabbath. There Matthew bought bread, some apples and a flask of ale. He then set off back across the City towards the Guildhall, and the Sheriff's lock-up.

Gaining entrance was somewhat easier than he had anticipated. None of the Sheriff's Officers was present, merely an ageing and slightly witless jailer. Matthew explained to the toothless old man that he had brought breakfast for one of the prisoners.

"Which one?" the elderly man wheezed.

"Tom Campion," Matthew told him. "He was brought here last evening."

The jailer might have been old, but he wasn't completely devoid of his senses.

"And what's it worth to me if I let you feed him?" he demanded.

Matthew placed twelve pennies into the wrinkled old hand, counting them one by one. He estimated that this would probably be more than the jailer would earn in half a week or more, though it was a tiny fraction of the money he had acquired from Lord Burghley. Very soon the white-haired guard opened a series of stout doors and Matthew followed him into the bowels of the building.

The lad was sitting in the corner of a cell, which was just as dark and musty as the one Matthew remembered inhabiting in this place himself. There was an iron bed but Tom Campion was sitting dejectedly on the floor in a corner, his knees pulled up under his chin, and for all his seventeen years he looked like a very small and very frightened child.

A look of recognition fell across his face as Matthew strode into the cell, carrying a lighted lamp, procured for an extra penny from the jailer.

"Master Prior," Tom exclaimed, his face brightening noticeably. "What are you doing here?"

Matthew perched himself on the edge of the iron bed.

"I've brought you some breakfast Tom. Now get up off the floor and sit here on the bed. You'll get God knows what down there in the rat droppings.

Tom did as he was told and was soon wolfing his way through the bread and washing it down with great gulps of the ale. When he had finished he said.

"This was very civil of you Master Prior. Very civil indeed, particularly bearing in mind that we only became acquainted a couple of days ago."

"Think nothing of it Tom," the writer replied. He looked around. "I've been in a cell like this on more than one occasion myself." He sighed. "Though I have to say I've never been in quite the pickle you find yourself in now."

"I've done nothing Master Prior," the lad assured him. "Nothing at all." He gave a downcast look. "I didn't even know that Master Thrace, my father, was dead until the Sheriff's men came to take me away."

"I'm truly sorry for your loss Tom. But if Bartholomew Thrace is....." Matthew pulled himself up in his tracks. "If he 'was' your father, how could it have taken you so many days to discover what happened to him?"

Campion looked a little furtive for a moment but then shrugged and said.

"Because I don't live with him and I never have. I live with my mother, at least I did until she died last year." He looked at Matthew pleadingly. "I'll tell you the truth of it Master Prior, because you thought about me this morning and brought food. But you must promise not to spread the story around in the Company if I get myself out of this mess, because I'm dog's meat with Mr Burbage else."

"You have my word," he confirmed.

"The truth is Master Prior that I'm a common bastard – though I didn't tell that to Mr Burbage when he gave me my apprenticeship. I used to sing in the choir at St Paul's, that's where Mr Burbage saw me and offered me my place in the company. He met my mother, just before she passed on, but he never asked about my father. As far as he is concerned I'm an orphan now.

"It's no crime to be born out of wedlock Tom," Matthew assured the lad. "But did your mother and father never live together?"

"Never", echoed Tom. "Well not for a long time at any rate." He looked to the door, to ensure that they were not being watched from outside but the door was ajar and the jailer was doubtless counting his new fortune. "They couldn't be married Master Prior because my father was a Roman Catholic Priest."

"What?" Matthew exclaimed. He recovered from the revelation, looked around again and lowered his voice to a loud whisper before continuing. "Have you any idea how dangerous it is to say such things in the present climate Tom?"

"But it's the truth Master Prior, honestly. Master Thrace, that is my father, was an educated man – he came from Cambridge. But times had been hard and he was working down at the docks when my mother met him. They stayed together for a while but when I was only weeks old he ran away to France, and came back wealthy and a Jesuit priest. He wouldn't have anything to do with us after that – well save for giving us the odd shilling now and again. We lived in

Whitechapel. My mother helped the gentry there - with their washing and such."

Was this fanciful nonsense? Matthew tried to be objective. He looked closely at the lad. There seemed to be little about Tom Campion that instinctively made him suspicious. The young man might have possessed a sort of self-cultivated naivety but if so he wasn't alone in that. This was an appearance deliberately fostered by some of the boy actors in all theatrical companies. It was intended to appeal to certain adult actors with 'specific' tastes. Matthew was aware of some of his own shortcomings as a writer, but he rarely doubted himself as a judge of character. Whatever the truth of Tom Campion's nature he certainly wasn't responsible for his parentage and doubtless he'd had to shift for himself a good deal. The fact that he had managed to procure an apprenticeship with Lord Strange's Men showed that he'd endeavoured to better himself, despite apparent adversity. Matthew looked at the lad again. The poor, scared young man before him certainly didn't look like a cold-blooded killer.

Matthew decided on a direct approach.

"Tom," he said, looking the lad straight in the eyes. "Did you go to Vintner's Row dressed in the green gown to kill Bartholomew Thrace? And come to that did you also try to break my skull with a wine bottle?"

Tom Campion's eyes were wide with incredulity.

"I didn't care very much for my father, mainly on my mother's account." he said. "But I swear to you Master Prior that I didn't kill him. And as for you – well I never even set eyes on you as far as I know, until yesterday."

"Very well," said Matthew. "If that is the case you should have little difficulty proving your innocence. Can you remember what you were doing on Wednesday morning last?"

"Certainly," said the lad immediately. I was catching eels in the Foss Stream, down below Whitechapel."

"Was anyone there with you?"

Tom's face fell. "Yes, two friends, Paul Usher and Nathan Smyth."

"And at what time did you go fishing Tom?" Matthew wanted to know.

"Oh very early. Probably about six – before sunrise at any rate."

"In that case you have no problem Tom. It was plain that your Father had only been murdered a very short time before I entered his shop. All you have to do is to get your friends to come here and swear that you were with them all morning."

Tom Campion looked crestfallen.

"That's the trouble Master Prior. I can't. Paul Usher and Nathan Smyth have both gone missing."

"Matthew was puzzled. "What do you mean by 'gone missing' Tom? People don't usually just disappear."

"No Master Campion, but they have. They were dragged from 'The Jennet', an inn down in Deptford by Queen's sailors, last Wednesday evening. I went to see them on Thursday but Nathan's mother was in a terrible state. She has no idea where they've been taken."

It was a tale Matthew had heard of more than once around the docks. With constant fears regarding the Spanish and despite the decisive defeat of the Armada, England needed ships, and ships required sailors. Life in Her Majesty's Navy was harsh and the wages low. As a result Captains had begun to resort to press-ganging to crew their vessels and lads around Tom Campion's age were prime targets.

Matthew made a mental note of their names. Of course, he told himself, it could be a fabrication but if so it was a naive one because it would be so easy to check out.

"I'll see what I can discover Tom," Matthew reassured him. "Have you seen the Sheriff yet?"

"No," the lad said, dejectedly, "I've been right where you see me now since they took me away last evening."

"Well he will see you Tom, and he will want to have a long talk with you. It's Sunday but this is a serious crime so he may come before the day is out. If not, it will be tomorrow for certain. My advice to you is to tell him the truth - the absolute truth, and if you are innocent you will have nothing to fear."

"Well said." The strains of a voice filtered in through the door. In the opening stood Jonas Kaye, who had obviously approached without either of them realising. He looked hard at Matthew. "I suppose you know that you shouldn't be here Master Prior, but I see you've brought victuals for the lad, and I call that full Christian on a Sunday morning, so I'll overlook the fact. Some of my fellow Officer's might take a different view," he added, "and I daresay the Sheriff himself definitely would, so it might be best if you made your exit now."

Matthew nodded his thanks and then turned his attention to Tom Campion as he turned to leave.

"Mark what I said Tom. Tell Master Kaye here the truth. You won't be gibbeted simply because you were born out of wedlock or because of your Father's religious leanings. You'll only suffer if you murdered him." He then turned his attention to Jonas Kaye. "Could I have a word with you Master Kaye?" He pointed to the door. "Outside if possible."

In the dank corridor and out of hearing of the prisoner Matthew asked.

"Can you tell me why you've arrested the lad Master Kaye? Presumably you had some logical reason for doing so?"

Kaye was still deferential. He clearly knew that Matthew had important people pulling his strings and he probably guessed that these were associated with the Privy Council. It didn't do for representatives of the Sheriff's Office to fall foul of the monarch.

"All I can tell you at the moment Master Prior is what we know; that the Sheriff received an anonymous letter, advising us that a costume held by Lord Strange's Men, presently at The Globe theatre, would lead us to the murderer of Bartholomew Thrace. Taking that advice together with your own statement it wasn't hard for me to work out what sort of apparel to look for." He now spoke conspiratorially. "I shouldn't tell you this but a few enquiries I made after receiving the letter led me to believe that Tom Campion and Thrace were not on good terms, and that the lad sometimes visited Thrace at his shop. One of the neighbours reported arguments between the two on more than one occasion."

"Did the lad tell you when you arrested him about the friends he was with last Wednesday Master Kaye? Assuming he's telling the truth he can't have murdered his father."

"He wouldn't be the first one to concoct an alibi that cannot be verified." Kaye observed. "It happens all the time." He sighed. "I'll do what I can to discover the truth of the matter, but even if they have been taken off to the Navy there's probably little to be done. They could be anywhere by now."

Matthew thanked Jonas Kaye cordially for his candour and left, asking permission to bring more food to Tom Campion on the following day. It was fairly standard procedure so he was advised that as long as he received the appropriate permission there should be no problem.

Out in the cobbled street, even the somewhat putrid air of the city seemed fresh and clean in comparison with the lock-up. Matthew gulped down a few breaths before he sat down on the stump of an old preaching cross outside St Thomas Jewry to think how to proceed next.

He knew, without doubt, that Bartholomew Thrace had been in the service, and therefore presumably the pay of Queen Elizabeth's first minister and spy-master, Lord Burghley. But by everyone's admission Burghley was a confirmed Catholic hater. Why would he want to have any truck whatsoever with a Jesuit Priest? And if a lad like Tom was so free as to tell an absolute stranger about his father's ordination, then Burghley, with his vast network of intelligence surely could not have failed to know. When he thought back a few days to the conversations he had engineered with a number of Thrace's neighbours Matthew realised that these people had all known about Thrace's Catholic sympathies.

He regained his feet and marched off in the direction of St Paul's, where he thought he may get a lead as to the whereabouts of Christopher Marlowe, who, according to John Acres, might be the only person in London who could offer him an explanation of some of these matters – that was if he chose to do so.

As he walked past the early morning church-goers Matthew thought hard about Marlowe's biography as he knew it.

Christopher Marlowe, Kit to those who knew him even reasonably well, had arrived in London just a few years earlier. He almost instantly became well known, both on account of his work, particularly his excellent plays but also because of his general behaviour.

Matthew had befriended Marlowe some years earlier. The two appeared to have something in common, for though Marlowe had received a university education he had seemed as poor as a church mouse when he took lodgings in Eastcheap, near to where Matthew himself lived. Even when sober, Marlowe was a force to be reckoned with. He'd once told Matthew that he had originally been singled out for ordination but for some reason that he had never explained fully he went on to develop a particular dislike for the Christian faith – though he constantly insisted that this was not the case. The truth was that Marlowe simply hated regimentation or orthodoxy of almost any sort, particularly in terms of religious practices. All of this would have been fine had he possessed the sort of nature that allowed him to hold his own thoughts in private, but that was far from the remit of Kit Marlowe.

On several occasions Matthew practically had to carry Marlowe home from one or other of the inns and stews in Southwark, either because the man had drunk himself into a stupor or on account of him having been laid out in some brawl. When in his cups Marlowe would tackle anyone, no matter how formidable. Nor did he attempt to stay out of trouble with the City authorities. On the contrary he provoked them at every possible opportunity. Yet despite his behaviour he seemed to operate with an impunity that many found utterly incredible. Almost everyone who knew him marvelled that he had managed to stay clear of prison – or even the gibbet, for so long.

There were many stories relating to his past prior to arriving in London. Some said he'd been in the Queen's army, fighting in the Netherlands whilst others maintained that he had travelled extensively in France. Whatever the truth of the matter he'd picked up some strange and dangerous ideas. Despite this, when he was sober he could be immensely likeable and he was generous to a fault. He was especially kind to ordinary folk and particularly to the poor and dispossessed. Most significant of all he wrote sensitively and with great intelligence. His plays were regularly to be seen in Southwark and were always well attended.

Matthew was heading for St Paul's because he was well aware that Kit Marlowe was often to be found there on a Sunday morning. The state of affairs that existed in and around this, the largest and formerly the most impressive of the City churches was a cause of wonder to Matthew himself and was the reason for Marlowe's regular appearances there.

St Paul's was not simply a Church, it was a Cathedral, and that meant that it fell under the jurisdiction of the ecclesiastical authorities and could not be regulated by the City Fathers. Normally this did not present a particular problem but in the case of St Paul's matters were very different. The truth was that the place was in severe decline. Some years earlier part of one of the towers had crashed down during a thunder storm. It remained in its broken state because those ordering the running of the place did such a terrible job. Most of them were making great profits from the building and its large churchyard but little or none of this was reflected in the state of the building itself.

The churchyard around St Paul's existed in the very heart of London. On every day of the week the whole area was crowded with market stalls, the holders of which all paid rent to the Church authorities. But this wasn't any ordinary market; it existed primarily for the sale of all writing requisites and most importantly for the purchase and resale of books.

Inside the Church itself every manner of impropriety took place. Two of the so-called Churchwardens were regularly to be found there, at the base of the broken tower. They would invite male passers-by to climb into its broken interior – though everyone understood what the ulterior motive actually was. The wives of the two wardens were each well known prostitutes and both were willing to offer those climbing into the tower a great deal more than a view of the City.

Ragamuffins and urchins of all kinds wandered around in the great building. Some of them slept there at night. The few parishioners who tried to keep services running normally in the building were regularly accosted and sometimes even assaulted by these vagrants. Little boys would piss on the sets of the Church floor before hiding, waiting to see people slip and stumble on the wet stones. All in all St Paul's was an utter disgrace, and one far beyond the ability of the authorities within London itself to remedy.

Christopher Marlowe, like other writers in the City, had little choice but to go to St Paul's churchyard for his writing implements and to obtain copies of books that were essential to his work. However, this was only part of his agenda. On almost every Sunday morning he would set himself up on a box in the eastern part of the area, close to St Paul's cross. From there he would shout at the assemblage, telling everyone that they were damned and that they had turned the Church into a den of iniquity.

Whether or not Marlowe actually believed what he was saying was difficult, if not impossible, to judge, for he was a man of mischief and probably revelled in the anarchy that was taking place within the Anglican establishment. In truth the man was just as likely to be downing pints of ale whilst spewing forth his stream of invective; sometimes pulling a woman of easy virtue onto his rostrum with him and giving her a tight squeeze, whilst at the same time extolling the virtues of abstemiousness and chastity.

Matthew turned into the gates to the west of the great church. Already the surrounding area was crowded with sellers of pens, ink, parchment, legal documents, books old and new and every other imaginable commodity that was of use to the writer and the scholar. People laughed and joked, eating hunks of bread and pasties purchased from vendors who, paradoxically were freed from the constraints of Sunday trading laws in London by virtue of their position on Church land.

By St Paul's Cross, around the far side of the building, was an area that had always been traditionally left clear for people who had some religious message to impart. It was suggested that this had been the site of the first Christian message to reach London and even despite the daily market the tradition of preaching at the spot was upheld. Here Puritan preachers in particular would call down the wrath of God on the unholy assemblage, whilst at the same time berating the Anglican Church authorities as being little better than Papists. It was amongst this number that Kit Marlowe was inclined to speak, though whether he did so partly in earnest or simply to mock the Puritans was impossible to know because he was as vitriolic in his condemnation of the Puritans as he was of more traditional Protestants.

Sure enough Christopher Marlowe was present, a tall, dark man with angular features and such a pair of piercing black eyes that the Devil himself might have envied them. He was apparently taking an Anglican stance on this particular Sunday and was busy arguing with one of the Puritan preachers. A large knot of people was gathered round, enjoying the spectacle.

"You Sir," said the Puritan, a stout man of middle years wearing black clothes and a tall hat, "are the antichrist. You will be damned to the darkest and most horrible recesses of hell. You do not know God sir," he bellowed, "and when the time comes God will refuse to know you!"

Marlowe wasn't in the least perturbed, and was clearly playing to the crowd, for he was not only an excellent writer but a capable public speaker, even if his message was sometimes contradictory and occasionally garbled by drink.

"Sir," he replied. "If Heaven is filled with odious little onion sellers such as yourself, then I would positively 'demand' to reside in hell."

The little man in the tall hat held up a bible.

"This is the law of God sir. Jesus is my salvation. He will smite you with the power of His hand for your sin and blasphemy. You are damned Master Marlowe. You are a fornicating drunkard, a whoremonger and a sacrilegious sodomite."

Marlowe was suddenly incensed. "Sodomite?" he yelled. "Sodomite?" He reached down and picked up a walking stick from one of the people nearby. "I'll give you sodomite you pompous, pontificating old fart!"

An immediate scuffle broke out and since the Puritan gentleman clearly had not come alone to St Paul's it soon became apparent that Christopher Marlowe was coming off worst in the encounter. Fists and feet were flying in all directions and it appeared that the majority of them were being directed at Kit. Matthew had to think quickly.

He cupped his hands around his mouth and shouted at the top of his voice.

"The Watch! The City Watch is here! Hi Hence! Be gone! The Watch approaches."

The reaction was immediate, with the protagonists and audience alike scattering in all directions. It may have been beyond the remit of the City to curb the commercial practices within St Paul's grounds but they would not hesitate to wade in and sort out any sort of fracas.

Marlowe was laid on the ground, protecting his head with his arms. He didn't look badly hurt. Matthew grabbed him by one arm and virtually launched him to his feet. Before the confused man had the chance to comment Matthew half dragged him from the Churchyard and away down New Change, across to the east. His Puritan attackers, realising that they had been duped gave chase. As Matthew looked back it now became obvious that there were full twenty men, most of whom looked extremely angry. The pair knew the city well and they dodged onto Watling Street across Bread Street and then down into Bow Lane. It was obvious from the din that they were still being followed but the chasers were not actually in view. Matthew dragged Kit Marlowe into the grounds of Aldermary Church and they crouched, panting, behind a crumbling tomb, the sound of singing behind them indicating that a Church service was taking place in the building.

The would-be assailants appeared and instead of searching for the pair they ran off north, up Bow Lane. When they were out of sight Matthew and Kit Marlowe stood up. Marlowe brushed down his dishevelled clothes and then shook Matthew by the hand.

"Well I don't know where you came from Mattie, but it looks as though you saved my bacon once again."

Indeed it wasn't the first time something similar had happened. Marlowe was very short tempered, whilst Matthew was more circumspect and usually able to talk or think himself out of a predicament.

"It appears I owe you a favour Master Prior," Kit Marlowe admitted. "If you hadn't turned up when you did they'd have given me a broken head for sure."

"Then that's fortunate", Matthew smiled, "because in truth I need some advice from you. Allow me to buy you a drink," he said, smiling even more broadly at the fortunate twist circumstances had offered him..

The two walked the short distance down to London Bridge and then on into Southwark, where there was drink a plenty to be found, even on a Sunday.

Chapter Ten
Intrigue

Christopher Marlowe was so well known amongst the brothels, low-life boarding houses and gaming establishments south of the river that some people referred to him as the 'King of Southwark.'. Almost every passing individual offered him the time of day as they strolled down narrow alleys, with houses, the upper storeys of which were so close their inhabitants could have shaken hands across the street. Some smiled as they offered Marlowe a greeting, others grunted an acknowledgement, but few ignored him.

They came at last to the Golden Cock, an establishment that looked even seedier than most of the drinking houses in the area. A crippled child crouched in rags at the entrance to the dive and Kit Marlowe took a small coin from his purse and thrust it into the waif's one good hand.

Inside, the room was a fug of smoke from a group of men drawing on tobacco in clay pipes. Matthew invariably avoided the habit, which had been inspired by the ships that now passed regularly from England to the Americas, returning loaded to the gunwales with the leaves of this strange plant, the smoking of which was said to 'Free the muse' but which Matthew found only numbed his into insensibility.

They sat in a corner of the smoky room and Marlowe shouted 'Mary'. An attractive young woman appeared from some dark corner, smiling at him

"Hello Kit," she said affably, a broad smile crossing her pretty face, "What's your pleasure today?"

"Mary," he replied, "You know that you will ever be my pleasure and my chief delight. But for the moment you can bring us something to drink."

"So Mattie," Kit said, when the girl had retired. "How can I be of assistance to you?"

Matthew had thought about this interview carefully. It would have been madness to confess to Marlowe that he was working for Lord Burghley. So instead he tried a different sort of approach.

"Well Kit," he said. "I had some small business a few days ago with a Vintner, a man by the name of Bartholomew Thrace."

He watched Marlow's face and registered the lifting of one eyebrow when the name of the Vintner was mentioned. But Kit remained silent, so Matthew continued;

"The only problem was that the business was never concluded – nor commenced for that matter, because I found Master Thrace dead with his throat cut."

"Well," said Marlowe dismissively, "We all have to die sometime Matthew. And Thrace was such a miserable, penny pinching old goat I don't suppose many will mourn his passing."

Strange, thought Matthew. John Acres had intimated that Marlowe and Thrace had been friends. He suggested as much.

Marlowe thought for a moment, narrowing his satanic dark eyes.

"I think friends would be an inappropriate term Mattie. Rather say we were..." He puzzled again for a brief second. "Rather say we were associates." Marlowe was nobody's fool. He looked shrewdly across the table. "I think you've a tale to tell Mattie. So why not relate what your dealings were with Master Thrace?. It can't have been simply to buy a bottle of Spanish wine or you wouldn't have got that nasty crack on the skull."

"How in the name of all that's holy did you know about that Kit?" Matthew wanted to know.

Marlowe smiled.

"I know many things Mattie. I have the eyes of a hawk, the ears of a bat, and, if gossip is to be believed, the cunning of a fox."

"In that case Master Raynard," Matthew went on, "Tell me how it was that a Roman Catholic Priest was selling wine and spirits right in the centre of London – and doing it with impunity?" It appeared that subtlety was a waste of time when dealing with Kit Marlowe. "And how was it that you and he were associated."

It could have been a dangerous question. Kit Marlowe didn't always take kindly to people prying into his business. But on this occasion it didn't appear to matter.

"That's simple Mattie. He was selling wines and spirits because he'd lapsed in his duties to the Holy Roman Church, and I knew him well because we were at the same seminary."

Matthew's jaw dropped.

"I'm sorry Kit, I think my ears must still be ringing from the sound of that mob. I thought you said that Thrace and yourself were at the same seminary?"

"That's exactly what I said Mattie", he confirmed, reassuringly. "Though of course you're a trusted friend and I'm sure you would realise why I don't want the fact to go any further."

Matthew sat bold upright in his seat. He was about to speak but the young woman returned with their drink. She set it down on the table, winked at Marlowe and then left again.

"May I take it then Kit that not only was the murdered Bartholomew Thrace a Priest of the Roman Catholic Church, but you are also?"

Marlow picked up the tankard and drunk deeply. Setting it down again he wiped his mouth with his forearm and said.

"You may Mattie. You may indeed."

"This is incredible!" Matthew heard himself saying. "This morning's debacle only goes to prove Kit that you can't take religion seriously at all. You mock almost anyone who's a believer and change your religious alliances more often than your jerkin. You've told me yourself that you hated religion so much you disobeyed your Father and refused to take the cloth yourself – and that was the Protestant Church."

"I certainly did Mattie," Marlowe confirmed, with a gracious smile. "Christianity has raped humanity since the belief came into being and the only thing that's more stupid than a man who stands in a pulpit and espouses the Christian message is the ignorant idiot who stays around to listen. Unless, that is, he does so only to pronounce the preacher a credulous fool."

"Then why in the name of St Barnabas would you want to become a Catholic Priest Kit?" At the very moment these words were out of his mouth Matthew realised how stupid he had been. It must have been obvious by his expression. Marlowe smiled as the look on the scrivener's face changed.

"You became a Catholic Priest not so that you could practice the faith, but so that you could inform on those who genuinely believed." He looked at Marlowe in disbelief. "You were working for the Privy Council?"

"Now there's a clever fellow," chided Marlowe. I went to Douai, in France, instead of doing my last year at university. Mind you," he added, Burghley saw to it that I still got my degree. I was at the seminary three years, and that's where I met Bartholomew Thrace."

"Who was also another of Lord Burghley's informants?"

"Oh Matthew you make it sound so vulgar. We were important Crown servants. And don't forget my friend, we're heroic too. It's a dangerous job. You've only to look at the murder of Bartholomew Thrace to understand that. We live in fear of having our throats cut every day of our lives – don't we Mattie?" He was smiling broadly again.

"You know that I'm working for Lord Burghley too, don't you Kit?"

"I guessed as much, and now of course you've confirmed it. But I have to say Mattie that I'm very surprised. I know you could roustabout with the best of us but you were never one for making waves, either religiously or politically."

"I'm not!" Matthew confirmed immediately. "I was dragged into something that I'd rather have nothing to do with, and at least partly on account of..." He thought about Rosemary and changed his intended tack. "And at least partly on account of someone who was close to my family."

Marlowe drank freely from the tankard before him and then asked.

"What have you been set to discover Matthew? The latest Jesuit conspiracy?"

"As a matter of fact I have, " Matthew confirmed. "Would you like to tell me how you know that?"

"It's all Burghley cares about. He sees Catholics, and Jesuits especially, hiding in every dark corner. Oh don't get me wrong Mattie," Marlowe continued. "There are plenty of them here in England. There are at least three seminaries, one in France, another in Italy and a third in Spain, all turning out Jesuit Priests who will ultimately return to England. But three hundred such institutions couldn't provide the number of Priests Burghley thinks he sees in any given day. He's probably got you on some fool's errand." He took another pull at his tankard. "God knows I've been involved in my share."

So many things regarding Christopher Marlowe now began to make sense. Matthew could not avoid mentioning one of them.

"That's why you speak your mind with impunity and get away with so much. You're being protected by the Privy Council. They don't arrest you because you're too valuable."

Marlowe's face hardened somewhat.

"I wouldn't exactly say that Mattie. It might have been true once upon a time but I know I'm living on borrowed time now. It won't be long before you hear that I've been found in more or less the same state as Bartholomew Thrace."

"You mean to tell me Kit that you think Lord Burghley had Thrace killed? I can't believe that. It doesn't sound very likely. In any case, the Sheriff's office think that Thrace was killed by his illegitimate son, a lad who goes by the name of Tom Campion and who is one of the boy actors in Lord Strange's Company"

Marlowe didn't look particularly surprised at this revelation either.

"I knew about Thrace's son. I think the lad considered that he and his mother had been badly wronged. As I told you, Master Thrace was a penny-pinching soul. It's quite possible that they quarrelled and the lad somehow got the better of him. To be quite honest with you Mattie I simply don't know who killed Thrace. Informers have many enemies – for example the relatives and friends of those who die because of the information they collect. But it's a fact that the more you know, the greater risk you pose to those running the country – Thrace knew a great deal, and I know even more."

Despite himself Matthew was becoming intrigued. "Like what Kit?"

Marlow's eyes narrowed again.

"You're not the man for this job Mattie. You're far too pleasant a fellow to be working for that rat Burghley. Act the idiot, leave the City and go home to Yorkshire. Do anything, but don't get into the pocket of the Privy Council. Believe me my friend, it's a very deep pocket, and those who fall in very rarely emerge again."

Matthew was many things. He'd been something of a womaniser, he was often in debt, he invariably ate and drank too much and was lax in his religious offices – but he was no coward.

"It's not that simple Kit. There are other people to consider. And in any case I would be a poor Englishman if I stood by whilst my country disappeared once again into the abyss of religious fanaticism."

"Oh you poor naive fool Mattie," Marlowe retorted immediately. "Don't you realise that the only time this country will belong to the people who work for its existence will be when all the religious bigots, all the political opportunists and every one of the idiots who thinks they have a head fitted for a crown have managed to destroy each other once and for all?"

"And you call me naïve Kit? What do you think would happen to the ordinary people if the English descended into civil war again?"

"Huh!" scoffed Marlowe. "They won't Matthew, believe me; they're far too apathetic for that."

Matthew caught the attention of the serving girl again and she disappeared to bring more ale. He leant forward in his seat, finally willing to ask the question that had been puzzling him ever since he'd known Christopher Marlowe.

"What exactly do you believe in Kit? I mean what really motivates you? It obviously isn't religion, and you don't seem to want preferment, or you wouldn't keep causing problems for the authorities. So what is it?"

Marlowe sat back and thought for a moment.

"It's excitement Mattie. That's all I care for – Excitement." He hesitated. "Well almost everything."

He didn't know whether to believe Marlowe or not but in any case he was getting further away from matters that concerned him immediately.

"You said an hour ago that you owed me a favour Kit, so tell me – as one spy to another. Do you think there is any conspiracy to murder the Queen and replace her with Lord Strange? And if so do you think Will Shakespeare would be involved in such a plot?"

Kit eyed Matthew across the rough-hewn table.

"And what makes you believe that such a conspiracy might really exist Mattie? I've told you the way Burghley's mind works. Why shouldn't this be simply another of his crackpot notions?"

"Well for one thing" said Matthew. "Lord Burghley considers, and is correct in his assumption, that there is a connection between Will Shakespeare's family and that of the Stanleys and in particular Ferdinando Stanley. Rose..." He broke off quickly. "One of my informants has confirmed that such a link does exist. And now Will Shakespeare is writing for Lord Strange's Company – which only became Lord Strange's Company when Shakespeare came onto the scene. Doesn't that all strike you as being rather odd – particularly since Lord Strange is a natural contender for a vacant English throne?"

The ale was making him rather less careful and a little more forthright.

"And incidentally Kit, what, if anything, do you know about Sir Thomas Gresham's House in Bishopsgate, and certain meetings that take place there?"

The girl began to approach again with the ale but Marlowe waved her away with a single gesture. He obviously didn't want anyone in earshot. The other drinkers and smokers had left during their conversation.

"Matthew," he said, almost sternly, but not with any anger or venom. "There are things that I can tell you, and others that I simply may not. I can't deny that you are correct in supposing that a vacant crown might be offered to Ferdinando Stanley. But what makes you think that he would want it?"

It was no real answer, but Matthew could tell for his expression that Kit Marlowe knew more about these matters than he was admitting. He became braver still, his curiosity now burning brighter than a midnight torch.

"And what makes you think he would refuse it Kit?"

Marlowe lifted his elbow onto the table and rested his chin on his slightly clenched fist.

"Mattie. I can honestly say that during the time I have been in London, you have been one of my staunchest friends. It is true that I haven't seen you all that regularly of late but when I arrived here in the City you were ever kind to me. You have proved your loyalty and companionship a dozen times over. So I'm going to reinforce some advice I gave you a few moments ago, and offer you another pearl or two of wisdom." He looked Matthew straight in the face, his gaze hard, his eyes fixed, black and resolute.

"Keep out of these matters Mattie. There are issues at stake here you cannot and should not understand. What you know already informs me that if you insist on following this course you will discover what you seek – and you may not be the better for it. But you can take my word for this. I see no Jesuit plot here, and no desire to remove Queen Elizabeth from her throne. Age will do that soon enough." he added. "And in any case has it occurred to you that it would suit 'certain people' if Queen Elizabeth reigned for at least a few years longer?"

Matthew was about to speak again but Marlowe held up his hand.

"There is no purpose in asking me to elaborate. I simply can't and won't tell you anymore. But now let me ask you a question Mattie. You almost mentioned a woman's name a few moments ago. 'Rose' you said, but it was only half a name wasn't it?"

Matthew probably flushed because Marlowe smiled, briefly, and then his face was stern again.

"Might the name have been Rosemary Mattie?"

"It could have been. But it isn't important."

"If the woman in question is Lady Rosemary Armscliffe it could be very important."

It was the turn of Matthew's eyes to narrow.

"How so Kit?" he wanted to know.

Marlowe let out a long sigh.

"If we are to do our jobs well, spies – like us Mattie, require friends, or at least contacts in the Privy Council, and at Courtl. Now bear in mind that I have been deep in Burghley's service for more years than I care to remember, both in my home-town of Canterbury and here in London. During that time it has been necessary for me to build up a great many contacts and almost everyone of note at Court is known to me. One of those people, a woman who is charming, honest and kind – all qualifications that make her totally unsuitable to be serving the Queen, is Lady Rosemary Armscliffe." He looked Matthew in the eyes again. "You know her don't you Mattie? She's from your part of the world, and you've been familiar with her for a long time."

"What makes you think that Kit?" Matthew wanted to know. "Plenty of people are from Yorkshire."

"I know it to be true Mattie because I've been reporting your movements to Lady Rosemary Armscliffe for the last five years or more."

"What?" Matthew asked, raising his voice probably more than was prudent.

"Through me she has observed your every movement, each play that you wrote and almost every poem of yours she could lay her hands on. And this has been the case since only a month or two after I arrived here in the City."

"But why?" Matthew wanted to know. "If, as you say, you trusted me as a friend and thought I had done you some service, why would you spy on me - for anyone?"

"Because I knew that it might prove to be in your interest one day." He laughed. "Don't look at me like that man? She's not been keeping an eye on you for any religious or political motive – I'm certain of that. Had I doubted her motives, or considered that she wished you any ill I would never have assisted her at all."

"I can't see any motive she might have had for monitoring my work and movements."

Marlowe laughed again, this time uproariously.

"You dunderhead Mattie. Must it be written in letters ten feet high on the side of a house? She's carrying a torch for you man."

Matthew didn't know what to say. It was preposterous. He found his voice eventually.

"That's absurd Kit. She's the widow of the Queen's Master of the Horse. Damn it man she's a Lady in Waiting and she serves Her Majesty almost on a daily basis."

"Didn't you ever hear the story of the elephant who fell in love with a mouse Matthew? It doesn't matter what position she holds. And if she isn't much more than simply sweet on you then my name is not Father Christopher Marlowe and I'm not a fully fledged Jesuit Priest."

"It's ridiculous Kit!" Matthew replied immediately. But was it? Rosemary had actually admitted, on that meeting at Hampton Court, that she had been keeping an eye on him. Only the previous day she'd intimated that she was more than familiar with at least some of his work. Rosemary had even made it quite plain that Matthew had become involved in Burghley's investigations at her instigation. But despite all this Matthew could not countenance such speculation. A match between her family and his might have been just credible back in Yorkshire, but Rosemary had moved into a very different sort of circle on the day she had become Lady Armscliffe.

"Well don't look so depressed," Marlowe said after a moment during which Matthew was lost in his own thoughts. "There are far worse things in life than having someone as rich and influential a Lady Rosemary Armscliffe watching out for you."

Matthew couldn't deny the accuracy of that statement, but somehow it didn't make him feel a great deal better. For one thing could he even be sure that the money he'd been given had arrived in his purse specifically at the behest of Lord Burghley. Might it not rather have originated in Rosemary's coffers? There was no doubt that he found her to be a tremendously beautiful, charming and entertaining woman but to become a 'kept man', the plaything of an extremely rich woman; that would be unconscionable.

Matthew voiced these concerns to Marlowe, whose smile disappeared, replaced by a look of genuine compassion.

"My poor friend," he said. "Life is short and brutal enough. Affection comes rarely. We don't always have any real choice as to its origin, or regarding where we must bestow it. Take the advice of a dead man Matthew, for that is what I shall be before many more months are passed. Seize the moment, and wring as much joy from it as you can, for in truth we are going to be feeding the flowers for a long time."

They sat for a while in silence until finally Marlowe said. "Well my old friend, though I have enjoyed our conversation tremendously, I will have to leave soon. I have an appointment to keep later this afternoon. If you are going back into the City I would welcome your company?"

They retraced their steps back across the river. The leaden sky was lifting in the early afternoon. To the east, from down river, a great ship, its sails furled was being towed up by three large rowing boats from the direction of Greenwich. At its masthead the flag of England fluttered cheerfully in the light breeze. They stood and watched it for a while.

"That ship is the Silver Plover," Marlowe told Matthew. She's back from privateering, and the gold in her holds will buy Sir Walter Raleigh out of the Tower."

Matthew knew, as did all England, that Queen Elizabeth's former favourite, Sir Walter Raleigh, had been imprisoned for daring to marry without Her Majesty's permission.

"Some say his own pride got him into the Tower in the first place," Matthew suggested.

"Possibly," Marlowe commented. "But for all that he's a good man; brave and heedless of his own safety. I am proud to count him as a friend Mattie – as indeed I am your good self. No," he went on, turning his attention to the ship again. "Sir Walter's only real fault is that our good Queen liked him too much. If there is any pride about in this world 'Gloriana' herself has the lion's share of it."

Christopher Marlowe knew the great Sir Francis Drake? Matthew looked at the man walking beside him. He was striking enough, with his shock of black hair and his demonic looks, but he was far too intelligent to behave in the way he did publicly unless there was some real gain to be had from doing so. Matthew was certain that it was more than a simple lust for excitement that caused Marlowe to appear such a hell-raiser. Yet despite all, the man was a total enigma. On the corner of Eastcheap they parted company, shaking hands warmly.

"Do not forget what I told you Matthew, for I am in great earnest. I don't have so many friends that I can afford to lose the least of them, let alone you." He smiled. "A simple country soul such as yourself, a man with a stout heart but a pudding for a brain wasn't built for a life of intrigue. Go back to your poetry and your plays Matthew Prior, and leave the spying to wretches like me. Men who have no honour to lose."

For the first time since he had known Kit Marlowe Matthew thought that he had come at least a little closer to understanding the man. All the same, Matthew had made a bargain to serve his Queen and his country and he hadn't been so long away from his sleepy manor that he could forget what every child of even the minor nobility was taught; that duty was all. Marlowe could see the fact in his face.

"Well if I can't persuade you to desist, even though I've done what little I am able to put your mind at rest, then all I can advise you to do Mattie is to keep to the wide byways and to watch your back."

"It's good advice," whispered Matthew's familiar into his left ear, "but not as good as the former council, to get out of the whole business and go back to Yorkshire."

"Thank you Kit," Matthew said. "But I have to go on. Even if what you say is true it's possible that an innocent boy will face the gallows for a crime he may not have committed. That at least is something I should investigate. And in all conscience," he continued, "even if what you say about Lady Rosemary is true I am honour bound to help her if I can. It is inevitable that until Will Shakespeare's name is cleared of any treasonable action, at least some suspicion may fall in the direction of Lady Rosemary, because of the family connections. And who knows, it might even fall upon my own if I disobey Lord Burghley's orders. No," he added, "If only for the sake of the truth Kit, I'm in too deep already to retire."

Matthew watched Kit Marlowe disappear into the distance and then turned to walk east, towards Whitechapel and the docks. He had business with Sam Hardacre, a man he hadn't seen for a year or two, but a character who might be of supreme use now.

Chapter Eleven
An Executed Priest.

Through most of the evening and on through a relatively uneventful Monday morning Matthew had considered the words of Kit Marlowe; his warnings about looking further into the connections between Lord Strange and Will Shakespeare and his observations regarding Rosemary. There may have been some substance to his advice on both counts but of course Marlowe was the master of subterfuge and obfuscation. The man had been accused by more than one person, and on diverse occasions of being an inveterate liar – so how could Matthew accept, carte blanche, the rudest part of what he had said? If anything his interview with the brilliant, but unquestionably Machiavellian Marlowe, had only served to deepen a whole series of mysteries that were beginning to complicate further Matthew's view of either situation. It seemed to Matthew that Marlowe clearly knew 'something', particularly regarding Shakespeare and Lord Strange. This had fired off Matthew's natural curiosity and he knew that it would be impossible for him to leave the situation alone, even assuming Lord Burghley would allow him to do so.

After parting company with Marlowe, Matthew had visited the docks below Whitechapel. There, amongst the crowded little houses, mainly occupied by boat-builders and dockers, he had sought out Sam Hardacre, a friend who Matthew had met almost the first day he had arrived in London. Like Matthew Sam was a Yorkshireman, a tough, weather-beaten old sea dog, now well into his fifties, who had made his mark skippering a bark that brought alum down to London, from the Northeast Coast of England.

Sam was an irrepressible story-teller who, a decade or so earlier, had frequented the inns and stews of Southwark. Tiring of the single life, and now based at the docks in London, where he had built up a small chandler's business, Sam had married a plump Cornish girl, a former serving wench from the White Goose. Together they had settled into domestic bliss and now, content with his lot, Sam Hardacre rarely visited Southwark.

The older man and his red faced bustling wife were pleased to see an old friend and received Matthew cordially at their dockside home. After reminiscences about old times shared, Matthew told Sam about Tom Campion and the loss of the two young men who could stand alibi for him. Sam had taken down the details and promised to make some enquiries. Matthew was aware that his old friend knew everyone of note in dockside London, naval and civilian alike. If anyone could locate Paul Usher and Nathan Smyth it would be Sam Hardacre. Sam agreed either to bring the lads to Matthew or alternately to the Sheriff's office in the City if he had any success. Matthew had remained talking to his old friends late into the evening and had arrived back at his lodgings around midnight.

Despite his late night, Matthew had arrived early at the theatre the next day, after once again taking food to Tom Campion, who was still being held at the pleasure of the Sheriff. Tom had still not been fully interviewed about the murder of his father and Matthew found the lad in low spirits. This wasn't surprising. As an orphan, Tom had nobody on whom to rely and he feared greatly for his position with Lord Strange's Men, even if he should be acquitted. Life as an actor was hard enough on the fringes of a City, the authorities of which contrived to do everything they could to ban theatre altogether. James Burbage would surely not welcome any slur falling on the company on account of the supposed actions of one of his players, a fact that Tom and Matthew alike knew only too well.

Without any real personal conviction Matthew had done all he could to lift Campion's spirits, telling him that he was making enquiries about the lad's friends and advising him, once again, to speak the truth. He left the musty dungeon with little heartfelt belief that Tom's full co-operation with the authorities would necessarily lead to genuine justice.

Early in the afternoon, some time before the actors assembled, Matthew had walked down to the Rose theatre, there to find Will Shakespeare already hard at work. Taking up his quill Matthew had begun to transcribe copies of the parts of The Tragedy of Richard III that Will had completed during Sunday. The rate of progress was astonishing. It was clear that Shakespeare had decided, wisely in Matthew's opinion, to follow the accepted norm when describing Richard III's character, making of him a clever but hideous and malicious opportunist – a man who was willing to go to any lengths to secure the throne, and to keep it at all costs. But Shakespeare's creation went far beyond the pale. Anyone possessing the slightest morsel of wisdom must see that a monster such as Will portrayed in the play could never have existed. Indeed, in some parts of the country and particularly in Matthew's own home County, Richard III, formerly Lord Protector of the North, was still spoken of with great affection. This state of affairs persisted despite the fact that there was nobody remotely old enough to have lived during his reign, which had ended over a century previously.

Shakespeare's prudence in taking for the theme of his play the observations of Sir Thomas Moore, formerly Chancellor of England and a staunch Tudor supporter, was to be expected. The man who had deposed Richard III, and whose forces had defeated and killed the former King, was none other than Henry VII, the grandfather of the present Queen. Matthew was familiar with the observation that 'history is written by the victor' and any playwright who valued his life would have been wise to recognise the fact.

No matter how quickly Shakespeare moved forward with his plot, he rarely, if ever made an alteration to anything he had already written. It appeared as if the whole story, speeches, characterisation and plot, was already lodged in Will's mind and that only the necessity of offering it to the public made it essential to transpose onto paper.

Eventually the actors began to wander into the theatre. Monday was quiet, with many workers remaining in the City in the afternoons in order to apply themselves to their respective tasks after their day of rest. As a result audiences tended to be small and the day was generally left free for one of the less popular plays. In this case it was to be a play written by John Rymer, a rather awkward and somewhat trite comedy based on an old Testament theme and entitled 'The Patience of Job'. It was tedious in the extreme and it had been neglected by most companies for a number of years. Every theatre company needed to have at last six full length plays in its repertoire at any given point in time and since most of the older actors had taken part in The Trials of Job earlier in their career, it was familiar.

This made it an adequate 'pot boiler' for a Monday afternoon performance.

The absence of Tom Campion under such suspicious circumstances seemed to be the main topic of conversation. James Burbage stormed about the place in a thunderous mood. It would have been impossible to keep a permanent understudy for each roll in every one of the six productions at present in the repertoire and that would mean a good deal of juggling of parts in the days ahead if Tom Campion was not released. Fortunately the young man had only a walk-on role in The Patience of Job and Burbage had elicited the services of Robert Meryl, a lad from St Paul's School, to fill in for the missing actor.

The part of Job himself was to be taken by Anthony Roper, one of the most experienced of the company's older actors. Despite the fact that the numbers attending the play were quite small Roper managed a superlative handling of the part, in direct contrast to his performance on the previous Saturday afternoon, which had been dull and lacking in commitment. Even off stage Roper seemed more jaunty. Upon his arrival he had greeted the other cast members, and even Matthew himself, warmly. As usual his daughter Jane was present, selling hazel-nuts to the audience members. At the end of the performance she and her father left the theatre almost immediately, hand in hand, smiling and obviously content in each other's company. There appeared to be no trace of the awkwardness that had been obvious in their relationship on the previous Saturday.

Some of the other actors stayed around for a while and Matthew paid full attention to the conversations that took place, mainly concerning the supposed innocence – or guilt of the presently imprisoned Tom Campion. Nicholas Tooley, who Matthew had noticed previously was apparently jealous of Tom's ability to play the best of the young female roles now that he could not do so himself, declared that Campion must surely have been charged falsely.

"I hope you are correct Nick, but how can you be so sure of that?" asked the affable Richard Tarlton.

"His innocence is obvious Master Tarlton. Rumour has it that Bartholomew Thrace, the Vintner, was killed by someone wearing the green gown, a person Master Prior here believed to be a woman."

"So?" Tarlton put in. "Why should that make young Tom innocent of the murder? He often wears the green gown on stage, as you know right well."

"That's my whole point Master Tarlton," laughed Tooley. "His portrayal of a woman is so poor it wouldn't fool anyone, let alone a person as knowledgeable and discriminating as Master Prior."

It was a bitchy remark, and had been intended as such, and so Matthew dismissed it from his mind immediately. It was clear from the conversations of the other actors that none of them had the remotest idea as to Tom's guilt or innocence, though the majority were sympathetic regarding the predicament in which the young man found himself.

As the theatre cleared Matthew busied himself finishing his tidying in the tiring house. Shakespeare was once again hard at work on his play, with the backstage curtains open, making the best possible use of the falling sun, which peered out furtively between gathering clouds, sending its beams sideways across the cockpit and up onto the stage. The pages of the manuscript now finished since Matthew had looked at it last lay in a pile, ready for him to copy them out. He picked up the sheaf of parchment and simply said

"May I?"

Will looked up.

"I'd be honoured to have your opinion," he said, smiling.

Matthew took the pages across to an adjacent table and began to read from the place where he'd left off copying. Some half an hour later, for Will Shakespeare had been no laggard prior to or during the performance, Matthew lifted his head.

"Well?" Will wanted to know. "What do you make of it? And don't be tardy when it comes to telling the truth. I respect your opinion Mattie."

The truth wouldn't have been likely to upset the playwright..

"It's extraordinary Will, truly extraordinary." Matthew was silent for a while, wondering whether he should voice his full opinions, but Shakespeare looked expectant, almost demanding the unvarnished truth.

"I have to admit," Matthew finally said. "I did have my doubts – oh not about your writing skills, I know those well enough already, but about the advisability of creating yet another play about Richard III. It's a popular subject and as you must know only too well there are several dramas about already using this theme."

"Yes I was aware that that was the case, though I have to say in fairness that I wasn't all that struck by the way some writers have handled such a complex character," Shakespeare said, almost apologetically. "So! How does my play compare with the others, at least to the point I've reached?"

Matthew was totally candid.

"It eclipses them all Will. It goes straight to the heart of the matter. History relates that Richard Plantagenet was a thoroughly evil and self-centred individual and you make no bones about the fact. You have him admitting it from the very first page. Though I have to say Will that I'm somewhat surprised."

"At what Mattie?" He could see the hesitation in the other's eyes. "No please, do tell me. Just because you are here as a copyist doesn't mean that I fail to recognise your own worth as a writer."

"Very well," Matthew told him. "I am surprised that you haven't left the slightest loophole of doubt as to the man's motives. I mean in all your other plays you draw wonderfully on the complexity of human nature, but here you don't even attempt to forgive Richard for anything. It's almost as if you are over-egging the pudding – as if you want the audience to realise that you are deliberately talking tongue in cheek. I mean in all honesty nobody could actually be what Richard Plantagenet is supposed to have been. But in your play, here he is – as large as life and twice as ugly."

Shakespeare had not stopped smiling.

"How perceptive you are Mattie." He replied. "Had I dealt with the story in the way my common sense intimated, I might easily have come closer to the real motives of the man. You know as well as I do that such a course of action would have finished my writing career, and might have endangered my life."

"So you did the exact opposite?" Matthew quizzed. "You made Richard so absolutely evil that the whole story becomes a virtual parody. You knew full well that such a monster could never exist, and you are aware that intelligent audience members will realise it too?"

Will Shakespeare lifted an eyebrow.

"Let us merely say Mattie that I will not be especially surprised, or indeed insulted if people leave the theatre genuinely wondering about the reliability of accepted historical accounts. In any case," he went on. "It is, after all, simply a story - and a tragedy at that."

Matthew took in this last throwaway statement. Despite Will's words it was clear that this man had a remarkable mind, and an approach to the writing of drama that was well out of step with all that had gone before.

It was an hour or two later that Matthew left The Rose. He had remained in the theatre, spending some time continuing the copying of the new play and had been complimented by Shakespeare as to the accuracy and neatness of his work. Will had announced his intention of going straight to his lodgings when he left the theatre. Matthew could not be certain that this would actually be the case and so, once again, he clandestinely followed the playwright across London Bridge and on up Bishopsgate Street. This time Will strode past the house of the deceased Thomas Gresham and eventually arrived at Hog Lane, Shoreditch, where Matthew knew the man's lodgings to be. Content that there was nothing else to see regarding Shakespeare, Matthew set his step south again, towards Southwark and The White Goose.

The place was busier than ever. There was a great deal of commotion coming from one particular corner, where a group of foreign sailors were playing a noisy game of dice. Elsewhere in the room Matthew took in the odd assortment of vagabonds and vagrants, pick-pockets and pimps, women of easy virtue, dockers, boatmen and apprentices from the City that made the place so worth visiting.

"Well met Mattie", came the voice of John Acres, who had followed him into the place and who now clapped him warmly on the shoulder.

The two found a corner away from the ribald antics of the crowded inn. Matthew was well aware from the look on his friend's face that John had been busy on his behalf and it didn't take the little man long to divulge at least part of the information that had come his way.

"I think I may have found the seat of your Jesuit plot Mattie," he confirmed, almost gleefully.

"How so John? And where did you come by such information?"

"From my cousin Walter - at Court. I met him this afternoon, here in Southwark. He'd been at the Rose as a matter of fact. So I brought him in here afterwards and plied him with ale." He laughed. "He's a terrible tell-tale and can't resist spilling the beans, so it wasn't hard to get him to tell me what he knew about Lord Strange's Men - and one of them in particular."

"Will Shakespeare?" Matthew asked, speculatively.

"No," John answered mischievously. Rather someone that you probably didn't suspect at all.

He remained quiet for a moment, teasing Matthew with his silence. An inebriated sailor stumbled nearby and fell awkwardly across their table. Their drink had not arrived and so no damage was done. As if it were nothing more than the alighting of a passing fly the two conspired to push him back into the scuffle beyond the table.

"Well don't keep me waiting you dolt. Who is it?"

"None other than Anthony Roper," John said, almost gleefully.

Matthew was sceptical but pensive.

"I don't know a great deal about Master Roper John, but he's hardly in a position to shake the nation to its core. He's simply one of the actors in the Company."

John Acres looked slightly disappointed. "Well if you don't want to hear what I've discovered......."

"No!" replied Matthew immediately. Carry on John. I'm all ears, and deeply indebted for your trouble on my account."'

His friend smiled again. "Have you ever heard of a man by the name of George Sale?"

Matthew sifted through his mind. Somewhere in the darkness a small candle glowed, and then he remembered. "I do believe I have John. It was something Rosemary – Lady Armscliffe mentioned to me. Wasn't George Sale a Jesuit Priest, captured recently whilst trying to travel to Lancashire?"

Indeed he was Mattie", John confirmed. "He was executed two weeks ago, though privily." He smiled again. "From what Walter says there are so many Jesuits being apprehended at the moment that Lord Burghley only allows a small proportion to undergo public execution. What was it Walter says? Ah yes. Lord Burghley fears that a plethora of Jesuits on the public scaffold might 'inflame the senses of the populace'".

"So what has, or rather had, George Sale to do with Anthony Roper?" Matthew asked, anxious to get to the heart of the matter.

"It appears," replied John., "that before he had gone off to a seminary on the Continent, George Sale had been a married man. He was a widower, though about the same age as Anthony Roper. He was formerly married to Roper's sister. They were brothers in law."

"Well," observed Matthew, after thinking about the situation for a while. "As I said to young Tom Campion only yesterday, we aren't responsible for our relatives, and particularly not those that come to us by way of marriage."

"True," admitted his friend, "but it goes rather deeper than that." Their drink arrived and John took great delight in keeping Matthew waiting as he quaffed half a flagon of ale at one pull. When he had finished he wiped his mouth in his sleeve and said. "Ah that's better. I'd a thirst on me like plough horse."

Matthew scowled playfully.

"You infuriating fellow," he said. "Are you going to carry on with your story or do you want the rest of that ale over your head?"

They both laughed and John eventually continued.

"Look Mattie this is strictly between the two of us. If it gets abroad that Walter has been talking to me about such matters we could all find ourselves deep in the mire." Matthew nodded his understanding and John Acres continued. "It appears Lord Burghley knows that George Sale was in contact with Anthony Roper almost as soon as he arrived in England, three or four months ago that would have been. Roper's family come from Suffolk." He narrowed his eyes and looked around, as if trying to recall something. "Walter did tell me the name of the place but I forget." He straightened himself in his chair. "No, no – I do recall, he comes from a small town called Southwold.. By all accounts, the old faith is still strong in those parts. But there's more still. Walter says Anthony Roper has a brother, a man by the name of James. He's a Catholic Priest too and teaches at the seminary in Douai."

"Does he indeed?" Matthew said, his eyes wide with recognition. "And Douai is the seminary from which George Sale travelled to England?"

"Exactly", John replied.

"If Roper has so many 'dangerous' Catholic connections, why is he still walking free John?" Matthew wanted to know.

"Yes I thought that was odd too. But as far as Walter knows Lord Burghley doesn't see Anthony Roper as any particular threat. He was certainly taken in for questioning when George Sale was arrested, but it seems as though the Priest told the authorities that he'd contacted Anthony Roper only on family business. He claimed that Roper had no knowledge of his true purpose in England."

"And Lord Burghley believed him?"

John shrugged.

"I suppose he must have done, otherwise he would have been on the scaffold with George Sale and we wouldn't be talking about him now. But it's equally likely that he's been left alone for reasons that only Lord Burghley understands."

"Well it's important information right enough John and I'm grateful for your efforts on my behalf," Matthew assented. "But all the same it doesn't prove a great deal. It's Will Shakespeare and our beloved patron Lord Strange that Lord Burghley seems most interested in. If Anthony Roper is any sort of fish in this pond he can surely only be a very small one?"

"Maybe so Mattie," John admitted, but it does show that there are definite Catholic connections within the Company."

"It does indeed John. It does indeed. And you can rest assured that I'll keep a special eye on Master Roper. He's a strange man altogether. Sometimes he's as tight as a fresh caught oyster and so silent and sullen you'd think him a dull fellow indeed. And then tonight, for no apparent reason, he was as friendly as could be to everyone." Matthew considered the matter and then said. "His daughter is an odd sort too."

"His daughter?"

"Yes. She's called Jane. She works at The Rose, selling hazel-nuts for James Burbage."

"So what's so strange about her Mattie?" John wanted to know.

"It's difficult to say John. She's quiet and shy, but I think there's more to her than meets the eye. I've a shrewd suspicion that she has some sort of relationship with Tom Campion, the lad who at present stands accused of murdering his father, Bartholomew

Thrace." He smiled. "If so it appears that her father doesn't approve. Perhaps he's simply over protective. But tell me John," he asked, changing tack. "Did Walter know of any connection between Anthony Roper and Lord Strange?"

"None at all. I asked him of course. And speaking of Lord Strange, he's in London at present."

"Really?", said Matthew. "I would have thought that being a Court favourite he would have been with the Queen in Northampton?"

"Apparently not. Though it doesn't matter...." He became conspiratorial. "....because the Queen will be back in the Capital in two days. She's cut short her stay in Northampton – and do you know why Mattie?"

Matthew thought he did.

"Would it have anything to do with Sir Walter Raleigh and a treasure ship named 'The Silver Plover?"

John Acres looked somewhat crestfallen.

"Oh," he said. "You've already heard about that have you?" After a short time he smiled again. "But I do have a further piece of information to impart which I wager you aren't aware of. Did you know Mattie that your contact and old friend Lady Rosemary Armscliffe is to be married later this year?"

It took a moment for the revelation to sink in, though when Matthew thought about the situation it wasn't too surprising. Not only was Rosemary a wonderful potential catch for any gentleman, for she held a sizeable fortune herself but she was also an extremely attractive woman. Matthew knew it, so how could others fail to notice the fact.

"No John", he said. "I didn't know that."

"Walter told me that it is the wish of the Queen herself that Lady Armscliffe should fasten her fortune onto that of Thomas Roach, Lord Newham."

Matthew pondered. "I can't say that I've heard of him John. Who is he?"

"It's clear that you don't keep up with what is going on at Court Matthew. Lord Newham is England's Ambassador to the Netherlands. He's wealthy enough and well up in the Queen's estimations by all accounts." He pulled a vinegary face. "Mind you I don't envy Lady Armscliffe that match. Lord Newham is sixty if he's a day and has already been married three times."

Matthew's heart sank, though in all honesty his disappointment was not so much for his own sake but for that of Rosemary. She had specifically pointed to the great difference in age between herself and the late Lord Armscliffe. Now it appeared that she was to be married off to someone even more venerable. He wondered why she had not mentioned the fact to him during their long conversations and then realised that it was, of course, none of his business. For all he knew she approved wholeheartedly of the match.

"When is the wedding to take place John?"

"Rumour has it that it won't be until the late summer Mattie because according to Walter, Lord Newham will not be returning from the Continent until then."

There was no denying that Matthew felt deflated. He soon grew tired of the noise and the smoke of the crowded room. After a few minutes he thanked John heartily for the information he had gathered and excused himself, claiming fatigue. Leaving the inn he walked slowly back towards the river, pausing to watch the waning moon peering out from behind wispy clouds, painting the ebbing water silver in the hollows of its many ripples.

Matthew was not given to being melancholy. It simply wasn't in his nature to brood. All the same, try as he might he could not get that dear face from the forefront of his mind. In his mind's eye he saw Rosemary as she had been at Hampton Court – stately and statuesque; and then at their second meeting, in the far more informal setting of her home in the Strand. All at once he was filled with a great and quite unaccustomed longing. Strings of words began to form themselves into stanzas in his head, and the stanzas became verses. He stood for a while at the parapet of the bridge, looking out towards the estuary, twenty odd miles distant. With a long, low sigh he took the mental verses, would-be sonnets for an affection that simply was not possible, and tossed them gently onto the falling tide.

With a leaden heart he turned north and strode off slowly towards Wyatt's Yard and his bed.

Chapter Twelve
The Alchemist

A new day had brought with it lighter spirits and a more sensible realisation of the way the world actually was, rather than the way Matthew might have wished it to be. He had woken to the joy of warm sunbeams cutting through the accumulated grime on the large window at the far side of his room. He had lain, listening to the stirrings of the City. Elizabeth Pugh, another tenant of the tenement where Matthew lived, was scolding her husband, David, beneath Matthew's casement, complaining about his constant snoring. This, apparently, had kept her awake throughout the whole of the night and which, she declared,

"Was loud enough to wake every sleeping soul in St Clement's churchyard."

Matthew had listened to the "Halloo Shoo – Shoo!" calls of drovers, bringing their animals over London Bridge and up into the City, together with the shouts of bread sellers and the crunch of heavy carts on the compacted road beyond the entrance to Wyatt's Yard. He was aware that his life had changed somehow irrevocably and that beyond these commonplace sounds existed a new world of intrigue and confusion. Perhaps he would not wish it any other way because recent events had brought a degree of excitement and a stimulus for his natural curiosity.

It wasn't long before he rose and dressed, ready to set his step once again towards the Strand. He had much to report to Rosemary, who, though it was obvious she could be nothing more to him had become a valued friend. The contemplation of her existence in the world seemed an extra ray of sunshine to push winter and its aching rawness to the back of his mind.

The two miles or so, through the City, along Fleet Street and the Aldwych had proved to be a joyful experience. It seemed that at every step there was some apple faced wench or rustic swain ready with a 'Good morrow Sir'. Even the crowded, refuse strewn streets of London had seemed to smile to a fresh day, with all the promise of new growth and nature's abundance lying around the corner.

But now, returning from the purer air and greener vistas of The Strand, he was back in the heart of the City once again. At the little lodge, hard by the entrance to Armscliffe House, Matthew had been given a note by one of Rosemary's servants.

"My wellbeloved Friend.

I think it possible that you may attend me today and so I leave this short note in place of my own presence. I apologise for this unforgivable absence and beseech you, if the hour of your arrival be early, to seek me at the home of Dr John Dee, who lives in the large house with the twin bays, overlooking St Martin's in Ludgate Hill. Should your hour of attendance be later, watch for my coach on the road, or wait for me at my home, enjoying in my absence all the comfort that my poor house can afford.

I remain you faithful friend and servant.

Rosemary Armscliffe.

Matthew had looked up at the sun and judged the hour to be no later than around nine, and so had retraced his steps back towards the City. On the way he had amused himself in wondering what business Rosemary could possibly have with the famous John Dee. This man, a doctor, philosopher, astrologer, mathematician and alchemist was a person of great influence and had been resident astrologer, not only to the present Queen, but also to her predecessor, Mary Tudor. Early in his career, for now he was an elderly man of some seventy years, John Dee had frightened sensibilities with some of his extraordinary claims, particularly regarding alchemy and had briefly been imprisoned for wizardry. Now, in his declining years, he was a figure of immense respect amongst a certain section of the intelligencia of London and still enjoyed a good deal of preferment from the Crown.

Matthew had never met John Dee personally, though he had seen the stately old man on many occasions. Dee was a great theatregoer and was known to be particularly fond of the work of both Shakespeare and Marlowe. One of Dee's servants, a personal aid by the name of Ned Cole, was an acquaintance of Matthew's. Ned had formerly helped to run the Rose theatre, though he had a natural penchant for mathematics and all matters associated with natural science. It wasn't especially surprising when John Dee appointed Ned Cole to his own household, particularly since the old man was now somewhat diminished in his physical powers, though apparently not his mental ones.

It was Ned who opened the door to Matthew, when he arrived, warm and invigorated from his long walk, at the large and imposing door of the great house in Ludgate. Ned was an interesting character in his own right, the son of a cobbler from Dee's own home city of Chester. From the most humble beginnings Ned had taught himself to read and write and had eventually served the students of Oxford University, in order to gain some semblance of knowledge in mathematics, Latin and Greek on the way.

"Why Matthew", he said jovially, as he threw back the door and bid the scrivener to enter. Ned was a man of similar age to Matthew, a neat individual, formerly gaunt but now grown somewhat portly from his cosseted life in the Dee household. He had fair hair and a neat beard sporting wisps of ginger.

As Matthew walked into the entrance hall Ned said

"Lady Armscliffe mentioned to me that you may call to attend her here this morning. She is presently with Dr Dee in his library but I have been asked to offer you hospitality whilst she is occupied. So what's it to be Mattie? A jug of ale perhaps?"

Matthew was grateful, dusty from the road and near parched with thirst.

The two talked for a few moments about life beyond the hallowed walls of Dee's home and workshop. Matthew explained about his present position at the Rose, Ned's old place of work, though of course without the slightest reference as to his real purpose for joining Lord Strange's Men. Ned admitted that he missed the hustle and bustle of life in the theatre, but seemed content enough with his present lot.

"I was just tidying away some items that Lady Armscliffe and Dr Dee have been inspecting in Dr Dee's laboratory." Ned said presently. "Perhaps you would like to see his most famous 'inner sanctum'."

This was not an invitation that Matthew would have passed up lightly. John Dee's laboratory was the very stuff of legend. Here, it was claimed; and the old man himself would not gainsay the suggestion, he had isolated the famous 'philosopher's stone'. Rumour had it that with this he had transmuted quantities of base metal into gold.

Ned gave some instructions to a minion, who appeared at the door at his summons, and then led Matthew through an antechamber into a large and airy room at the back of the house, looking out over the private garden and an uncultivated burgage plot beyond.

There were several large tables in the chamber, each one containing greater and seemingly more mysterious pieces of equipment. Matthew's eyes took in a series of retorts, flasks, lamps, tubes and crucibles. In a far corner was a large iron stove. Everyone in London knew of the existence of this stove, which was reputedly the place where Dee had placed small wax balls, containing chunks of lead, together with pieces of the philosopher's stone. When he had removed them the next day the wax had melted and the lead had turned, in its entirety, into pure, shining gold.

As Matthew gazed in absolute awe around the room the servant reappeared, now carrying a jug of ale and a large tankard. He set then down on a small, empty table near the hearth and then retired.

"Help yourself Mattie", Ned instructed him, turning to a series of glass and pottery jars which lay open on the table nearest to the door. All the receptacles appeared to contain powder of one sort or another, and in a great variety of different, vibrant colours. Matthew had poured himself a flagon of ale and now stood looking quizzically, though unsure of himself in such surroundings he remained at a distance.

"These are some of the ingredients Dr Dee uses in his work Mattie," Ned explained. "He and Lady Armscliffe were discussing them earlier. This blue one," he said, pointing to one of the large open jars before him, is a powdered form of copper and the deep red one here is made from the bodies of innumerable small, dried insects, which can only be found in the very interior of the African Continent.

Matthew was transfixed. "What does he use them all for," he asked after a while, "Medicines?"

Ned laughed.

"Some of them," he said, "but Dr Dee is a great experimenter and his work lays often far beyond the horizons of my limited understanding."

Matthew now approached the table and gazed with increasing fascination at an array of colours in the various pots and jars the like of which his eyes had previously never beheld. A few he recognised, such as the metallic blue of powdered lapis lazuli and the warm fiery yellow of amber, but others were bright, lucid green, lustrous black and one jar containing powder of a stunning turquoise hue.

Ned invited Matthew to inspect the powders at closer quarters before he put them away.

"They're all relatively harmless Mattie," he commented; "except for this one." He held up a fluted clear jar, containing a pearly white powder. Unlike the other containers it was securely stoppered.

"Matthew knew a little about alchemy, having read what treatise on the subject he could obtain. He looked carefully at the powder in the jar Ned was holding.

"I've read," he said, "that the philosopher's stone is actually a powder that looks much like this."

"For all I know it is Mattie," Ned smiled, "though I've never seen it myself. "But you can be sure that this is not it. This innocuous looking powder is so deadly that Dr Dee tells me that there is enough in this small receptacle to kill half the population of London. Even a few grains inhaled could be quite deadly. It comes from the Americas and is said to be the distilled essence of the root of a tree so hideous that it has come to be known to Europeans as 'the Medusa tree'. And as with that famed lady of Greek legend, none may even gaze upon the tree with impunity."

Matthew shuddered and turned his attention to the various components of the chemical apparatus. He looked towards the door, ensuring that Dee himself had not entered unseen.

"Tell me Ned," he asked and then added apologetically, "Though I doubt it not if Dr Dee says it is so. Can he really turn lead into gold?"

Ned's smile faded.

"I believe he can Mattie. Though I think that if this experiment alone lay at the core of Dr Dee's work, as people suspect, he would rather have been a tanner. It is the essence of self knowledge that lies at the heart of the alchemist's striving."

Their conversation was cut short as Dr Dee himself, together with Rosemary, entered the room.

"Matthew," she said breezily. "How good of you to come and escort me home. Have you met Dr Dee?" she wanted to know.

Matthew looked at the old man and wondered if there was actually any truth in the alchemists claim to be able to preserve youth and vitality. He had heard it said, in tavern conversations and in aimless chit-chat prior to performances in the theatre, that some people believed Dee to be several centuries old, despite his own admission to only seven decades. Certainly many thought that the depth of learning enjoyed by this elderly man would surely take more than one natural lifetime to amass.

Dee was a little bowed by age, but his hand was steady and his gaze fixed and penetrating. He was a handsome man for his age, with blue eyes and a fine head of stone grey hair.

"I have never had the pleasure," Matthew admitted, "though of course I've seen Dr Dee on numerous occasions. Sir," he said, bowing reverently, "it is a great honour to make your acquaintance."

The man's voice carried the slightest trace of his Northern origins.

"You are too kind Master Prior. Here sir," he went on, moving towards Matthew and offering his hand. "I perceive you are from North of the Trent. On that account alone I would call you an ally, but the matter is sealed in the knowledge that you are a confidant of Lady Rosemary here, who I would sincerely claim to be the most learned and beautiful lady in London."

Matthew took the proffered hand and gripped it warmly.

"Well," Matthew said to Rosemary, as they sauntered in the sunshine, down Ludgate Hill in the direction of The Fleet. "You have some important and fascinating friends Rosemary."

Rosemary had dismissed her carriage and sent it back to The Strand, preferring to make the most of the pleasant weather and to walk home, with Matthew, dismissing his protestation regarding her safety with "You Master Prior, represent all the protection I shall need."

"I've known Dr Dee almost since the day I arrived in London," she told Matthew. Whenever I have the time I go to see him. Some people find him difficult but he has always encouraged my desire to learn. In the absence of my own father down here in the South, Dr Dee has sometimes played the part of a surrogate."

Rosemary was wearing a gown of bright russet silk. Now in a public setting, as befitted a Lady in Waiting of the most famous Queen in the world, she reflected the glory of the Court of which she was part. She was a good two hand spans shorter in height than Matthew and she looked up at him, smiling, as she spoke. About her head was a glass beaded net, which held her hair in place and when the gentle breeze blew across her and towards him, Matthew could perceive the faintest odour of damask roses. The silk of her gown rustled as she walked and she turned often to smile at passers-by.

Matthew explained to her what he had discovered since they last met, rehearsing in detail all Marlowe had told him, though choosing not to mention his knowledge of the interest she had shown in him during the last few years. He also explained about the arrest of Tom Campion for the murder of Bartholomew Thrace, of the missing alibis and his attempts to find them.

"And Master Shakespeare?" she wanted to know. "Have you come to any deeper conclusion regarding his place in all these affairs?" She sighed. "If indeed he has one at all."

He pondered for a short while.

"I would say this Rosemary. Kit Marlowe told me enough to lead me to believe that there is some sort of connection between Will Shakespeare and Lord Strange, beyond that of playwright in residence and Company patron." He snorted, "Though Master Marlowe talks in riddles half the time and it is extremely difficult to know when he is telling the truth, and on what occasions he merely means to obscure it."

"And what form do you believe this 'connection' takes Matthew?" she enquired, as they gained the top of Ludgate Hill, looking west, out over the silver river, with the high buildings of the Temple in the foreground.

"That I cannot say Rosemary. But you can rest assured that now my interest is aroused and I know we are probably not chasing phantoms, I shall not stop until I get to the truth."

They had paused for a moment but now they continued walking in the direction of the Fleet, the site of a former tributary of the Thames, now mostly culvetted but still hideously filthy and pungent during the heat of summer. He told her about Anthony Roper and of his relationship with George Sale, information that caused her to pause once more.

"That is interesting indeed Matthew. They say George Sale was a good and kind man, a person of some fortitude by all account. He went to his execution praying for those who were tormenting him." She looked thoughtful. "It is certainly a hard thing that men should die for their faith. I am sure, no matter what names we give to God, that such is not his intention for us."

"Amen to that," Matthew agreed. "Though regarding Anthony Roper I find it difficult to believe that he could be at the forefront of any plot to murder the Queen. He has no access to her person. He also has a daughter to protect, a responsibility that he seems to take very seriously. And though he can be irascible at times he doesn't look at all the type of man to me who would be party to murder."

"So where do you intend to push your investigations henceforth," Rosemary asked, looking up at him and squinting slightly into the sun, which was now almost full risen to its daily zenith.

"Well in the first instance I would like to know whether or not there is any truth in the alibi that Tom Campion has for the time of his Father's murder. If he is in earnest then we are back at the place we began, for we do not know who murdered the Vintner. As far as Will is concerned I shall stay on his tail. If he visits Sir Thomas Gresham's house again I could do worse than to discover why he goes there at all, and whom he meets."

She threaded her hand through his crooked arm.

"Whatever you do Mattie make sure you remain safe." She looked at him affectionately. "I would be deeply upset if my actions were to lead you into any sort of danger."

Matthew's next sentence came unbidden, for in truth it was a matter he had intended to stay away from altogether, but the words were out before he had chance to stop them.

"One of my informants also told me that you are betrothed, to Thomas Roach, Lord Newham."

She looked a little shamefaced.

"I'm sorry Mattie. I should have told you myself."

"Not at all," he protested. "In truth it is none of my concern. I should not have mentioned the matter at all."

"Indeed you should," she chided, "for you are an old and dear friend, come once again into my life and friends do not keep secrets from one another. The Queen told me of this plan some days before she went to Northampton." She sighed. "I was shocked Mattie, as you can imagine. But as I also told you, we are not our own masters. She looked into the middle distance and appeared to be stifling a tear. "And me more than most it appears."

"If you are not happy with this arrangement Rosemary," he said, "Can you not find some way to defy the Queen in this matter?"

"If only I could," she replied. "Her Majesty is filled with horrors on a daily basis by Lord Burghley. You and I may be co-operating to try and uncover a plot which even now might be a product of his own imaginings, but it is clear to me that Lord Burghley doesn't entirely trust me either."

"But that is nonsense Rosemary", Matthew exclaimed. "You've given every evidence of being faithful to your monarch and your country. Certainly far more than most people ever do – including Lord Burghley I would warrant."

"Perhaps," she replied. "But I am blood tied to Lord Strange, who seems to be Lord Burghley's chief interest at the moment. Her Majesty declares that my alliance with so Protestant a Lord as old Sir Thomas Roach would show conclusively to Lord Burghley that myself, and by implication my family, are above reproach."

"In other words she is blackmailing you into this marriage?"

"That's an ugly word for so beautiful a day Matthew. And besides, Monarchs do not have it in their vocabulary. She may dispose of us all as she thinks fit. She is the Queen of England after all."

There was a silence between them for a moment.

"But let us not worry about eventualities that have not taken place yet," she managed with a sort of smile. "August is some way off, and who knows what the winds of fortune may blow our way in the meantime." Now her face broke into a broad grin. "Lord Newham is so old and so fat that he may well expire with the gout before he can even regain English soil."

He laughed with her, though he wasn't convinced. The day was growing warm. Matthew took off his cloak and threw it across one shoulder, his other arm still linked with that of Rosemary. From her sleeve she drew what looked like a long, narrow tortoise shell box. With a deft flick of her hand the little box broke in two and out of it came a semi circle of folded parchment.

"What on earth is that?" he wanted to know.

"It is a fan Matthew, though not a type with which you are likely acquainted. It came from the Far East and was a present from my father."

"May I look at it?" They stopped in the road and he investigated the exquisite craftsmanship of the ingenious device. The case was indeed made from tortoise shell, but inlaid with mother of pearl and semi-precious stones. The folded parchment was painted gaily with scenes quite unlike anything in European art. There were pictures of dancing women and on the reverse side were depicted the form of animals that Matthew could not even recognise."

He handed the fan back to her.

"It is extremely beautiful", he told her.

"Yes it is," she admitted. "And I don't believe there's another as fine anywhere in England. My father came by it at significant trouble and expense. And merely on account of it being a present from him I would not give it up to anyone – not even the Queen of England herself, though she has admired it many times."

She demonstrated the use of the fan, cooling her face with it and then deftly swishing it away into its ornate case.

By now they were well along Fleet Street, with houses and small patches of land on the right and the vast complex of buildings that represented The Temple. St Clement Danes stood before them, its ancient tower slumbering in the noonday sun. All too soon they had arrived at Armscliffe House and it would not be long before Matthew would be expected at the theatre for the afternoon performance. They stood together by the entrance to the house.

"Tell me Matthew – if you will forgive me for being so bold. Would you be in the least upset if I was to follow the Queen's instructions and marry Lord Newham.?"

What could he say but the truth? Should he draw her into his arms here and now, in the public highway, and tell her what a shameless, terrible thing it would be for someone so young, so intelligent and so vibrant to be married to the old fossil he believed Sir Thomas

Roach to be? Would it even be wise to pass any heartfelt comment at all? She was his better in breeding and station, no matter what Kit Marlowe had said to the contrary. He had nothing at all to offer. No title, land or possessions and not even any name except that of a little known family whose ancestor had probably held Duke William's horse at Hastings.

He looked down at her – that honest, fair face, which in only a few short days had become so crushingly important to him. He burned inside with fury at the thought of anyone but himself knowing or possessing her in the future and yet he knew that her life was not her own. Like him she was merely flotsam cast up on a shore that was owned exclusively by Queen Elizabeth – the great Virgin queen. Nevertheless his father had brought him up to believe that an honest question positively deserved an equally honest answer.

He turned towards her, taking her forearms in his hands and looking squarely into her eyes.

"Rosemary, I would be much more than upset. I would be destroyed."

For a long time she held his gaze before she spoke again.

"Then mark what I have said Matthew. There are some months between now and August. A great deal of water will have tumbled down that shining river between now and then." She smiled and standing on her toes kissed him lightly on the cheek. "We must put our faith in God," she admitted. "But God is inclined to help best those who are willing to help themselves."

She released herself gently from his hands and slipped in behind the tall iron gates. In a moment she was gone.

Chapter Thirteen
Trouble Brewing

Needing to call at his lodgings to pick up his writing implements before walking once again to the Rose theatre, Matthew quickened his pace on the return journey. The parting conversation had offered at least a glimmer of hope. Perhaps, he told himself, in some way or another all would be well regarding Rosemary and himself.

"And pigs might grow wings and take flight" his familiar commented.

Matthew had little time to pay it any attention. His head was a whirl of opposing possibilities and apparent realities as he turned off Eastcheap into the secluded shade of Wyatt's Yard. The very last people he expected to see there were Sam Hardacre and young Tom Campion, who were both waiting patiently by the door leading to his lodgings.

"Well met Matthew," smiled Sam, holding out a hand and shaking Matthew's own with great gusto. "See, I've done your bidding; and in short order too you'll have to agree." He gestured towards Tom Campion.

Matthew opened the door and ushered the two men up the stairway and into his apartment.

"I'm pleased enough to see you Sam," he said, moving pieces of paper and items of clothing from the sparse furnishings. But I'm afraid I've nothing to offer you in the way of refreshments."

"Ah the life of the bachelor eh?" Sam announced, his short, stocky body rolling with laughter. "I remember it well Matthew. You should get yourself a good wife. You'd have wine and ale a plenty then."

"So," said Matthew, as Sam and Tom seated themselves. "How do you come to be here Sam, and with Tom in tow to boot." It crossed his mind that he should report Sam's speedy success to Lord Burghley, for the ex sea captain was obviously speedier at going about his business than Matthew himself was turning out to be.

Matthew glanced at Tom but the lad was silent, like a mesmerised rabbit caught at night by the light of a lantern in the middle of a mown meadow.

"Well Matthew it was like this," Sam told him. Early yesterday morning I went abroad and made some enquiries, relating to our conversation of Monday evening. It didn't take me long to track down your two missing lads, the more so because I already had an idea where they might be. It occurred to me that there was only one vessel in the River at present that might be forcing hands into service, and that's a naval warship by the name of 'the Scorpion'. She's skippered by Captain Rufus Jones, a Norfolk man and as rum a cove as you'd expect to meet in many a long day.

I thought as how I'd missed them, because I was told that the Scorpion was taking the next tide out of the River and then on to the Mediterranean. But I was in luck. Captain Jones had decided to lay in at a dock beyond Greenwich for some last minute repairs. It didn't take me above half an hour to row down there. I found the Scorpion at anchor – a fine ship," he added.

"And Tom's two friends were aboard?" Matthew wanted to know.

"Indeed they were Matthew. Trussed up down below like two Christmas geese. When I told Captain Jones that these lads were wanted for questioning by the Sheriff of London he set about blustering and fussing like they was made out of pure diamond." Sam snorted.

"But he let them go, as I knew he'd have to."

"And you brought them back to London? Sam you are a miracle worker."

"I don't know about that Matthew but I had a devil of a job even getting those two lads to even agree to see the Sheriff. They probably supposed they were in bother for something or other – you know what young men are like? In the end they agreed, mainly because they were so pleased to be set free; and then when I did persuade them to come with me, we had another problem, trying to get anyone at the Sheriff's office to listen to their story."

"But it's Wednesday Sam, and all this took place yesterday."

"Aye, right enough. We stayed there all night; just settled ourselves all comfortable like in the Jailer's little lodgings until someone with authority turned up this morning. It was a gentleman by the name of Kaye I think."

"I know him Sam," Matthew said. "And he listened to the story."

"That he did Matthew, like a goodun. And when it was told he went straight down to the cells and released young Tom here."

For the first time since Matthew had met them in the yard Tom Campion spoke.

"Thanks to you Master Prior, and of course Master Hardacre here too, I'm a free man again. Master Kaye admitted that I could not possibly have murdered my father once Paul and Nathan spoke up and told him that I was catching eels with them all that morning."

"Well I'm pleased and not a little surprised to hear that justice has been done Tom. And as far as you are concerned Sam, my old friend, I owe you a great debt."

"Poppycock!" asserted Sam. "I only done what any Christian soul would do for a friend. But now if you don't mind I'd better be on my way. I sent a message to my Bessie last night to let her know where I was but she's terrible for worrying and she will probably have it in her head by now that it's me who is locked up at the Sheriff's pleasure."

Sam sauntered off jauntily in the direction of Whitechapel, whilst Matthew and Tom walked down over London Bridge, pausing to buy food and drink before finally arriving at The Rose.

On the way Matthew noticed, with some little sense of concern, that there were more people of a 'particular' sort in the alleys and byways than might usually be expected to be the case on any average weekday afternoon. Knots of young men had gathered on many of the street corners, and especially on London Bridge. They stood, gossiping and drinking around the doorways of taverns and strolled in sizeable groups towards the bear baiting and bull baiting pits, close to the theatres in Southwark. These were exactly the sort of precursors Matthew had noticed prior to the riots caused by apprentices in and around the City only a week or two before.

James Burbage was already present at The Rose when they arrived and was so pleased to see his errant actor returned he asked almost no questions, probably preferring not to know the full truth of the matter. As soon as he was satisfied that all charges against the young man had been dropped he was content enough to allow Tom to go and prepare himself for the forthcoming performance.

A few minutes later Will Shakespeare walked in, carrying another sheaf of finished pages for Richard III. Since the other actors had not yet arrived and it would be some time before the audience began to wander in, Matthew spent a few minutes perusing Shakespeare's latest additions. The play was drawing towards its crescendo and Richard was positioned with his troops, at the top of Ambion Hill at Market Bosworth in Leicestershire. The writing was as superb as always but there was one fact that stuck out in Matthew's mind, namely the importance placed by Shakespeare upon the Stanley family at various points throughout the play. Matthew knew the story well enough and was aware that the vacillating tendencies of the Stanleys at the time of the Battle of Bosworth certainly did sway the battle in Henry Tudor's favour, but they achieved this objective at the very last moment.

In reality the Earl of Derby and his brother had not enjoyed much in the way of preferment from Henry Tudor when he mounted the throne as Henry VII. The reason for this seemed to be that King Henry believed at the time, and never ceased to believe that the late commitment of the Stanleys to his cause had very nearly cost him his life.

These considerations made, Will's placement of the Stanley's within the plot was that much more difficult to understand. The Earl of Derby and his brother enjoyed a far more central role in the story than could be accredited to them by the known facts.

In addition it gradually began to dawn on Matthew just how apposite the penning of this new version of Richard III's story might seem to be in the present political climate and especially bearing in mind the supposed plan to replace Queen Elizabeth with Ferdinando Stanley, Lord Strange. The play depicted Richard III as a tyrannical and despotic monarch, who was eventually overthrown by Henry Tudor, a man whom the play treated as a dashing and brave young nobleman. Matthew scratched his head. Was it his imagination or might some people draw parallels between the events of the play and the present situation in England?

Queen Elizabeth had begun her reign as an extremely tolerant monarch, but that state of affairs certainly had not perpetuated. Those of differing faiths from the expected State norm or persons who disagreed with the Queen's political motives were now being quite ruthlessly harried and in some cases executed. Was Will Shakespeare deliberately drawing the attention of his intended audience to the plight of England now, perhaps as a preparation for some sort of struggle for the throne? Indeed, was the part of Henry Tudor in the play intended, in a modern sense, to identify with the young Lord Strange, who practically everyone recognised as possessing all the qualities of a perfect knight? Further to this it occurred to Matthew that in his version of Richard III Will Shakespeare had Thomas Stanley, first Earl of Derby, actually placing the crown around Henry Tudor's temples. The inference might be that the Stanleys were so powerful they could 'bestow' kingship. Did that also mean they could remove it if they wished, as indeed had been the case at Bosworth Field?

There was no real time to contemplate such matters because quite soon the actors began to assemble in the theatre. Matthew was standing on the stage when Anthony Roper arrived. He looked calm and relaxed, once again hand in hand with his daughter. Only at the moment he caught sight of Tom Campion did his expression suddenly change. Jane too looked shocked for a moment, until accosted by the young man, who walked immediately over to speak to her. In a second an obvious chasm opened up between father and daughter and Jane, somewhat awkwardly, but quite definitely, fell back into her former preferential treatment of Tom. This was a puzzle. It would have been clear to anyone that Anthony Roper had no liking whatsoever for young Tom Campion, a state of affairs that might easily have been explained by Roper's knowledge of who Tom's father had been. Why would Jane, a young woman who quite clearly relished the company of her father, and who seemed to respect him in almost everything, embark on a relationship that she must have known would anger him so much?

After a few moments Tom was called back to the tiring house by James Burbage, leaving father and daughter together in the pit. Shouted whispers were the result and from his vantage point, Matthew could see the young girl dissolve into tears. The only words he could hear her utter between her sobs were:

"You don't understand father. You don't understand."

Matthew forced himself to turn away since there was work to be done: laces to fasten on the actor's costumes and properties to prepare for the play, which was to be Shakespeare's Henry VI part iii, another of the histories in which Matthew knew Will had given the Stanley dynasty an impossibly large role, bearing in mind the true historical context.

Burbage had disappeared from the tiring house, probably gone to check the numbers of people passing through into the pit and gallery. All of a sudden he thrust aside the curtain from the stage and burst in.

"Jesus," he said, "Lord Strange is here. He might have let me know he was coming."

"Had you no idea?" Matthew asked.

"Not a clue. Of course I was aware that he was presently in the City." He raised his voice enough to quell the quiet clamour of a busy tiring house just prior to a performance. "Listen men," he announced. "I've just seen Lord Strange and his entourage enter the theatre. You all know that he is patron of this company and that without him we could not perform at all. I want you all to be on your mettle tonight and I don't want to see anyone putting a foot wrong." There were surprised murmurs from the assembled players. "Lord Strange is a great gentleman," Burbage went on, "and he has a great love of the theatre. Oh!" he added as an afterthought. "Don't dash off immediately after the performance. He may just want to meet some of you."

Within a few short minutes the audience began to settle and the actors commenced. As always this particular play was well received. Matthew had no actual role to undertake and so was condemned to remain in the tiring house for the duration of the entire performance. There were many entrances and exits, with frequent changes of costume for members of the cast, so Matthew had little time to consider anything, save his duties throughout the performance. At its close, as had been the case throughout, there was rapturous applause from what was obviously an extremely large and keen crowd. Within moments of the epilogue Burbage was tidying up the younger actors and eliciting silence from the veterans. He disappeared into the body of the theatre and returned in a minute or two.

"Well done lads," he smiled. "My Lord Strange wishes to compliment you personally on your performance tonight, so I want you to line up on the stage, men to the left and boys to the right. Make it neat and tidy and stand up straight. Off you go then."

Matthew had been given no particular instruction, so he hung back. The curtains between the tiring house and the stage were drawn back and the actors lined up as instructed. There was a small knot of people at the back of the cockpit, some of whom were obviously dressed in sumptuous clothing – the glint of silver and gold in the late afternoon sun was unmistakable. James Burbage walked down the stage steps and across the pit, joining the small group. A few moments later the assembly began to walk towards the stage. Matthew dodged back into the shadow of the tiring house and Burbage and his guests disappeared, temporarily, from his view.

There was a clatter of booted feet mounting the steps from the pit to the stage. First into Matthew's view came James Burbage, talking deferentially to someone behind him, the man who must obviously be Ferdinando Stanley, Lord Strange himself. After another moment or two he came into view, a tall, lean man with a regal bearing – and unmistakably the same individual who Matthew had observed greeting Will Shakespeare warmly only a day or two before, outside the house of Sir Thomas Gresham in Bishopsgate!

Lord Strange walked slowly along the row of actors, commencing with the youngest and working his way towards the time served veterans. He had a word or two for every cast member, and each bowed as he moved to stand before them. His approach was informal and friendly, with a joke or two for actors he obviously recognised and had met before.

Will Shakespeare was standing more or less directly in front of Matthew himself. Matthew had fully expected a warm greeting to pass between Lord Strange and Will at the appropriate moment, but nothing could have been further from the truth. Lord Strange smiled as Shakespeare bowed and then simply said:

"Well done Master Shakespeare. It appears that you are becoming a force to be reckoned with in English Drama."

"Thank you My Lord," was Will's simple reply before Lord Strange moved on. There was not the slightest hint of recognition from either direction and anyone watching would have sworn that there had never been any sort of informal contact between the two men prior to this meeting in the Rose.

"Matthew," said James Burbage quietly, as Lord Strange and his attendants stood talking informally on the front of the stage. "My Lord Strange has invited me to dine with him. I'm taking Master Shakespeare and one or two of the other senior men with me. I'd be obliged if you could see to securing everything here before you leave."

Matthew nodded his understanding. The assembled Cast was dismissed and the curtains pulled across the tiring house so that they could change into their everyday clothes. James Burbage hurriedly paid out the shares to the players and then gave Matthew money and a list, so that he could hand out wages to the Vendors.

Anthony Roper was changed in a flash. Jane had waited in the pit, with her fellow sellers of food and drink, so that Matthew could deal with each of them in turn. No sooner had be handed Jane her pennies than Roper arrived.

"Come Jane," he told her. "We must be on our way. There's going to be trouble in the City this evening."

Young Tom Campion was also present by now.

"I had hoped Master Roper," he said politely, "that I might be allowed to take Mistress Jane to dinner this evening – to celebrate my release. We would of course be accompanied by Mary, Mistress Jane's friend here." He pointed to another young woman, whom Matthew knew to be a cousin of Nicholas Tooley, who herself worked in the theatre.

It all seemed above board and acceptable. Jane was not a girl and worked for her living. Surely she was coming to an age when she could be expected to enjoy a degree of independence?

Despite the people present Anthony Roper snarled out his reply in the most uncivil terms. He drew close to the young man and looked him full in the face.

"I know what you are Thomas Campion. You may have fooled my daughter here, but you won't pull the wool over my eyes. I forbid you to show any sort of familiarity towards Jane." He was silent for the briefest of moments, never allowing his gaze to drop from the young man's eyes. "Mark my words sirrah," he spat eventually. "And if you do not I cannot be held responsible for my actions."

By this time poor Jane was beginning to sob again, looking at Tom Campion apologetically. The people standing close by had either stared open-mouthed at the incident, or else turned away politely. At the end of his outburst Anthony Roper took hold of his daughter's arm and led her, protesting and weeping, from the theatre.

Of course it wasn't Matthew's business, though he would quite happily have sought out Tom Campion for an explanation but by the time he had finished his necessary duties the lad was gone out through the entrance and into the streets beyond.

It had been a long afternoon and Matthew was hungry, so after leaving the theatre he began to walk the short distance to the White Goose, intending to dine there. It appeared that his evening would be his own. There was no point at all in trying to register the movements of Will Shakespeare, who had left with James Burbage and Lord Strange's party, for heaven knew what destination.

Normally, at the termination of a play, the area around the Rose cleared quickly, as audience members either sauntered off to eat or drink, or simply to return to their homes and businesses. Such was not the case on this afternoon. Matthew noticed that the Fleece, the Rubicon, Boston Tavern and several other of the drinking houses around the theatres and the baiting pits were unusually busy for this time in the afternoon, with patrons spilling out onto the pavements. In addition people stood together, in groups, in the small open spaces amidst the tight streets and alleys. There appeared to be a distinct lack of the ribald conversations and general banter that typified Southwark at almost any time of day, and instead there were a thousand brooding whispers that were ominous and glaring in their implications. Trouble was in the air, and it was as palpable as the breeze that was beginning to blow up from the river.

None of Matthew's close friends were in the White Goose. He managed to secure a seat at a table by the window looking out onto Cargo Street. As he ate his meal he watched events begin to unfold. Snatches of conversation filtered across to him. He heard one old man say to another.

"I 'eard that the 'prentice boys of the Goldsmiths are at the Guild Hall, demanding more bread and better wages."

From another corner he could hear dockers talking.

"I'm telling you Jabe", a surly and petulant looking fellow said to a friend. "It's the Frenchies we have to deal with. They cause nothing but problems wherever they go."

Trouble was a beer that could brew itself. Matthew had seen it happen in the past. Occasionally the populous seemed to be seized by a common skittishness, the origins of which were impossible to identify. Under such circumstances generally suppressed fears and grievances tended to spring to the surface.

Gradually the quiet whisperings began to grow in intensity.

"It's the Spaniards from their holdings in the Netherlands I've heard," one of the serving girls told a customer on a table close to Matthew's own. "They're intent on razing the City to the ground."

"Well I was told this afternoon," the customer confided, "That they've sent another Armada, and that it has been seen in the Channel, off Wight."

It seemed as if each person had his or her own particular theory to explain a state of unrest that was actually fuelling itself. Matthew began to grow a little concerned. His route home must take him over London Bridge, always a place of great concern to the authorities if trouble began to break out. His only other option was to either try to secure a boatman or to remain in Southwark until things calmed down.

Gradually, in the distance, and above the rising clamour of remark and counter-blast within the body of the inn itself Matthew could begin to discern shouts. A young man burst breathlessly into the room and yelled, at nobody in particular.

"The fire-raisers are out. And the watch is fighting with a big crowd near the Bridge."

During the previous disturbances, and quite unaccountably, several important buildings in the City itself and in the suburbs had been damaged by fire, started by unknown arsonists and for no apparent reason. A sailor from Flanders had been accosted by a crowd outside Lamb's Tavern, in Leadenhall, near to such a blaze, and simply because his English was poor he had been accused of fire-raising and had almost been lynched by an unruly mob. Fortunately the City Watch had intervened in time and had rescued him.

Perhaps understandably, fear of religious insurrection encouraged and gave focus to the latest outbreaks of civil unrest, a fact that wasn't helped by a temporary shortage of wheat, which itself had lead to escalating prices for bread. This situation was already being remedied, with additional supplies of grain being shipped in from the Continent. Any sensible observer would realise that it would take a few days for bread to become more freely available and for prices to steady. But Matthew knew that mobs don't possess much in the way of sense and, as he listened, mutterings about the situation were rife, even though there was good, new bread for anyone in the inn who took the trouble to ask for it. Illogical as it might be, even this situation was blamed on one religious or national faction or another.

Paying for his food Matthew walked out into the darkening night. The noise in the distance was growing louder. He could perceive angry cries and the splintering of wood. It came from across the river, in the general direction of the City. Through the crowded streets of Southwark people were hurrying this way and that. Amongst a few, panic was beginning to set in, and Matthew's knowledge of history told him that alone could sometimes lead to disaster.

The closer he came to London Bridge, the more the seriousness of the situation became obvious. The small groups of young, disaffected men had now joined forces, forming what could only be described as mobs. Some of these hung around the southern approaches to London Bridge. Shopkeepers were busy trying to secure their properties as best they could with boards and shutters. In the shadows Matthew could make out men carrying clubs and a few even sported swords. Some of them could easily have been these same shopkeepers, merely intent on protecting what they had – but their presence added to what was obviously a tinderbox.

In the churchyard of St Overy's things were somewhat quieter, but local residents stood around the building talking, obviously tense and nervous. The church itself was open. Matthew entered. Already there were a number of dark figures, crouched like bundles near to the altar, old women praying for the deliverance of their homes and families. A number of people were gathered in the base of the bell tower. Matthew pushed past them and in the growing darkness he climbed the stone steps that led to the belfry. The stone rail, with its many grotesque gargoyles, was lined with onlookers, but there was a gap, looking out to the north, from high above the crowded roofs below.

A great mob, many with lighted torches had gathered on the northern side of London Bridge. Although nothing of their conversation was audible, their sheer presence was impressive and frightening enough. Somewhere in the City, probably in the area of St Paul's, bright streaks of orange and yellow indicated that a fire was burning fiercely. There were others to be seen in the docks to Matthew's right. His gaze took in the full panorama of the City and as it wandered to the left, and therefore to the West, he could see another two fires burning beyond Westminster. He took a sharp intake of breath. These fires must surely be to the west of The Temple, and probably at the bottom of Fleet Street, or in The Strand itself.

"Rosemary!", he said to himself. In only a few moments he had quitted the bell tower and was hurrying down the steps. He rushed out of the church and made straight for the river. The Bridge was almost certainly impassable, but he had to get across somehow, and as quickly as possible.

Chapter Fourteen
A City in Turmoil

He had no problem finding someone who would be willing to row him across the river to Westminster. It seemed that the boatmen enjoyed the only trade that could benefit from the unrest, since only the most foolish individual would have chosen to cross the Thames on foot under such circumstances.

As they pushed out from the jetty away to his right he could clearly see the clashes that were taking place on the bridge itself and on its southern flanks. Torches held by the rioters silhouetted the ramshackle army of apprentices, vagrants and doubtless a fair sprinkling of people with their own particular grievances, clashing with the City Watch and other men in uniforms which could only have been those of the Queen's own soldiers.

In the centre of the river all became eerily quiet for a few minutes. The smudge of flames and smoke, both from the City and further out, between it and Westminster, seemed like some sort of silent tableau. The fires were obviously growing in intensity and Matthew's anxiety for Rosemary's safety grew by degree as the oars creaked and the water splashed behind them.

A few minutes later the buzz of distant conversation interrupted his private concerns, as the looming giants of Westminster Abbey and the Palace suddenly towered over them. Matthew had instructed the boatman to take him to Westminster for a very specific reason. It lay to the west and south of the City. It would mean him having to walk a mile or so back to the Strand, but would also offer him the chance to review the situation without becoming involved, supposing that the riots had already spread to districts west of St Paul's and Fleet Street.

Immediately Matthew had quit the boat the oarsman pushed off into the stream again, obviously only too anxious to make as much money as he could while the going was good – or bad. Matthew scrambled up a small bank and walked across the open ground towards the massive form of Westminster Abbey. Torches were burning brightly outside the southern entrance and there he could see a large group of people gathered, though they were obviously not more rioters. On the contrary, as he drew close he could see that they were ordinary citizens, doubtless trying to ascertain exactly what was happening and feeling safer in a group, congregating hard by the one building that gave them a sense of security – their cathedral.

Some of them saw Matthew approaching, and were anxious to know what news he might have, coming as he had so recently from the seat of the problems. He had little enough time to blurt out some sort of account, for the fires directly before him, with another a little way to the right gave him great concern. He had to get to Armscliffe House as soon as possible, to do whatever he could to ensure Rosemary's safety and to offer her his continuing protection – if she wished it.

Taking the path to the north side of the abbey he began to walk up Whitehall. It was becoming much more populous of late, though when Matthew had first arrived in London Whitehall was nothing more than farm plots and small dwellings. Now there were shops and business. People gathered in the streets, around torches and braziers. They talked anxiously one to another as he passed, a few stopping him and asking what he knew, for reliable information was in short supply. On he went, the vast grounds of St James' Palace on his left, one of the preferred residences of the Queen when she was in London.

It gradually became obvious as he walked, that one of the fires he had noticed from Southwark was actually located between Whitehall and the river. He didn't recognise the building, which was now fully alight but its proximity to the river made it likely that it was some sort of warehouse. The other blaze was now before him and to his left, out across the rooftops.

He quickly arrived, half walking, half running, at Charring Cross, once a village outside the environs of the City but now a suburb and teeming with people. Many of them milled around in the road. A large group of men, woman and children fell silent as he approached. One of them hailed him nervously and he replied.

"That's alright." Matthew heard the man say to one of those standing with him. He's no foreigner."

Turning onto the Strand Matthew breathed a sigh of relief. He could now see that the large fire that lit up the sky before him was burning some short distance to the north, probably in Covent Garden. The large houses, the frontages and gardens of which lined the Strand appeared to be quite untouched. As he passed one of them he could hear a series of large dogs barking, and he sensed watching eyes following his movements. Soon Armscliffe House came into view, with a small group of people standing before its large gates. Matthew was temporarily alarmed to notice that some of them were armed.

As he grew closer the light of the torches made it possible for him to recognise one of the men, who was brandishing a pitch fork. It was the servant who had shown him in to Armscliffe House on the occasion of his first visit there. The man was also Rosemary's ooqohman. If ho oould moko out tho faooo of thooo guarding the house, all 'they' could see was the shadowy form of a man looming up at them from the dark. Suddenly a cry went up in the still air.

"Who goes there? If you be a friend stand and declare yourself. If not then be prepared to defend yourself, for we are all Englishmen here and right determined to defend this house."

Matthew stopped in his tracks, surveying the makeshift militia. There were five or six men, some armed with scythes, others with bailing hooks or forks with vicious looking tines.

"My name is Matthew Prior," he shouted back. I am acquainted with your mistress and have come here from the City, anxious to help protect my friend and see her safe."

There was a light burble of conversation before the voice rasped again.

"Come forward Sir, but keep your hands out in front of you where we can see them."

Matthew did as he was told and after a moment the servant he had recognised said.

"Aye lads, that's Master Prior right enough, let him pass. Welcome Sir," he said to Matthew. My mistress is not abed for she was out here encouraging us, like good Queen Elizabeth herself only a few minutes ago. And 'tis a happy coincidence that you are here, for she was expressing her anxiety as to your own safety in these troubled times."

He trotted before Matthew through the high gates. The large front door of Armscliffe House was open, and there, framed by the gentle glow of the rush lights and candles behind was Rosemary herself. The servant reached her a good dozen steps before Matthew did and obviously announced his arrival to her. Almost pushing the servant aside in her anxiety Rosemary was out of the door and in Matthew's arms in a second, her tears of joy at seeing him falling cold on his cheek in the night air.

"Oh Mattie, Mattie. I've been so worried about you. We've had such news from the City and I knew that the troubles centred around Eastcheap and your lodgings."

"Be calm Rosemary," he told her, equally happy to see that she was safe. "As you can see I'm hale and hearty, and I see that my visit was pointless," he teased, "for you have your own army to keep you secure."

She smiled up at him.

"And a wonderful array they are," she admitted. "I doubt not that they would fight off the whole Spanish army if necessary."

"There's no army," said Matthew, "except that of the Queen, fighting alongside the City Watch to keep order near the bridge. As far as I can tell the problem is caused by a few dozen hot-headed youths, with a sprinkling of general malcontents thrown in for good measure."

"But what of the fires?" she asked, pointing at the flames in the distance.

"I know it looks bad Rosemary, but I saw the whole spectacle from a church tower in Southwark. There are only a few fires, doubtless each started by some individual with his own axe to grind and merely taking advantage of the situation. Believe me there is no invasion as far as I can see, though I don't doubt there are people around who will make these problems work to their own advantage, Will Shakespeare and Lord Strange may be amongst them for all I know. Incidentally Rosemary I met Lord Strange tonight."

"Really?" she said. "Where".

"He came with his entourage to the Rose. And the most interesting fact of all Rosemary is that there is not the slightest doubt that he was the man who greeted Will Shakespeare outside Sir Thomas Gresham's House a few nights ago. What is more he acted as if he'd never met Master Shakespeare before."

"Come into the warm," she said, reluctant to let loose his arm. As they strode into the doorway she said to one of the servants. "John. Please fetch us some mulled wine, and take some to the men at the front of the house."

he led Matthew through to her sitting room, which was warm and bright, with a large log fire burning in the grate, for the evening had grown cloudy and not so warm as of late. Matthew gazed at the young woman, who looked as beautiful and radiant as he had yet seen her. Her wide, open eyes danced in the firelight and her face was flushed with the excitement and the evening air. She seated herself on a settle and Matthew sat on the seat opposite and yet close to her.

The wine arrived and Matthew drank a goblet down greedily, not realising how much he had tired himself with his haste to arrive at Rosemary's side. It was hot, red and spicy, infused with cinnamon and cloves.

"Do you remember," he said, his mind rolling back across the years. The time your family came to us at Stanton Prior one Christmas Day. I don't suppose you do. It was a long time ago."

"I recall it perfectly well Mattie. We had been to Church, and to visit the poor in the village when we decided, on impulse, to walk across the hill and visit you. And I know why you have recalled it too. Your mother ordered mulled wine for us that afternoon and I had rather too much I'm afraid."

"Yes I know!" Matthew agreed. So much in fact that you stayed at Stanton Prior with us until St Stephen's Day. And when the time came to leave, you sat up in front of me on my horse."

"So I did," she said, perhaps blushing a little. "But only once we were out of sight of the house. It wasn't a very ladylike thing to do was it?"

He remembered the canter back around the hill, along the ice-laden paths, amidst trees, still heavy with haw frost even at midday. He had sat well back in the saddle, with a very young Rosemary before him, his right arm holding the reins and his left arm crooked around her slender waist.

He looked across at her, not so different for the intervention of the years. Despite her station she appeared now every bit the country-woman that she was, with her simple clothes and starched white apron. Wisps of hair fell from her cap and tumbled down onto her brow. He reached across to brush one aside with his finger and she clasped his hand in her own.

"If I wasn't already in love with you Mattie, I think that day would have sealed it. You were so gallant – you still are."

He withdrew his hand gently. Propriety surely demanded that he should quit Armscliffe House soon, and return to his lodgings, though the thought of trying to stay clear of the problems the City was encountering wasn't appealing.

Perhaps she read his mind, for she lifted the jug and poured more wine into his goblet. They spent the next hour sitting by the light of the fire, talking of summers and winters long gone, of picking brambles in the autumn and climbing to the heights of the dale's rim in the heat of August, hunting for bilberries amongst the new shoots of heather. They remembered terrific storms that raced up the valley from the direction of

Cumbria, of paired kestrels high in the sky, clutching talons, tumbling and turning hundreds of feet in an orgy of togetherness and about sultry summer nights when the air was alive with the sound of crickets and nightingales.

All too soon it seemed to Matthew that he had no choice but to leave. When he announced his intention, though less than willingly, Rosemary started from her dreams in an instant.

"What? You intend to go home Mattie? Tonight? With riots in the streets? No", she insisted, "It wouldn't be safe Matthew. Like as not you would either be assaulted by the rioters themselves, or else arrested by the Watch." She was standing now, agitated again and quite clearly worried for his safety. "Besides which," she insisted. "You risked life and limb to come here to protect me tonight. It would hardly be chivalrous of you to go back to the City and leave me here would it?" she finished, drawing close and looking up at him, for now he too was standing.

She remained tense, until she could tell from the expression on his face that he had relented. In an instant the gap between them dissolved. Perhaps it was the wine or the common reminiscences of their childhood home, or perchance it was the full blossoming of some magic that had sparked between them from that first moment at Hampton Court. Whatever the explanation it seemed to Matthew that it was the most natural and wonderful thing in the world to take her in his arms again.

The City looked bruised and shaken under a leaden sky as he arrived back at his lodgings late in the morning the next day. Everywhere were piles of broken glass, uprooted cobbles and stones taken from the edge of the river to be used as projectiles. Men employed by the City were already out in the streets, repairing the damage and clearing up as best they could. The fires, though fierce, seemed to have been limited in scale and had been contained to specific buildings, close to the Guildhall and near to St Olave's Church.

Wyatt's Yard was quite untouched by the disturbance and his own lodgings were secure. His neighbours were pleased to register his return. They told him that a group of young men, fuelled by ale imbibed south of the river had come up into the City to the Goldsmith's Hall, intent on taking their grievances out on someone. They had found the Hall locked and shuttered, so had vented their anger on the streets surrounding it. The City Watch, soldiers from the Sheriff's own small force and men from the Queen's army, garrisoned at the Tower had moved quickly to stop the disturbances. They had closed London Bridge, trapping even more potential rioters in Southwark and then had herded the mainly drunken demonstrators into closed yards and narrow alleys within the City itself. By the early hours of the morning it was all over. Two or three people had died and many had been arrested, but nobody expected that this one night would see an end to the matter.

Matthew walked down early in the afternoon to the Rose. He had copying to complete and only prayed that the theatre, together with its many costumes, properties and scripts had remained intact. It had and in fact there was little sign of the previous night's events within Southwark itself. When the actors began to arrive he could tell that they were all worried men, James Burbage the most. The City authorities had already issued decrees declaring that if the troubles that had been fermented in the taverns of Southwark continued the theatres would be closed.

James Burbage had wondered whether it might be more prudent to close the Rose for this one day, if only to prove that he was doing his part to try and keep people at home until their tempers had abated. In the end, he told Matthew he considered it more prudent to go ahead with the performance as usual. He could not predict how people might react if the palaces of pleasure were suddenly barred to them. They may even take their anger out on the Rose itself.

All conversation amongst the cast was about the riots of the previous night. Each person had his own tale to tell but it appeared that most of them had been safe at home before matters really began to get out of hand. Once again Matthew noticed the preferential treatment afforded to young Tom Campion by Jane Roper, though she was continually casting worried glances in the direction of her father. Roper himself seemed to have ceased his verbal protests regarding the relationship and merely glowered at the pair. The performance itself was badly attended, with sensible people staying at home until matters calmed down.

It had been possible for Matthew to copy the remaining parts of Richard III before most of the actors arrived. He knew full well that James Burbage was anxious to apportion roles and for the actors to begin learning their lines. The performance of the play, due to take place before the Queen herself, was only two or three weeks off and Burbage wanted it to be as flawless as possible. At least in part the continuing existence of the Company might depend on her influence with the City authorities. Will Shakespeare himself had stayed more or less silent on the subject of the riots, though he had been as polite as always to Matthew. He was obviously pleased that the new play was finished and that his first critic, Matthew himself, painted it in glowing colours.

It would have been impossible to check the whereabouts of Master Shakespeare on the previous evening and in any case he had been in the company of James Burbage and some of the actors as well as Lord Stanley. All the same things were hotting up and Matthew determined to follow Will again when he left the theatre. With this in mind he again stationed himself in the inn opposite the Rose. It was too chilly to sit outside and it was some time before the playwright sallied forth into the early evening. Paying for his drink Matthew followed Will at a distance, until he walked into a quiet tavern, on Crandon Street. There he partook of a meal, whilst Matthew stood in the shadows of a house opposite, watching the small groups of young men who were beginning to gather near to the entrance of inns. Others were wandering back from the bull baiting ring and the cock fights to join their obviously aggrieved and plotting companions.

Eventually Will appeared at the door of the tavern and began his walk away from Southwark and back to the City. On the north side of London Bridge the City authorities were already in evidence but Shakespeare walked quickly by them and continued on his way towards Bishopsgate. On this occasion however he did not continue on towards Shoreditch, but halted outside the tall gates of Gresham House. There he stood for some minutes, whilst Matthew took up his former hiding place in the gate of St Helen's Church. Two other men soon arrived and had the briefest of conversations with Will. Matthew did not recognise either of them. One was obviously older, short and stocky, with dark clothes and a large ruff. His companion was probably in his middle twenties, a much taller man. Both bore themselves like gentlemen and appeared to know Will Shakespeare at least tolerably well.

In only a few moments the three passed through the entrance gates of Gresham House and beyond Matthew's view.

Within the space of the next few minutes Matthew saw at least fifteen or sixteen other men enter the house. A few bore the look of artisans or merchants, but there was also a fair proportion of gentlemen amongst them. At last, from the direction of the City came a figure he recognised immediately, even despite the failing light. It was none other than Ferdinando Stanley – Lord Strange himself. He walked purposefully towards the house and then disappeared in through the gates.

Matthew moved out of the shadow and strolled along the front of Gresham House, as if he were nothing more than a simple passer-by. The doorway was lit and open but there were two men standing there. Judging by their attire they were not servants, and whether they were or not it appeared that at least this entrance to the house was blocked to him.

Waiting until the two were looking away from the road, Matthew slipped past again and dodged into St Helen's churchyard. Walking down the length of the high wall that divided the Church property from that of Gresham House he eventually came to a portion of the wall that had suffered damage from tree roots. In places the mortar had fallen away, offering significant hand and footholds. Looking around to make absolutely certain that he was not being observed, Matthew hoisted himself to the top of the wall and then sprang down on the other side, between two large elm trees.

Arriving at the side of Gresham House Matthew walked around part of the building, looking for another entrance. He was out of luck, all were locked and barred. There were no lights shining out from windows, which was odd because there was obviously some sort of gathering taking place inside. On the far side of the building he noticed a small chink of light emanating from a ground floor casement. Pulling himself into a semi-upright position he peered in through the gap. It was now obvious that the windows of this room at least had been covered on the inside with dark hanging drapes. Nevertheless the small gap near the very bottom of the casement, allowed him a fairly good view of the room.

It was a large hall, ornate and strongly built of huge timbers. Around three sides ran a minstrel gallery. It was devoid of everyday furniture but at one end there was a sort of platform. Upon this were seated three men, one of whom Matthew could see was Lord Strange himself. Two further men kept station at a door on the other side of the room and each carried a large sword.

All the other men Matthew had seen entering the building, and a good few others who must already have been present before he arrived were seated on benches, ranging back down the room from the platform. Only a few candles illuminated the scene but there was a large lamp suspended from the roof, which burned wanly above the platform.

It was difficult to hear what was being said because of the thickness of the glass but odd words did filter through. What seemed to be taking place might have been some sort of religious ceremony for Matthew heard the words

"In the sight of the Great Creator" and "Most

ALAN BUTLER

illustrious and mighty Protector". The next part of the proceedings were lost on him, since they were not spoken in a loud tone of voice. Certain of the party took up positions in various parts of the hall, some carrying staffs and others motifs that Matthew did not recognise.

The man who occupied the centre seat of the three on the platform eventually stood and began to speak in a louder voice. As some of his words filtered through the glass Matthew shuddered. He was intoning some sort of speech, which detailed the fate that would fall upon

"anyone who should report the proceedings, rites and ordnances of this august gathering to the profane."

Perhaps thankfully he could not make out the full list of prescribed penalties, though it was obvious that they included strangulation and ritual disembowelling.

Matthew wasn't at all prepared for what came next. The two swordsmen by the door moved aside and the door opened. In came two further individuals, flanking a third. This unfortunate man was blindfolded; his hands were tied and he was naked to the waist. He was led to a position below the platform and forced to his knees. It was now impossible to hear what was being said but one of the swordsmen moved into a position alongside the blindfolded man. His head was forced forward and the sword was raised.

In an instant the whole scene disappeared to Matthew and the world went black. It took him a second or two to realise that he his eyes had been covered with some sort of fabric. Strong hands gripped him by the arms and shoulders. Before he could cry out a gag was placed across his mouth and then his hands were forced behind his back and secured with rope.

His captors uttered not one word as he found himself being led around the edge of the building. He was forced to climb a series of steps and then the change in temperature on his face told him that he was now inside Gresham House. Twenty or more paces further on his captors stopped him, made him turn left and then led him a few more paces before turning him round and forcing him to sit on some sort of hard bench.

He heard the men retire from the room and the door shut behind him. Was he alone? It was impossible to tell. For some minutes he remained in this position, daring not to move.

"Well you've really done it this time Matthew!" The voice of his familiar came tumbling into his mind. He couldn't really disagree and in any case he was in no position to argue the point. "If only you had left London when you could, or better still never come here in the first place," it droned on, inside his head. But it didn't have the chance to gloat as much as it might have, for Matthew heard the door open again and sat up straight to greet whatever fate awaited him. It seemed likely that, as with the wretched man he had observed in the hall, he could expect to have his head struck off with a single blow.

"If only you had listened to me....." the familiar was saying, but its insistent nagging was drowned out by a more tangible voice, as the gag was removed from his mouth.

"What is your name and what business do you have here?" The voice wanted to know.

Matthew decided on a direct approach. He was as good as dead in any case, so he could hardly be any worse off for speaking the truth.

"My name is Matthew Prior and I am on the Queen's business" he said, with a force and a clarity that surprised even him.

The door closed again and once more it appeared that he was alone. His mind's eye turned to pictures of

Rosemary, as he had seen her only a few hours before. How would she ever discover the fate that had befallen him? He was desperately sorry for that, though grateful that his life had seemed to carry a new purpose since she had re-entered it.

Once more he heard the latch and was aware that someone had entered the room. His blindfold was removed and his eyes gradually adjusted themselves to the candlelit interior of what appeared to be some sort of anti-room. When he looked up, it was into the impassive face of Will Shakespeare.

"Are you a spy Mattie?" Will asked quietly and deliberately.

His answer came instinctively and immediately.

"If by spying you mean am I trying to protect the life of my Sovereign and the security of my nation then yes Will, I must indeed be a spy."

"And what makes you think," Shakespeare wanted to know, "that any man here tonight wishes any less?"

Now Matthew thought before speaking.

"Well for one thing the fact that I am sitting here against my own intent, with my hands pinioned behind my back. And perhaps also the consideration that I have just witnessed some poor wretch being foully done to death; an individual who doubtless happened across your 'ceremony' in the way that I did."

For the briefest duration a slight smile hung about Shakespeare's face and then he composed himself again.

"Nobody has died Matthew. We are not in the habit of killing our own brethren. What you witnessed was merely part of an ancient ceremony – no more."

"And who are 'we'?" Matthew almost demanded, for it seemed at that moment that he had little to lose and could at least hope to satiate his curiosity before he was dragged hence to meet his fate.

Chapter Fifteen
The Safety of the Realm

I'm going to untie your hands now Mattie," Will Shakespeare told him. "But do bear in mind that there are armed men beyond that door, so there is absolutely no point in you trying to escape."

He walked round and loosened the cords restraining Matthew and then resumed his seat.

"Your arrival here tonight is not exactly a shock to us." Shakespeare told him. "We have been deliberately very cautious of late and that is why we discovered you outside the house. We even left you a means of observing what was taking place within."

"You deliberately set a trap for me?"

"We had little choice Mattie because we were fairly sure that you would not heed the warnings you had been given to stay away."

"Marlowe," Matthew said, almost to himself.

"It doesn't matter 'who' Mattie. But we had better get to the business at hand. I've been chosen to speak to you because you already know me, but what I ask of you comes from the elected leader of our...... he paused and obviously sought for the right word " our fraternity."

"What I am going to ask of you is simple Mattie. It is this," he said earnestly. "If I can satisfy you that neither the Queen, nor the realm have anything to fear from the gathering you have witnessed here tonight, will you give me your word, as a gentleman that you will never breathe a word about what you have witnessed?"

"How do you know you can trust me to do so?" Matthew found himself saying.

"I don't for certain," came the reply. "However, we already know a great deal about you Matthew. Although you do not realise the fact you have some important friends, here, in this house. They have already vouched for your integrity and I, even on our short acquaintance, am willing to do the same. But you must make this commitment or the consequences could be beyond my control."

Matthew might have agreed immediately, but he thought about Rosemary.

"I cannot entirely fulfil your requirements Will, but if you will allow one slight modification, then I believe we can proceed."

"What is that?"

"There is another; a person who I would gladly trust with my life and that of all those I hold dear. Whatever is vouchsafed to me now I must be free to repeat to that person. However, you have my absolute guarantee that the individual of whom I speak would take this trust to the grave if necessary."

Shakespeare did not hesitate.

"If the person of whom you speak is Lady Rosemary Armscliffe, then I agree to your terms, though you should bear in mind that even then there are only certain things I can tell you."

Matthew was shocked to realise that Will, and presumably this whole gathering knew so much about him, whilst for his own part he had been completely in ignorance of its existence.

"Then you have my word Will, Matthew assured him. "Though only if I am convinced that you are in earnest and that you are not part of some intended insurrection, determined to wrest the crown from Her Majesty and to place it upon some less worthy head. If that indeed were the case you had better make an end of me now, for though I am not anxious to meet my maker I will not see this land plunged back into civil war and religious mayhem if I have any power to prevent it."

"And you have my word Mattie that nothing could be further from the mind of any man here tonight."

Matthew looked Shakespeare full in the face.

"There is much about you that has puzzled me Will, ever since I came to work with you over a week ago. But first, prey tell me what is this strange gathering?"

"It is an old and illustrious brotherhood Mattie. So old in fact that its origins are lost in the mists of time. If you knew where to look you would find groups of men such as the one you see tonight meeting in secret, in various places throughout Europe and beyond. This gathering, and all others of its sort, is composed in the main of men of great influence..."

"Such as Lord Strange?" Matthew interjected.

"Yes," Will agreed, "though in this assembly he has no title except that which his personal effort and time served experience afford. There are no lords here Mattie."

"And what is your purpose Will? Why do you meet in dark corners? Surely such behaviour can only foment suspicion and doubt?"

"Perhaps. But as an institution we do not seek to become part of any establishment except our own. Each man in this fraternity has a life beyond it and each takes the truths espoused here back into his respective position within society, be he a peer of the realm or a master printer. As for our purpose, we seek to pass on timeless truths and to make men realise that whilst power and influence are transitory, the common betterment of humanity is the true object of life. Our fraternity is a fountain of learning and wisdom. Within its ranks you will find those well versed in commerce, natural philosophy, architecture, mathematics and statesmanship. We seek only a fairer and more cohesive society."

Matthew shrugged slightly.

"It sounds a little like Thomas Moore's Utopia to me," he commented. "I've lived long enough in the world to know Will that, at base, each man looks out for himself. Give the average individual a sniff of power and any real ideals fly out of the window. If the history of England proves nothing else it supports the theory that man is born to selfishness and greed."

"True," Will agreed. "But it does not have to be that way. The fraternity you observe here tonight is not isolated. It is part of a great movement and one that, with God's Grace, will assist in healing some of the wounds of the past. We have no allegiance politically – merely a desire to see fair dealing for all citizens. We hold to our own specific religious beliefs, which although not alien to Christian thought are not part of it. What we definitely possess en masse is experience. This fraternity grows stronger in every way with each new initiate. We possess extensive libraries and seek to make knowledge available to all. Unbeknown to society at large our richer brethren donate large sums of money to the betterment of humanity, though not specifically through alms Matthew, because that is short-sighted giving. Our legacy is knowledge, and once in possession of that, humanity will shift well enough."

"What then is the name of your institution? When did it come into being and why is it necessary to be so secretive?"

Will smiled.

"You can have the answers to these and many more questions Mattie, but only if you are willing to become a part of the fraternity yourself. Knowledge about what we are, where we originated and our specific intentions is for initiates only. We are a 'secret' society through choice."

Matthew stood and walked over to the dark window. Only the faint glimmer of some distant lantern, partly obscured by the bows of large trees filtered in through the glass. He watched it for a while and then turned back to face Shakespeare.

"You already know a great deal about my purpose for coming here this evening," Matthew proposed, "For otherwise you would not have been aware of my association with Lady Rosemary Armscliffe. And I don't doubt, he went on, that you are also aware of my involvement with Lord Burghley?"

"All quite true," Will admitted. "You would be surprised if you were to learn just how deep within society our influence is felt."

"That being the case you must also know Will that you, and specifically My Lord Strange, are suspected of planning regicide and usurpation."

"Not only are we aware of it Mattie. It is a state of affairs that is partly of our own manufacture."

"But that's preposterous Will. Why should you actively foster such suspicions? Surely there is nothing to gain by doing so, except to create greater suspicion?"

Shakespeare looked into the middle distance for a moment before replying.

"I cannot make you party to all our purposes Matthew. Suffice it to say that we would rather attention was focussed on a potential situation we 'can' control, rather than a whole series that we cannot. But I can tell you this. It is the consideration of this fraternity and so many others like it the length and breadth of these islands, that the Crown of England should come to

James VI of Scotland when the present Queen passes to grace. Only by this means can England and Scotland be united under one crown. Further to this King James himself has assured us that religious and political tolerance will be the bench mark of his reign."

"And you believe him?"

"Why should we not Mattie? He was brought to birth partly at our behest and he is one of our number."

Matthew might have personally believed every member of this strange collection to be a credulous fool but he was extremely relieved to learn of their common support for James. It seemed quite plain that only James, son of the executed Mary Queen of Scots, himself a Protestant but with a strong Catholic background could heal the deep wounds that both England and Scotland had suffered in recent decades. Matthew didn't really care what the ultimate objective of Will's fraternity might be but if Will was speaking the truth it was almost certainly composed, at least in part, of very powerful individuals. This must definitely be the case if they could include kings amongst their number. His immediate considerations were tinged with a natural cynicism but for all, his natural curiosity had been roused.

"Might I ask you a personal question Will?"

"You can ask Mattie. Whether I make a satisfactory reply depends entirely on 'what' you ask."

"Then how did you personally become involved in this.... in this fraternity, as you call it?"

"That's quite simple. Through my father, who was already initiated."

"Then he was not a Catholic sympathiser?" Matthew asked, almost to himself.

"I consider my father to have been extremely wise Mattie. He believed that many of the troubles this realm was heir to had been brought about because of differing religious adherences. He personally held to none of them but that is a quite different story. When I was eighteen, and despite the fact that I was already married, he despatched me to Scotland and to High Germany. There I met some of his former acquaintances and friends, who hold to a religious imperative that, at heart, is every bit as secret as the gathering you have observed here tonight. They are masters of philosophy and great experimenters. These people understand the very 'essence' of life and wish to use what they know for the betterment of the world. By remaining exclusive they do not open their beliefs to dilution or distortion."

"Which brings us back to Utopia?" Matthew suggested.

"Perhaps Mattie. Though if we cease to at least strive for knowledge, high ideals and spiritual understanding do we not lessen ourselves in our own eyes and those of our Creator?"

There was no way to argue with such a statement. At heart Matthew could not find any real fault with Will's words, even if his doubting human soul attempted to do so.

"And these people of whom you speak form the core of this fraternity?"

"In part Mattie. Though it would be true to say that they 'introduced me' to it. Now!" he said. "No more questions Mattie, for as I have already told you, only initiates may learn the truth of our brotherhood. Perhaps one day you will be numbered amongst them but for now you must go home Mattie because there is likely to be unrest in the City again tonight."

"And your brotherhood is doing nothing to ferment it? You give me your word?"

"I do Mattie, and I can go further. The gentlemen here tonight are gathered partly to discuss how our combined and individual influence can lessen the present tension. The very least that we can do is to put pressure on the members of the Guild of Goldsmiths to reach some compromise with their wayward apprentices. This is the way we so often work Mattie. Our influence may not be obvious, but it sometimes proves to be important."

"I cannot say that I will be particularly unhappy to quit the life of a government spy Will," Matthew told him. "However, if I cannot report this assembly and your words to my Lord Burghley – and I have given my word that I will not, how on earth am I to satisfy him that there is no genuine plot to place Lord Strange on the throne?"

Will smiled again.

"From what I am given to understand Matthew your apparent prowess as a spy and an investigator will not have seemed so great to Lord Burghley. After all, you still have no idea who murdered Bartholomew Thrace, which was virtually the first task given you." He changed tack for a moment. "And let me assure you Mattie, before you ask, nobody here tonight was associated with that foul deed either."

"It there anything you do not know Will?"

He burst out laughing. "A great deal for certain Mattie. I use what little talent I possess to provide the means by which audiences can come to understand some of the philosophy that is so important to my life, but like the next man I often fail through my own incompetence and ignorance." He looked sincere. "It is unlikely that you will be troubled much by Lord Burghley. All you have to relate is the truth. You cannot find any evidence within Lord Strange's Company of complicity with any plan to murder the Queen or to replace her on the throne of England."

Back out in the slight chill of the night Matthew turned back towards the City. In the distance he could hear shouts and the ominous sound of breaking glass. As he walked cautiously down Bishopsgate it seemed evident that the road ahead of him was quiet. The problems, the scale of which he could not ascertain, sounded as if they were centred on the old City itself, away to his right.

As he finally gained the entrance to Wyatt's Yard he could see the bridge ahead and observed a large and impressively solid line of liveried men protecting its northern end. He turned to his right, where streaks of red and orange told him that, once again, the fire raisers had been at work. Thankful at least that he had not personally found it necessary to run the gauntlet of either protestors or protectors, he opened the door of his lodgings, walked inside and fastened it tight behind him, blocking out the unruly night. As he climbed the stairs to his chamber he was certain that he had endured more than enough excitement for one day.

He enjoyed a fitful night's sleep and lay awake in the dark for long periods, at first slightly alarmed by the commotion taking place in the distance, wondering momentarily if the disturbance was louder and the trouble heading in his direction.

Later, when the City had quietened, Matthew reflected on the events of the last few days, thinking of how his life had altered. Not that he appeared to have achieved a great deal. True his efforts had at least resulted in him being fairly sure that there was no plot to murder the Queen, or at least if there was it did not emanate from Lord Strange or the theatre Company which bore his name. Despite his natural tendency to 'doubt' Matthew was convinced that the story he had received from Will had been genuine. Had the gathering at Sir Thomas Gresham's house been intent on overthrowing the Queen, Matthew himself would hardly have been left alive when he was found there.

Besides this simple fact, everything he had learned of the late Sir Thomas Gresham; his beliefs, aims and objectives seemed to tie in well with the shadowy fraternity that met in his property. Matthew could see all too clearly that Sir Thomas Gresham's bequests of what amounted to a free college, imparting education that was available to anyone, irrespective of rank or station was exactly the objective that Will had laid out as being the driving force of his philanthropic brotherhood.

If he was to take Will's story at face value, that was an end to the situation, though of course, he told himself, it couldn't be because there was one significant factor that had not been addressed. Tom Campion had not killed his father, Bartholomew Thrace – but someone else had done so. For his own part Thrace had been a trained Catholic Priest, albeit one specifically planted to work for Lord Burghley and the Privy Council. He had also been a spy and an informer. Will had specifically stated that his fraternity had nothing at all to do with the murder and, on balance, once again Matthew was inclined to believe him. Matthew had been trusted with what amounted to a huge secret. It stood to reason that those who vouchsafed their business to him were men of integrity – or he surely would not have been laid in his own bed now.

Nevertheless he didn't care for loose ends; they ran contrary to his nature. However, it seemed likely he would have to do admit defeat in this case. Anyway, he told himself, Thrace obviously had so many potential enemies almost anyone could have ended his wretched life. Having gleaned what sort of an individual the Vintner had been Matthew could not force himself to be as troubled by his untimely end as had been the case on the horrible morning he had discovered the body. He thought once again about the lifeless, staring corpse, of the hideous gash to the right of Thrace's neck, trailing off to a superficial and angry scratch on the left side. In his mind he went over what little he could recall about the person in the green gown, of their struggle and the events that followed. There was something here that he was missing – some vital clue that might, even now, lead to the apprehension of the killer.

Slowly but surely certain suspicions began to mature in his mind. He put them to one side, reasoning that one or two of them could be addressed on the morrow at the Rose. The copying he had been employed to undertake was almost finished, and so, it appeared, was his need to work with Lord Strange's Men. After due consideration he decided to maintain his position with the company for a few more days at least. After that he could quite plausibly suggest to James Burbage that he had other fish to fry and that in any case his usefulness to the Company had come to a logical end.

Finally, after the sun had risen and was probing manfully through the grime of his windows, Matthew decided that any further effort to sleep was futile. It suddenly occurred to him that his insomnia might well have been the due to the fact that he had eaten nothing since the middle of the previous day. He dressed quickly, intent on inspecting the last evening's damage to the City and finding himself some breakfast into the bargain. Picking up his purse he was suddenly struck by the realisation that his new found wealth might not be as safe under the floor in his lodgings as he had thought only a few days ago. The fire raisers abroad in London had so far been very indiscriminate in their choice of target and living so close to a main thoroughfare his own lodgings might be at risk.

Reaching into a trunk and rummaging through its contents he pulled out a second leather purse, with a tight draw-string. Taking the golden sovereigns from below the loose floorboard he placed them in the purse, pulled the string tight and pushed it safe down inside his shirt. The purse he sported at his belt carried only a small amount of money, but probably enough to satisfy a cutpurse or a more determined criminal that it was all the cash he was carrying.

The air was noticeably warmer as he gained the street and the deep blue of the sky prophesied a fine spring day. It was still very early but a good many people were already about in the City. Up the Gracechurch he walked, until he came to the place where it was crossed by the Cornhill. Turning left, he walked past the end of Birchin Lane, where the smouldering ruin of one property and broken glass all around bore testimony to this having been one of the areas where trouble had flared. On Threadneedle Street there was more damage and signs that some shops had been looted. Old Jewry on the right seemed to have been singled out for special destruction. Two houses had been burned and barely the front of a shop or business remained undamaged. That wasn't surprising. Anti Semitic feeling needed little excuse to rear its head in London.

Matthew entered a tavern and ordered a sizeable breakfast. When he had eaten his fill he left the inn and set out on the journey that was by now becoming familiar to him, towards Fleet Street and, eventually, The Strand. At the end of Cheapside the great bulk of St Paul's towered over him. He walked through the churchyard, where even now market stall-holders were beginning to set out their wares. Once on Ludgate he noticed more evidence of damage but any signs of disturbance had disappeared before he arrived in Fleet Street. He was pleased to register this fact for though common sense told him that Rosemary was as well protected by her household as she could be by him, he had remained anxious on occasions throughout the previous night.

By the time he arrived at Armscliffe House he found the place in a state of ferment. Servants were loading trunks and boxes onto a large horse-drawn cart and further horses were being brought round from the stables at the rear of the house to be harnessed to Rosemary's carriage. Rosemary herself was issuing instructions to one of her women in the hall as Matthew walked in through the open front door. The maid caught sight of Matthew over Rosemary's shoulder and smiled at him, which caused her mistress to turn on her heels. Her face broke into a broad smile and she moved towards him, suddenly stopping herself in her tracks and dismissing the girl.

When the maid had gone Rosemary embraced Matthew.

"Good morrow Mattie," she said cheerily. "As always it is my greatest pleasure to see you here, but I am afraid that our meeting today must be short."

He smiled

"Really?" he said. "And why is that prey?"

"I had word last evening that her Majesty has come south again. In truth she was expected two days ago but the trouble in the City caused her to pause. Even now she is coming to Hampton Court and not to St James', which is doubtless thought to be too close to the riots for comfort."

"You are summoned there to serve her?"

"Aye Mattie, so it may be some days before I can see you again." Suddenly she looked downcast. "Why is my life not my own?" she asked, almost angrily.

Matthew took her two hands in his.

"Hush my love," he said. "The situation is frustrating, but it spoils such a beautiful face when you are glum. Do you have a moment to speak?" he wanted to know.

"If I could Matthew I would devote my every moment to hear anything you have to say. Alas that is not possible at present. But let us walk in the garden, for now that you are come I am inclined to let the Queen wait upon my arrival."

He explained to her the events of the previous night, though making light of the danger he had believed himself to be in, for fear of alarming her unduly. She was as surprised as he had been to learn of the true reason for the association between Will Shakespeare and Lord Strange, but also like him relieved to discover that the supposed plot was almost certainly without foundation."

"Well that is good news indeed Mattie. Of course I will keep your confidence and you can rest assured that I will inform Lord Burghley that you can find no reason to doubt Lord Strange's Company, or indeed the man himself. In truth I am happy at this news, for though my mind was filled with doubts inspired by all this intrigue, I always judged Lord Strange to be personally loyal to the Queen."

He could see from the agitation of the servants that all had been prepared and felt guilty about detaining her longer.

"I must bid you goodbye for the moment," he told her. "For I am certain that Her Majesty will not take kindly to your absence."

She looked up into his face.

"I have been very happy whilst the Queen was out of London Mattie," she said.

"As have I Rosemary," he agreed.

Her face became set and she spoke deliberately.

"I have made up my mind Mattie, that I will talk frankly to the Queen about her intended match for me. I could never be happy with such a man. And in any case," she continued with mock coyness. "There may be someone who loves me more than the Ambassador."

"I don't doubt it," he agreed. "Every man in London I shouldn't wonder."

She smiled and then pulled a face at him for his teasing but a moment later she looked serious again. There was even a trace of venom in her voice.

"Mark me Mattie. This match will not be. Queen or no Queen. I have done my duty since I was little more than a child and now it is over."

"You must not lead yourself or your family into any sort of danger Rosemary," he said, "and certainly not for my sake. I have nothing to offer you except a few sovereigns tucked here inside my shirt."

"What do I care for money or position Mattie? I would rather live in a hovel with you than in a palace with any other."

They walked together around the side of the house and he helped her up into her waiting carriage. There were no more words, just longing looks and involuntary, half- stifled tears. With a crack of the whip and a lurch the vehicle began to move forward. Matthew stood for full five minutes in the dusty road, watching as the carriage rolled away into the distance, then he turned forlornly on his heels and walked away.

Chapter Sixteen
Realisation

Will Shakespeare was not present at the Rose theatre. He had no role to play in the afternoon's production. Matthew had applied himself strenuously to all the copying that both Will and James Burbage had required and now he found himself with very little to do, except to help when he could and most importantly – to watch.

The most intriguing situation was the apparent relationship between Tom Campion and Jane Roper. When he had observed them together previously it had been at times when they were also beneath the gaze of Jane's father, Anthony Roper. Now he had the opportunity to see them when they were alone. All other cast members were in the tiring house but Tom Campion had donned his costume early. He had walked out of the crowded backstage space and into the cockpit, where Jane was preparing herself for her own afternoon's work. By chance Matthew was in the gallery, collecting cushions and taking them back to the place from which they were distributed to patrons for the performance. Neither Jane, nor Tom Campion could have had the slightest idea that he was present. As the young man approached the girl, Matthew quietly seated himself and watched.

This is indeed a strange sort of romance, Matthew told himself. The two spoke in whispers, so it was impossible to know exactly what was passing between them. Their conversation lasted full five minutes. Jane's face was, by degree, sad, perplexed, angry and indignant. Not once did she appear to offer Tom Campion the merest hint of a smile, nor any gesture of encouragement. The normally affable face of Tom Campion was set and severe. He glowered across at the girl, spitting words in her direction that were obviously deliberate and from his expression, stern. Suddenly she appeared incensed by some specific remark and lifted her left arm, as if to strike him. Tom Campion caught the girl's wrist in his hand and held it fast. He looked straight into her eyes and laughed, so loud that Matthew could hear it from the gallery. He kissed her full on the mouth then threw her arm to one side and walked off, leaving the girl once again in floods of tears.

One of the other vendors walked over to her and attempted to offer some comfort, but Jane simply shrugged off the concern and walked to the back of the cockpit, where she remained in the shadows until the commencement of the performance.

Back in the tiring house all was hustle and bustle. The young men of the company, like young men everywhere were not inclined to be tidy, often leaving their day clothes strewn on the floor for someone else to retrieve. As Matthew moved to pick up a discarded doublet, Nicholas Tooley, already costumed for the performance walked towards him. Nicholas wore a long gown of deep blue. Once again the performance was to be Romeo and Juliet. As the would-be Lady Capulet drew almost level with Matthew, young Nick caught his foot in another item of discarded clothing and fell forward. He was not a heavy individual and Matthew, already on his feet, managed to prevent his forward motion, grabbing hold of the lad before he had the chance to make contact with the floor.

"Have a care madam," Matthew laughed.

"I thank you for your pains sir," Nick replied in kind, "but would kindly request that you remove your hands from my person." As he moved away it was if a lightning bolt struck Matthew. In an instant a jumble of mixed possibilities came together in his mind with startling clarity. He looked across to where Anthony Roper was busily preparing himself. Roper was by no means a large man, in fact not much different in stature from Tom Campion. Like the boy actors Master Roper was clean-shaven and, Matthew reasoned, he could, with difficulty have squeezed himself into the green gown.

Heaven knows, he thought; this man had more reason than most to wish Thrace dead. Anthony Roper had proved in the last few days that he possessed a mercurial nature. He could be brooding and dark and was given to spontaneous fits of rage. All in all he appeared to be a prime candidate for the killing of Bartholomew Thrace, a fact that seemed to have been overlooked by the authorities. But then the truth about Anthony Roper and his association with the executed Priest, George Sale, was known only to Lord Burghley and the Privy Council, who had almost certainly not shared what they knew with the investigators at the Sheriff's office.

Matthew watched the man closely as he finished donning the elaborate costume of the Prince of Verona. Roper picked up his sword and scabbard, pulling the belt around his waist and then adjusting the straps, so that the weapon hung at the required angle on his left hip. The audience was in place and the performance about to begin.

Quite suddenly, and with an inspiration that came upon Matthew like a bolt of lightning the whole situation fell into place in an instant. Without a shadow of the doubt Matthew knew full well who had killed Bartholomew Thrace, but he could do nothing about the situation until the play was over.

At the end of the performance, to a less than full house the actors changed, most determined to go home before the City once more turned itself to the anarchy of the preceding nights. Matthew busied himself with tidying up but glanced across to where Anthony Roper was dressing. The man had a face as sour as five day-old cream. He glowered constantly at Tom Campion, who returned only a self-satisfied smile. After a short while James Burbage entered with each actor's share of the takings. There were a few low grumbles, because the trouble in the City had meant lean pickings, which was of little use to the married actors, most of whom had families to feed.

Matthew was busy trying to extricate a less than helpful Nick Tooley from his costume and was surprised to see, when he looked up, that Tom Campion had already quit the tiring house. The copyist received his own meagre share from Burbage, watching Anthony Roper all the time. The man was rushing to don his clothes and waiting impatiently for his own share. When he had received it and pulled on his boots he pushed out through the curtains and onto the stage. Matthew followed as discreetly as he could.

Roper scanned the cockpit, which was now completely empty of patrons. The vendors were standing in twos and threes, talking and waiting for their own turn to be paid. Anthony Roper was clearly very agitated. He stormed up to Mary, the young woman who was a friend to his daughter.

"Mary," he said curtly. "Where is Jane?"

The girl looked shamefaced and a little scared.

"She's gone Master Roper, a few minutes ago."

Roper's face reddened.

"Was she in the company of Thomas Campion?"

With a downcast look the girl merely nodded.

"Then by all the saints," Roper bellowed. "I shall not be held responsible for my actions."

Anthony Roper threw his cloak across his shoulders and stormed out of the theatre, with Matthew only a few steps behind. There was no opportunity to alert the authorities, in fact not a moment to talk to anyone if he did not wish to lose track of Roper's intended direction, because he was sure that Anthony Roper had determined upon some violent course of action.

Roper walked quickly and with a purpose. Through the narrow alleys of Southwark he went, past groups of young men, some of whom had attended the performance in the Rose and who now took up their positions of the last couple of afternoons, waiting for dusk and whatever mischief they had planned. Pushing past loiterers and drovers, whose geese hissed and cackled as he walked amongst them, Matthew struggled to keep Roper in view. He crossed London Bridge and then turned right onto Thames Street. Eventually coming to the Tower of London the obviously agitated man skirted the building, walking quickly up Tower Hill and then along the full length of East Smithfield. Now the river was on the right, sporting the motley collection of wharves, jetties, dry docks and storage buildings that had inhabited this area since time out of mind.

Some half a mile further on, and still walking quickly, they came to more open country and a dilapidated and seemingly abandoned long wooden jetty. A few craft were tied up against the wooden piles by frayed ropes, hulks most of them, ancient river craft long since abandoned and forgotten by their owners. There appeared to be nobody about at first. Anthony Roper stood for a second at the landward end of the wooden pier, jutting out like a sore finger into sparkling water of the mighty Thames.

He scanned the various boats, one or two of which were holed and had settled onto the river bed. Matthew held back slightly. There was nowhere to secrete himself this time because he was out in the open. If Anthony Roper should look behind him Matthew's presence would be observed immediately. But the other man did not cast a glance over his shoulder; he was too busy looking for something specific on the jetty.

Then it came suddenly. The sound of a raised and frightened voice – the tones of a woman.

"No", the voice cried. "Get your hands off me Tom. I won't do it anymore, I swear I won't."

It was unmistakably the voice of Jane Roper. A second later came Tom Campion's reply.

"Oh yes you will my girl, and you know what will happen to you and your precious father if you do not?"

Roper fixed his gaze on a particular hulk, a hundred paces hence. It looked like a converted cargo boat, with a hut-like structure on its deck – not an elegant craft but rather less decrepit than its neighbours. He started to run towards it, padding heavily along the boardwalk. In his anxiety he was less than careful. At about the third or fourth step his right foot crashed through a rotting timber and he fell forward. Desperately he struggled to free his foot from beneath the shattered board. Meanwhile his daughter had begun to scream – horrible, tortured screams, framed by the almost manic laughter of Tom Campion.

Matthew was galvanised into action. He began to run along the jetty, though more carefully than Anthony

Roper, keeping to the edge and away from the most rotted wood in the centre. The screaming continued as he drew level with Roper, who was cursing, swearing and full of panic, writhing to free his foot and in his anxiety only making matters worse as the toe of his stout boot became wedged even tighter under the more solid timber. All the while, for what seemed an eternity, the screaming continued, and then, at the instant Matthew stood looking at the peculiar craft, which had been made into a sort of floating house, there was silence.

A door at the rear of the cabin suddenly opened and Jane Roper, her dress torn at the shoulder, her hair dishevelled and her face as white as driven snow, stumbled out. Behind her came Tom Campion. He stopped just beyond the door. The young man bore a glazed look on his face, looking straight ahead, holding out a beseeching hand towards the young woman who was cowering in the rear of the boat, hard against the gunwales. Dropping his gaze his hand withdrew to his own body, making contact with the handle of the dagger, the blade of which was embedded deep into his chest. With no trace of horror or shock Tom Campion looked at the weapon and then stared once again at the young woman, who was beginning to sob hysterically. He drew one last breath, as if intending to speak to Jane, and then he fell forward onto the deck. His body quivered once or twice and then he lay completely still.

As Matthew took in the scene, and in particular the figure of the wretched young woman, crouched low, cowering like a hunted and hiding animal, he could see the dark marks of bruises on her forearms and at her shoulder, where the tatters of her dress had fallen forward, exposing the upper part of her breast.

Anthony Roper had freed himself from the broken boards and, in a second, he was on the boat with his daughter.

"Oh Father," she sobbed, throwing herself into his arms. Roper embraced his daughter, who, after a short while quietened. Anthony Roper looked round. He wasn't angry any more, though still red from his exertions and breathing heavily. He turned his face to Matthew.

"How come you to be here Master Prior?" he asked in a measured tone, still cradling his daughter.

"I followed you from the theatre Anthony," Matthew admitted, climbing onto the deck of the boat. He bent forward to inspect the young man. A large pool of blood was seeping out from beneath the body. It ran in a small rivulet towards the far side of the deck. There was no doubt at all that Tom Campion was dead.

As Matthew glanced up he could see that not only Anthony Roper, but also his daughter was now staring down at the lifeless form. The girl bore a look of abject terror and her father seemed almost paralysed.

"Come away," said Matthew kindly. "There's nothing we can do here. He led the pair off the deck and back down the jetty to solid ground. There they seated themselves on the grass in the late afternoon sunshine. High above the fields, away to their backs, Matthew could hear skylarks twittering, a sure sign of the high summer that was fast approaching.

"Why did he attack you Jane?" Roper asked, carefully removing the girl's hands from her face and gently lifting up her chin so that she was looking at him."

She took a couple of deep breaths to quell her sobs and said, with difficulty.

"Because I would not let him have me again." Once more she began to weep.

Roper looked over his daughter's head, back in the direction of the lifeless body.

"By my oath it is good that he is already dead Matthew," the man said, through gritted teeth. "The only sorrow is that I did not get here soon enough to do the deed myself."

Within a few minutes the girl was calmer, the initial shock of the struggle and her reaction to it slowly ebbing from her.

"I knew from the moment I saw them together that it was wrong." Anthony Roper confided, still cradling his daughter. "But Jane seemed to respond to his advances. All the same it was obvious that she was growing daily less happy. When they disappeared so quickly from the theatre I determined to come to where I knew they must surely be and to settle the matter with Tom Campion once and for all."

"How did you know where to find them?" Matthew wanted to know.

"I made it my business two days ago to question some of the younger people at the theatre. They told me that Tom Campion lived down here on an old boat. After some persuading Mary told me that Campion brought all his conquests here. "He looked around, "Probably because it's so quiet and deserted." After a short while he looked at his daughter again. "Why Jane?" he beseeched. "Why did you have anything to do with him in the first place? You knew who he was, 'what' he was!"

Jane was silent. Matthew looked at her kindly.

"You didn't have any choice, did you Jane?"

The girl looked away and Roper asked.

"What do you mean Matthew? She didn't have any choice?"

"Exactly what I say. She had no choice because Tom was blackmailing her. If Jane wanted to keep herself, and you out of trouble – at least in her comprehension, she had to do whatever Tom Campion wished. Isn't that right Jane?"

They both looked at the girl who remained silent for a short time but who then nodded.

Anthony Roper looked puzzled so Matthew said.

"Young Master Campion didn't have much time for his father, but that didn't mean that the man wasn't useful on occasions. I'll wager that Tom confided in his father that he had a fancy for Jane and I would also bet that the Vintner, though apparently stingy with his money, was more forthcoming with his advice. For his part Tom used what he discovered to gain control of Jane." He looked at the girl again. "He told you, didn't he Jane, that if you did not do exactly what he wished, you and your father would fall foul of the authorities for your involvement with your Uncle, Father George Sale?"

For a moment Jane looked surprised but then she took a deep breath and said.

"Tom told me that the Privy Council would have my father arrested, because of Uncle George and my father's brother John, at Douai."

Matthew said quietly.

"It was all lies Jane. Your father was in no danger. The Privy Council knew all about him and since he was not arrested, they must already have decided to leave him alone."

"What?" the young woman said, a look of incredulity on her face.

"It's true," assured Matthew. So you see Jane, you didn't have to kill Bartholomew Thrace at all."

It took some time for Matthew's words to sink in but eventually Anthony Roper responded.

"What are you saying Matthew?" he demanded, his voice raised in anger and indignation.

"Jane thought up a way to rid herself of Tom, whilst at the same time disposing of the man who had betrayed her uncle and brought about his execution. Didn't you Jane?"

She stared blankly ahead and said nothing.

"This is preposterous Matthew," Roper protested, the blood coming to his cheeks. "She killed a man yes – Tom Campion. But you yourself are a witness to the fact that she did so in self defence."

"I have no doubt that she did Anthony. As you say we can both bear testimony to the fact. However, the killing of Bartholomew Thrace was no 'spur of the moment' act. It was thought out very carefully. And if I hadn't intervened, Jane's plans would have worked perfectly."

The girl looked at him, round eyed, her face smudged and dirty.

"You intervened?" she said.

"Yes Jane – God forgive me." Matthew confirmed. "I believed Tom when he said he hadn't killed his Father. I managed to free the two lads who represented his alibi. It was you Jane who had arranged for them to be taken aboard the warship. The captain is a man by the name of Rufus Jones, and I would be surprised if he isn't an acquaintance of your family Anthony."

"Indeed he is. He is a valued friend. I've known him for many years," Roper admitted.

"My involvement in these matters literally ruined your plans Jane. You have a good head on your shoulders, and had it not been for me, all would have turned out exactly as you had wished."

"I don't understand?" Roper admitted, looking puzzled.

"Jane borrowed the green gown from the costume store in the tiring house at the theatre. She went that morning to the shop of Bartholomew Thrace. I don't know what passed between them but I do know that at some stage she came up behind him and cut his throat."

"No!" yelled Roper, letting loose of his daughter and turning angrily towards Matthew. "She could never do such a thing, not my Jane."

"She made sure that she dipped the hem of her gown into Thrace's blood. Of course she had intended that nobody should observe her, that wasn't part of the plan at all. What she really wanted was the soiled gown, which she could place back in the theatre. Unfortunately for me, and also perhaps for Jane, I came on the scene. She panicked and hit me with a bottle, though I firmly believe she never intended me any real harm. Did you Jane?"

Almost immediately she said.

"No Master Prior. You appear a kind man to me. I would not have injured you for the world."

"She put the gown back in the theatre and then alerted the Sheriff's office. She knew they would readily accept Tom Campion as the chief suspect for the murder of his father – he had argued with the man on many occasions, a fact well known to many people."

"This is incredible," Anthony Roper said. "But how in all this world could you have known that it was Jane."

"I didn't know for certain," Matthew replied, "not until Jane confirmed it for herself just a moment ago. But I did suspect strongly. You see my first instincts were that Thrace had been murdered by a woman. After all, the murderer, though I didn't get to see the person in detail, was wearing a woman's gown. But when suspicion was cast in the direction of Tom Campion I allowed my own instincts to be swayed and I told myself that anyone can wear a gown, be they male or female. And I was correct, but what I hadn't thought about was the fact of how different they would 'feel' when wearing it?"

Roper still looked puzzled, so he continued.

"It only really fell into place this afternoon at the theatre." Matthew told him. "Young Nick Tooley was playing Lady Capulet. He tripped in the tiring house and fell against me. It wasn't too dissimilar to the tussle I had with Thrace's attacker – but he felt quite different beneath my hands. It was at that moment that I remembered the attacker's waist and breasts. Christopher Tooley's bust was padded with rags, but not that of the person who hit me with the bottle. And a young man has no real waist to speak of, which my attacker definitely did. On top of that you can add the fact that I knew Thrace's killer must favour their left hand."

"How could you possibly know that?" Roper asked. You only saw the attacker for a moment by your own admission."

"Once I knew for sure that the killer of Thrace was a woman, it became obvious that he must have been attacked from behind. He was a strong man. I don't know any woman slim enough to get into the green gown who would be able to overpower such a man as Thrace. No, he was approached from behind his back. The killer grabbed him around the forehead with their none- favoured hand. Whilst he was unaware what was happening the attacker yanked his head back, and then slashed his throat. But the cut ran from right to left, so the knife had to be held in the killer's left hand. I even suspected you for a while Anthony, but on stage you wear your sword on your left, and that means you are right handed."

Anthony Roper stared at his daughter, who had remained impassive throughout the revelations. She took his quizzical look as an invitation for her to speak.

"He as good as killed my mother's brother," Jane said, with barely a trace of remorse in her voice. "And heaven alone knows how many other innocent people he helped to send to their deaths. I thought that if he was gone, and if Tom was accused of his death, we would rid ourselves of all our problems." She stared into Matthew's eyes. "I'm not ashamed of what I did Master Prior. You can't judge me for it. Only God has that right."

"How long had Tom Campion been abusing you Jane," Matthew asked.

"Two months or more," she replied, looking away, her eyes beginning to fill with tears again.

Matthew could not comprehend what this young woman had suffered, and all in order to keep her father safe from what was obviously an unjust system; one which castigated people on the strength of their religious beliefs and even because of their relatives.

"Is this true Jane," Roper asked his daughter. "You know that if it is, you have committed the mortal sin of murder?"

"Then may God have mercy on my soul," she replied. "And though now the truth is out I will pay for my crime, I do not regret what I did."

Anthony Roper turned once more to face Matthew.

"Do you wish us to accompany you back to the City Matthew, to the Sheriff's office?" he wanted to know, his voice cracked with emotion.

Matthew gazed at him; a broken man with a daughter who had been assaulted and taken against her will, probably day after day. After having received a deeply religious upbringing and knowing the shame that was being heaped upon her hourly, who in all conscience could have suggested that she should not take such actions as she deemed necessary to end the torture? It was obvious that she believed the law to be powerless and uncaring. What would her death achieve, except to quite possibly condemn her father too and find them both meeting their end on the public scaffold?

"You have a brother Anthony, in France?" Matthew asked.

"Yes I do. And other relatives too. Most of my family fled there when things became difficult for our faith here."

"Then you must go to them immediately, Matthew told him. I will make certain that the death of Tom Campion is not discovered immediately, and by the time anyone could possibly grow suspicious, you will be long gone."

Anthony Roper looked downcast.

"Matthew, it costs money to get out of England and across the Channel. We have very little."

Matthew looked at Jane, who lifted her gaze to meet his. She was a pretty girl, probably kind by nature and quite innocent until fate and Thomas Campion had forced themselves on her. He sighed and reaching into his shirt, he pulled out the leather purse. Handing it to Anthony Roper he said.

"There are gold coins in here Anthony. More than enough to get you across the Channel and on to your relatives. There may even be sufficient for you to settle yourself into some sort of business once you arrive."

Anthony tipped the sovereigns into his hand.

"But this is a fortune Matthew. I have no way of knowing when, if ever, I could return the loan."

"It isn't a loan Anthony. It's a gift from the Privy Council. Call it compensation for what they've done to your family."

Shortly after, Matthew waved Anthony Roper and his daughter off down the path, towards the docks. Anthony had his arm around his daughter, who was wearing his cloak to cover her damaged clothes. Matthew knew that the pair would soon find a boatman willing to row them to a place from where they could take ship for France.

"You fool! You stupid bloody fool", his familiar fairly shouted in his ear. "You've just given the only fortune you've ever owned to a murderer. I despair, I really do. I mean to say..."

"Oh be quiet," Matthew shouted out loud.

He then turned his attention back towards the boat. Searching through the cabin he found a tinder-box and dry stuff. Rummaging through a trunk he discovered rags and pieces of parchment, some of which contained the words of Will's new play, the role that Tom Campion would have been expected to play.

"Needs must" he observed, looking at his own neat handwriting. He went outside and surveyed the landscape and the river. There was nobody about and the Thames too was quiet. Walking back into the cabin he struck the flint until a spark caught. He then piled the rags and the parchment onto the flames. When they had begun to crackle and burn he lifted Tom Campion's dry bedding towards the small blaze. He then quit the cabin and climbing over Tom's body he jumped ashore. In an incredibly short period of time the cabin was well alight, the pitch on the timbers melting and bubbling, feeding the ferocious and hungry flames.

His last act was to free the ropes at the prow and stern of the boat, before pushing hard with his foot until the small craft broke free of the jetty. It gradually gained pace as it floated out towards the centre of the great stream, moving quickly on the falling tide. It was fully alight now and would surely sink before anyone could approach it.

Now his tally of failure was truly complete and nobody would ever know exactly how and why both

Bartholomew Thrace and Tom Campion had met their deaths. No plot; no intrigue; no murder; and in the case of Tom Campion, no body either. Added to all of this was the fact that he was now also a pauper again. All the same, there was one blessing that occurred to him as he walked back towards the Tower of London. If Lord Burghley allowed him to keep his head, he would never be chosen to go spying for England again!

Chapter Seventeen
Epilogue

"Why did I ever agree to this," Matthew said to himself. The gown he had been given to wear was too long, his boots pinched and he was more nervous than he had been on the night he was apprehended at Sir Thomas Gresham's House. The play had already begun and the great hall of St James' Palace was crowded with members of the Court. Close to the stage, specially created for the occasion was a raised dais, atop of which sat the Queen herself. She had entered the hall only a few minutes prior to the start of this, the first ever performance of 'The Tragedy of King Richard III."

Matthew had stared at the Queen from behind the curtain at the rear of the acting area in absolute awe. Nobody could have called her a handsome woman, in fact she looked far more like some chalk-faced doll than a normal person but she certainly was striking. She wore a diamond studded head-dress, above curls so auburn they clearly had to be a very expensive wig. Her gown was voluminous; countless yards of the finest burgundy silk, intricately over-sewn with thousands of seed pearls, semi-precious stones and ribbons fashioned into every conceivable design.

Like most citizens of London Matthew had seen the Queen on at least a few occasions, though generally when she was riding by in a carriage, being carried atop a glorious litter or glimpsed from the bank of the Thames when she passed on her famous state barge. From a distance she was impressive, but in close proximity she seemed a phenomenon.

Not that Matthew held the Queen in particularly high esteem at this moment in time. There had been few opportunities in the last two weeks for him to see Rosemary at all, since her Majesty had first call on her, both day and night. They had managed to speak for a few minutes by the river at Hampton Court, and again, just a day or two before, as the whole of the Queen's retinue moved to St James' Palace, on the western fringes of the City. It had been deemed safe for the monarch to return now that all semblance of trouble in the capital had died down.

When he had been able to snatch a conversation with Rosemary and in the letters she had sent to him, Matthew could hardly fail to realise that she was anxious and fretful. Although Rosemary had spoken to Queen Elizabeth on numerous occasions concerning her proposed betrothal, the monarch had always found some way to side-step the issue or had promised to give the matter her undivided attention at a later date.

Only as the Queen departed from Hampton Court, en-route to St James' Palace did Rosemary receive the answer she had been waiting for, and it wasn't the decision she wanted to hear. Strangely enough despite her previous concern regarding the matter, Rosemary seemed unusually sanguine when Matthew had met her on the road. At her invitation and along with an entourage that stretched for nearly half a mile, Matthew rode with Rosemary in her own carriage, far back in the procession and well away from the Queen herself.

"At least I have an answer Mattie, and I know what is expected of me." She had smiled at him and put her hand on his, with her other hand waving from the open window at a few locals, gathered on a lovely May morning to watch the Queen ride by. "Her Majesty considers that it would be 'politic' for the match to be made. That is almost all she said on the subject."

"You must do what you know to be right Rosemary," he had told her. It was true that he found himself now deeply and irrevocably in love with this woman but from the start he had been more than aware of the gulf that lay between them. In truth he would have sacrificed anything to make Rosemary his own, but the situation was futile, and the more so with this most recent decision of the Queen.

"I have never exactly 'liked' the Queen," Rosemary had told him, at the same time smiling broadly for those standing at the side of the road. "But all that has changed."

"Well she is the Queen," Matthew commented.

"Now I absolutely hate her."

He had turned to her, squeezing her hand.

"I beg of you my love. Don't make yourself unhappy in this way. We are what we are and there's no help for that."

"Oh I am not unhappy Mattie," she had said. "I am quite resolved. It is still only May and August is three months away. Who can say that even a passing breeze may not waft Good Queen Bess to her eternal rest before then?"

Trying to divert her thoughts, and his own, he had explained his discovery of Thrace's killer and how he had dealt with the Ropers, that day by the river.

"How typical of you Mattie and how absolutely kind. I think you to be quite the most sensitive and caring man I have ever met. You are," she had affirmed, looking at him with adoring eyes, "far more of a gentleman than any of the fawning and ingratiating creatures at Court."

Now the day had come. On several occasions Matthew had spied Rosemary, attending to the needs of the Queen, placing necessary objects, sweetmeats and wine on the table beside her. Rosemary knew that Matthew was behind the tiring house curtain and on two or three occasions had cast a glance in the direction of the stage as she passed.

He had been more or less coerced into taking several small parts in the play, though he insisted that he should have almost nothing to say. He knew where to stand during the various scenes, and how to react to the speeches of others. Beyond that Matthew was simply animated stage scenery, which was more than enough as far as he was concerned.

Matthew had been prevailed upon to remain for the moment in his position with Lord Strange's Men, particularly since the sudden and unexpected disappearance of both Tom Campion and Anthony Roper. It was now generally known that Tom's floating home had disappeared from its usual mooring but as to the whereabouts of the young man himself, or the Ropers, there was only idle and completely inaccurate speculation.

The idea of permanently being attached to a company, even to work alongside a man as affable and brilliant as Will Shakespeare was not to Matthew's liking, though now his fortune had disappeared with the Ropers to France he was, in truth, glad of a steady income. Will had never mentioned anything about the encounter at Gresham House, either in public or in private, and so Matthew had stayed clear of the topic too.

With a great fanfare the play commenced. Little by little, act by act the story of this tyrannical monster was played out in front of the Court and the Queen. Matthew looked nervously out on those occasions that he was personally on stage. It seemed that the whole audience, including the Queen herself, were enraptured.

The penultimate scene of the play was set at Bosworth field, the site of Richard III's final battle and the scene in which his death was portrayed. Matthew was on stage, though not playing a specific character. He came under the heading of what Will Shakespeare described in the manuscript as 'Divers other Lords.' It was not a long scene but long enough for Matthew to have time to observe the audience, and in particular the Queen. It had been a warm day and the number of people crowded into the great hall, together with the many lights by now burning all around the room had elevated the temperature. Matthew could see a number of audience members sporting fans of one sort or another. The Queen was obviously feeling the heat too because in the silence as the actors positioned themselves for the short last act of the play he heard her call.

"Lady Armscliffe. Would you pass me a fan? I don't seem to have one with me."

Matthew was already in his correct stage position, as were the rest of the cast, but the Queen of England had given an instruction that could be heard all around most of the hall; protocol demanded that she should be settled before they recommenced.

Rosemary came forward, and offered the Queen the same ornate tortoiseshell fan that Matthew had seen her use herself. This, she had told him, was one of her most treasured possessions. What was it she had said?

"...I would not give it up to anyone for an instant – not even the Queen of England herself."

It was surely therefore very strange that Rosemary should behave in such a manner. She was standing by the dais, looking up at the Queen and bearing a more fixed and determined expression than Matthew had seen cross her face previously.

The Queen took the closed fan, inspecting the ornate manufacture of its case. Whilst she did so the cast waited patiently for her to indicate that she was ready for them to continue. Meanwhile Matthew's mind went back to a strange comment Rosemary had made on the morning he had accompanied her from Hampton Court to St James' Palace.

"Who can say that even a passing breeze may not waft Good Queen Bess to her eternal rest before then?"

Queen Elizabeth moved the fan in her hand, preparatory to opening it. As she did so Matthew remembered the strange but intriguing hour he had spent in the house of Dr Dee; of the vast array of chemical powders in jars, that Rosemary and Dr Dee had been inspecting. In particular he brought to mind the white powder in the clear fluted jar, about which his old associate, Ned Cole, had said:

"Even a few grains inhaled could be quite deadly."

He looked again at the strange expression on Rosemary's face and he knew, with startling clarity what she was about to do.

If circumstances had permitted him time to think deeply about the situation, which in later days he would, then his actions at that moment may have been different. As it was he had no more that the briefest span of time to try and preserve the life of the Queen, and yet also protect Rosemary. If he leapt down from the stage and wrested the fan from the Queen's hand the truth would almost certainly come out, as it would if he was to alert her verbally. The only way he could think of to remedy the situation was to divert the monarch's attention away from the fan.

Swallowing hard he stepped forward, at the same second the Queen opened the fan.

"It is my considered opinion," he declaimed, to the total astonishment of those standing beside him on the stage. "That though this play is a masterful piece of writing, penned by a veritable genius, it fails completely to point to the true character of the man who succeeded Richard III on the throne of England. The real tyrant here," he shouted, "was Henry Tudor!"

There was a stunned silence. The Queen put the fan down on the table beside her. For some moments it would have been possible to hear an ant scurrying across the floor of the great hall. Then, suddenly, the voice of one of the Lords of the realm, sitting not so far from the Queen rang out.

"This is treason," he cried. "That man is a traitor."

"Treason, treason," the cry went up from around the hall. Almost immediately two of the Queen's guards leapt onto the stage and held Matthew fast.

Queen Elizabeth at first appeared perplexed, but then her face took on a more quizzical look.

"What is your name fellow?" she demanded.

Matthew worked to gain enough saliva in his mouth to utter any words.

"It is Matthew Prior," Your Majesty.

"Are you tired of living sir?"

"Indeed no Your Majesty."

"Then your wits must be deranged. You must surely be aware the Henry Tudor, the great lord and even greater king of whom you speak was the father of my father."

She had not picked up the fan again, but she might at any moment.

"I know very well your Majesty, of your relationship to this individual. But for all I hold to my opinion."

The Queen took in a deep breath.

"Guards," she said. "Take him to the Tower. If he is sane, he will hang. Should we discover that he is mad, he must be committed to some asylum. Either way it is clear that he is potentially dangerous."

Before the guards could move, Rosemary had snatched the fan from the table and standing back from the dais, in the space between the Queen and the stage, she held the open fan in front of her.

"May it please Your Majesty. In knowledge of the service I have offered you these long years gone I beseech you to listen to what I am about to say." She looked at Matthew tenderly. "This man is neither dangerous or traitorous. In fact he should be ranked amongst the very highest of your most faithful subjects and servants. In his actions this evening, though clearly endangering his own life he has endeavoured to save your life, and mine also." Rosemary lifted the fan and turned it in her hand."

"No", Matthew shouted, his voice echoing around the lofty timbers of the hall. He struggled to break free of the guards, but they held him fast. Rosemary shook her hand, breathing deep from the current of air created by the ornately painted parchment of the fan. After only seconds her hand slipped to her side and the fan dropped from her grasp to the boards. She turned to Matthew and smiled, before crumpling to the floor like a doll made of rags.

The Queen was galvanised into action. Almost nimbly for a woman of her years she stepped down from the dais and walked the step or two to where Rosemary was lying.

"Guards," she shouted. "Take Lady Rosemary to my own chamber and then fetch my physician to her." She turned her attention back to the stage. "Until I know the tale of what has taken place here keep that man under close arrest, but do not molest him in any way."

Matthew was half dragged from the hall. On the instructions of the Captain of the Guard he was taken to the basement of the Palace, and there placed in a cell. For some time he sat forlornly, feeling numb and unreal; only too aware that had just contributed to destroying that which meant the most to him in life. After a few minutes the Captain of the Guard arrived again. He ordered the door of the cell to be opened and said to Matthew.

"You are to come with me now, and quickly."

Back up the stone steps they hurried, through corridors and doors, until they came to a bed-chamber. The Queen herself was seated by the bed, upon which Rosemary was laid. Queen Elizabeth said nothing as Matthew entered, and he bowed upon seeing her. Matthew also caught sight of the man who must surely be the Queen's physician. He was standing at the foot of the bed, with a solemn look on his face. There were tears in the Queen's eyes as she stood, looked briefly in Matthew's direction and then swept out of the chamber through another door, followed by all other persons present in the room except for Rosemary and himself.

Matthew approached the bed. Rosemary's eyes were open and she smiled when she saw his face.

"Come close my love." She said, struggling to lift her arm. He took the cold hand in his own and knelt by her side, the tears welling up in his eyes.

"Oh Mattie, please do not weep for me. This is the best solution to my dilemma. How could I have lived in a world that had you in it and yet be separated from you?"

"Please don't go," he said, squeezing her hand. "Oh!" he sobbed. I have killed the person I love the most above all else. What a wretch I surely am."

"You are a brave, honourable and truly wonderful man Mattie. Whatever happens you must know this. I have loved you with all my heart and soul since I was nothing more than a child. No incident in my life, no matter how significant has taken my mind away from Matthew Prior for more than a few minutes at a time." She fought for her breath and Matthew held her hand yet more tightly. "I consider myself supremely lucky to know that if only for a few short weeks, you felt for me that same emotion that has inhabited my breast from almost as early as I can recall."

He looked down at her. No element of her beauty was diminished. Her eyelids fluttered.

"Try not to grieve for too long Mattie. You have liberated me. At last I am free. With the Good Lord's providence we shall meet again, in a place where no earthly monarch holds sway. Adieu my heart, my life."

Her grip slackened in his hand and her arm became heavy. The trace of a smile played around the corner of her mouth, then she closed her eyes and was gone.

It was two weeks later that Matthew found himself back in the great hall of St James' palace. He had not been detained after Rosemary's death and some anonymous servant of the Crown had brought him a command to attend her funeral. With no specific knowledge of Rosemary's own wishes on the subject, the Queen ordered her to be laid to rest in a quiet corner of the nave in Westminster Abbey, not far from her home in the Strand, which she had loved so much. The Queen did not attend the service, though many of the Lords and Ladies of the Court did. Not knowing any of them Matthew stood alone and when the service was over he walked drunkenly along the Strand, past Armscliffe House and on into the City.

The days had passed in a blur. He had worked little, slept less and walked endlessly and aimlessly about London and its suburbs. Then, early one morning, when every shrub and tree was exploding into full, honest blossom, the Queen's Yeoman arrived at his lodgings. With little ceremony, but some deference, they took him to St James' Palace.

Now he stood in the great hall. The stage was gone and the dais on which the Queen had sat on that horrible night had been pushed back against the wall. It bore the throne, upon which the Queen was seated.

To his great surprise, for he was certain that he was being brought to his death and genuinely did not care, he was announced from the wide entrance at the back of the hall. The Queen was studying some papers but at the call of his name she looked up and put them aside.

"Come hence Master Prior," she instructed. "And as for the rest of you it is my command that you clear the room. I would have a private audience with this fellow."

Lord Burghley was standing close to the throne and looked for a moment as if he intended to protest. One glance from the Queen brought about a change of heart. Along with the rest of the assembly he bowed and retired. Matthew walked forward wearily and stooped low when he reached the dais.

Queen Elizabeth waited until the last of the courtiers and guards had left the hall. She looked down at him pointedly, but not unkindly.

"I have cleared the hall Master Prior because it is my painful duty to do something that no monarch should ever have to do."

He looked at her with a puzzled expression.

"It is my duty as a woman who has known the pangs of love, if not as the Queen of England..." She paused but then went on. "It is my duty to apologise. In my anxiety to run this great ship of state I have neglected to protect the rights of one who was ever faithful to me, and upon whose assistance I now realise I relied too

much. My grief is heavy to bear indeed Master Prior."
She managed half a smile as she rose and walked
down the steps towards him. "Heavy to bear", she said
again "but I dare say only a small proportion of your
own."

Queen Elizabeth, though great in station, was not
large of stature and she looked old and vulnerable,
despite the splendour of her gown and jewels – a
human being like himself. She stood only a few inches
from him, the ageing Gloriana.

"There is not so much genuine love in the world
Master Prior that we can afford to destroy the smallest
part of it. I have done many things in my life which I
have come to regret – but I think few that shame me
more than this."

She turned to her right and took several paces, her
hands in the attitude of prayer and close up against her
face. She then turned and looked at him.

"I cannot push back the sands of time Master Prior. I
am a monarch, with a realm to run and so life must go
on. But know this; the Queen is in no way unmindful of
the sacrifice you made on her behalf and does not
doubt in the slightest your loyalty or your courage. In
the knowledge of this," she continued, walking back to
the dais and mounting the steps again. "I must take
such actions as are incumbent upon sovereigns when
they occasionally find true pearls amongst all these
swine."

She seated herself again.

"I have ministers galore, all vying with each other to
'please me' and to 'serve me'. I could choke on the
sweetness of their honeyed words and still be no better
informed as to what is happening out there, beyond the
walls of this or any other of my palaces. The best of my
advisers has an eye to his own fortune and
preferment." She looked beyond him, into the middle

distance. "It might interest you to know Master Prior that in her last moments, once Lady Armscliffe had explained how, and why, she had tried to poison me, and before you were called to the chamber, she told me a good deal about you – and I believed all she said."

I believed it so well," she continued, visibly growing in stature and once again taking command of the regality that set her apart, "that I am become convinced that I cannot afford to be without a man of your calibre Master Prior. However, if I bring you to Court I risk spoiling what you are, and negate the value of the service you can afford this crown." She gained her feet and looked down upon him. "Kneel before your Queen," she commanded.

Surprised, Matthew nevertheless did as he was bid. The Queen lifted the sword of State from its stand near to the throne. Walking once more down the steps she raised the sword and touched him with the tip of its blade on both shoulders.

"For the sake of one who loved you so," she announced; " and to serve the needs of a troubled and often badly advised Crown, arise Sir Matthew Prior, Lord Dalworth."

He regained his feet, stunned by what had taken place, his mind in a ferment. Queen Elizabeth put down the sword.

"Matthew," she said kindly. "I cannot give back what my inattention and impatience has taken away. You are the best of Englishmen but I am not willing to compensate you by bringing you here to live amongst this nest of vipers. The lands I grant you do not belong to the Crown. They are my personal property and therefore mine to dispose of as I see fit. However, I do not wish anyone here at Court to be aware of how you came by this land and property. To that end I have made it my business to create some new kin for you."

"I'm sorry your Majesty," Matthew said falteringly. I do not understand."

"A man by the name of Sir Roland Mathers administered the Dalworth Estates on my behalf. He was titled in his own right and had extensive land around the village of Hempleton, close to Dalworth, which is hard by Scarborough, in Yorkshire. He died some two months ago and since he was a widower and had no direct issue, his lands have been divided amongst his surviving relatives. You, Sir Matthew, are his second cousin and will inherit Dalworth and the title it carries."

"But I have no cousin named Mathers, Matthew protested."

The Queen betrayed a brief half smile.

"I, Sir Matthew Prior, am the Queen of England, and I say you have. The truth of these matters, and the fact that I personally elevated you and gave you these estates, will be known to none, except my private secretary, you and your Queen."

"But Your Majesty......" Matthew began to protest again. It was as far as he got because she interrupted him.

"You will not live on your estates Sir Matthew. At least not for now. It is my desire that you stay close to London, until such times as I tell you differently. In future you will take instruction from me, and from no other."

He didn't care a great deal for Queens at that moment, and less for this one more than most. Neither did he worry over much about his own position, or even his life. His natural instinct was to tell her so – this Virgin Queen, whose behaviour had caused him to as good as kill his own heart's love. And then he gazed down at her face. She was looking back at him, with such earnest pleading that she was suddenly little more than a vulnerable and over-dressed parody of a woman. She grasped his hand in her own for a fleeting moment.

"Please?" she said, in a low and imploring voice. "For the sake of a dear friend we both loved in our respective ways and for a pitiable woman growing old with few people she can trust..." Her voice trailed off to a virtual whisper. "Few people she could ever trust?"

With a heavy step, and with tears now on her cheeks she gently embraced him. Her arms lingered around his shoulders and then she moved away and slowly climbed once again to the throne, where she straightened her skirts, seated herself and donned once again the mantle of Queen.

"Get you hence Sir Matthew and do your best to enjoy this glorious summer's day more than affairs of state allow your Queen to do" He made no more protest but simply bowed low and turned to leave. As he did so the Queen said. "We shall meet again Sir Matthew Prior – be certain of it!"

ABOUT THE AUTHOR

Alan Butler is a long-standing writer of both fiction and nonfiction books, as well as plays, poems and songs. He is probably best known for his many 'alternative' history books that in recent years have brought him to a wider audience on account of his many appearances on television documentary series. Alan travels extensively but is never happier than when sitting at his own desk, in a small town on the Yorkshire coast of England and allowing himself the luxury of accessing his imagination.

The character Matthew Prior lodged in Alan's subconscious for years before he ever found life in this, the first novel about him. Alan says of Matthew:

"Matthew Prior is now as real to me as any friend I have known in my life. It seems as though I am aware of every twist and turn of his nature and nothing gives me more pleasure that exploring his world. I hope readers come to have the same regard for him that I do."

WITHDRAWN

CPSIA information can be obtained at www.ICGtesting.com
Printed in the USA
LVOW10s1707030815

448642LV00006B/758/P